# GUTS & GLORY: STEEL

In the Shadows Security, Book 5

---

## JEANNE ST. JAMES

D1514326

---

**Acknowledgements:**

Photographer: FuriousFotog

Cover Artist: Golden Czermak at FuriousFotog

Cover Model: Mac Robinson

Editor: Proofreading by the Page

Beta readers: Whitley Cox, Andi Babcock, Sharon Abrams & Alexandra Swab

———

———

Keep an eye on her website at http://www.jeannestjames.com/or sign up for her newsletter to learn about her upcoming releases: http://www.jeannestjames.com/newslettersignup

Author Links: Instagram * Facebook * Goodreads Author Page * Newsletter * Jeanne's Review & Book Crew * BookBub * TikTok * YouTube

## A Special Thanks

To Alexandra Swab for assisting me with Steel's blurb. Your help, as always, was invaluable!

Also, thank you to ALL my readers who belong to my readers' group:
https://www.facebook.com/groups/JeannesReviewCrew/
You all encourage me to keep writing!
Love to you all!

# A Note to Readers

Dear readers who are MMA fans:

The MMA fighting in this book does not follow UFC guidelines/rules. UFC may currently be the top MMA promotion organization but it's not the only one. There are many more out there. Please keep that in mind when you're reading.

I never thought I'd be writing about an MMA fighter, especially a female one. But here we are! I learned a lot during my research (I was an MMA virgin). I hope you enjoy Kat and Steel's story as much as I enjoyed writing it. They are TRUE fighters and now one of my favorite couples.

## Kat's Motto

*When they say you can't, prove that you can.*

# Chapter One

*Strength is what we gain from the madness we survive.*

STEEL PULLED the toothpick out of his mouth and flicked it across the bar at Moose to get his attention. "Who's the new girl?"

Moose straightened up from behind the bar and narrowed his eyes on Steel. "Why?"

"Because maybe I want a motherfucking lap dance, that's why."

The manager of Heaven's Angels Gentlemen's Club barked out a laugh. "You're too motherfuckin' cheap to pay for a lap dance."

Steel twisted his neck to look at the woman on the stage who was working the pole like a fucking pro gymnast. And looked like one, too. A lot of guys didn't like a muscular woman, but that just left more for him. Because it no fucking doubt did it for him.

He wasn't like his veteran brothers and fellow Shadows, who went for the softer, curvy, cuddly type. Fuck no.

Though he had to admit, their women had some great tits.

But then, so did the woman who worked the men who sat along the stage, encouraging them to tuck their last dollar into her G-string. Though, Steel doubted her tits were real.

Didn't matter. He'd still let her crush his cock with those thighs. Or those implants.

He liked when women had enough muscles to crack a walnut. Or his balls. And with strength came endurance, meaning they could ride him for a long time, while he just sat back and enjoyed the show.

He grinned. "Give me another fucking toothpick."

Steel could hear Moose's sigh, even over the loud music which was rocking the joint. The big biker threw a box of toothpicks onto the bar in front of Steel. "That box has your fuckin' name on it. No one in this decade, except assholes, chews on fuckin' toothpicks."

Steel gave Moose the finger, while saying, "Chew on this." He tucked a fresh pick into his mouth and slid the box across the bar top toward the Dirty Angels MC member. Moose didn't need to know the reason for his habit.

One of the servers stopped in front of him, blocking his view of Moose. That didn't matter, either, since Tawny was much prettier than Moose. And she wore a tight leather corset, not a leather cut. *And* had a bottle opener tucked between her generous cleavage.

"Hey, honey. Haven't seen you around in a while."

"Been busy." He leaned over the bar, so she was sure to hear him. "Hey, who's the new girl?"

Tawny's eyes slid over to the stage and back to Steel. "Why?"

Steel sat back, shaking his head. "Really?"

Tawny raised her tawny eyebrows at him. "Yeah, really."

Steel swore he heard Moose laughing behind her. He frowned. "Get me a beer."

"Please," Tawny added.

"Last I checked, Tawny, you're a fucking server. Your customer shouldn't have to say please for you to *serve* them."

"You might not have been here in a while, Steel, but I see you haven't changed. You're still an asshole."

"Can't expect miracles."

Tawny leaned over the bar giving him a good view of her tits. "Her name is Cherry. And I hope she makes you swallow your own fucking dick. Get your own goddamn beer." She stomped away on her four-inch heels.

"You hear that?" he asked Moose, who was now leaning back against the counter, his thick, tattooed arms crossed over his chest, a huge smile on his bearded face. The man was a big boy. Not only tall, but almost half as wide.

"Heard it."

"Well?"

"Well what? I agree with everything she fuckin' said."

"Great customer service," Steel grumbled.

"You get a pass here, Steel, only 'cause of who you are. That's the *only* fuckin' reason. Now, if you really wanna pay for a lap dance, Cherry ain't cheap. She's got skills that're worth every fuckin' penny. Got me?"

"Got you. How much?"

"Fifty for fifteen. But that fifteen will be good enough to make you blow your load."

Steel whistled low, yanked his wallet out of his back pocket and threw the money at Moose. The biker grabbed it, jerked his chin up at one of the DAMC prospects working as a bouncer and then pointed at Cherry.

The prospect did an answering chin lift and moved off.

"VIP Red Room. Fifteen minutes. Make sure you tip her well."

Steel grinned and slid off the stool.

But Moose wasn't done yet. "You know the rules. No fucking touchin', Steel. Or will have one of the prospects toss you the fuck out an' then all you did was blow your fifty."

One of those young prospects wouldn't be enough. "Just want to inquire about her workout routine," he tossed over his shoulder with a wink as he headed toward the private rooms at the back of the strip club.

Ten minutes later, he was staring at Cherry's bulletproof ass as it was bent over in front of him and she was shaking it. It hardly wiggled.

No surprise his cock was as hard as her ass.

But it was the way her muscles flexed that got him off the most. And when she turned and climbed onto his lap...

*Yeah.*

Maybe he wasn't allowed to touch her, but nothing stopped the *ladies* from touching their customers. It was their choice and apparently Cherry saw something she liked.

The only thing she still wore was a thong, which was no more than a string up her ass and over her hips, and obscenely high heels.

As she ground down against his cock, he groaned, then was surprised when she shoved his face into her tits with a hand to the back of his head.

Yeah, maybe this was worth fifty bucks. She was definitely getting a tip.

"You want the extra special?" she asked, her voice husky.

The extra special?

He pulled his head away from her tits, dropped his gaze to her crotch and then closed his eyes, his heart racing.

*For fuck's sake, don't tell me she has a dick.*

*Don't have a dick.*

*Don't have a fucking dick.*

"Are you tucking?"

Cherry stopped grinding against him. "What?"

"Are you tucking your dick?" His voice might have cracked when he asked that.

"My dick?" she repeated with her eyebrows now dropped low and pinned together.

"Is that the extra special? You having a dick?"

Cherry jumped off his lap and before he could stop her, slammed both palms into his shoulders, knocking both him and the chair backward. He hit the ground hard, his head bouncing off the floor with a grunt.

"You asshole!" she screeched, picked up her scraps of clothing and flung open the door. "He's an asshole!" she screamed at the prospect who had been standing outside the door.

"Fuck," Steel muttered, untangling himself from the chair.

He heard a snicker and saw the prospect's head quickly disappear from the open doorway.

Just as he got to his feet, his cell phone buzzed in his back pocket. He pulled it out and saw it was a text from Diesel. Did Moose call the big man already about what just happened? There was no way.

*Fuck.*

He opened the text. It was typical D. Short and to the point.

*Here. Now.*

He assumed "here" was the warehouse and "now" was non-negotiable.

It was close to nine o'clock. It was late for the boss man to be working, so it had to be important.

———

"Moose ain't happy with you, asshole."

"That's why I'm here?"

"Fuck no."

"So, does Cherry have a dick?"

"How the fuck do I know if the fuckin' bitch has a dick? Got three kids an' an ol' lady, you think I got fuckin' time to watch snatch swing around a goddamn pole? Then I got you six to deal with. Always tryin' to fuckin' take work on for fuckin' free. Like we're a fuckin' charity. Well, we ain't."

"Okay then, why am I here?"

"'Cause a payin' job fell into my fuckin' lap an' I'm assignin' it to you."

Steel sat up straighter in the chair in front of D's desk. Or what should be D's desk. It was covered in loose crayons, rag dolls and a couple stray pacifiers. "What kind of job?" Steel hesitated and wrinkled his nose at the sudden stink. "Did you shit yourself?"

"Fuck," D muttered and lifted a month-old sleeping Scarlet up to his nose. "Fuck."

"There's got to be a clean diaper in this mess somewhere," Steel said, glancing around the office that was jam-packed with baby and toddler shit.

"You wanna change her?"

Steel's eyes snapped back to Diesel's. "No fucking way."

When Violet was born, D wouldn't let anyone touch her. Now at kid number three, he wasn't so worried. In fact, he might even hand her over to a stranger just for a diaper change.

He didn't blame the big man. The moment changing shitty diapers was added to his job duties, Steel was out. "Where's Jewelee?"

"Home. Tryin' to get some fuckin' sleep."

"Well, now what?"

"Fuck," D muttered again, hauling his big body out of his office chair and handing a stinky Scarlet off to Steel.

"I don't want her!"

"Just hold her 'til I find a fuckin' diaper."

Steel held the baby as far away from him as possible. "Like ya, kid. But not when you've crapped your pants."

Diesel looked like The Hulk smashing up a city as he dug through shit on the floor searching for a diaper.

"Didn't you bring a diaper bag along?" Steel bit back his laugh at picturing D with a pink diaper bag hanging over his bulky tattooed arm.

"Fuckin' forgot."

Steel smirked. "That'll teach you."

D grunted and kept digging. Finally, he found an open box of diapers, snagged one and after pushing shit off his desk—Steel had to turn away, so he didn't gag—D cleaned up his girl and changed her, all while muttering curses.

When he was done and after he settled himself and Scarlet back into his chair, he got back to business like the big badass behind the desk hadn't just wiped a baby's ass.

"Got a call from a guy—"

"A guy?"

Diesel cocked a brow at him.

"I'll shut up."

"Don't think you fuckin' can," Diesel grumbled. "Got a call from a guy 'bout doin' some personal security for a girl."

"A girl?"

Diesel gave him a look and Steel raised his palms. "Go on."

"Girl's got a stalker. Can't shake 'im. Guy doesn't know who it is. Got the pigs involved an' nothin' so far. Worried she's gonna get hurt or takin' out. Guy's her manager."

"For what?"

"She's an athlete or some such shit. Who fuckin' cares? Payin' good. Will put a nice chunk of scratch in your fuckin' pocket for more lap dances by chicks with dicks."

"So, she does have a dick?"

D closed his eyes and shook his head like he was trying not to go into beast-mode.

Steel thought it was smart to let that subject drop. "Do I need to find the stalker?"

"No. Just protect 'er 'til the pigs do their job."

"Which means, we don't know how long this will take," he muttered.

"Fuck no. That's why I'm sendin' you instead of any of the others. Got no ball an' chain. Can stay until it's over or they run out of scratch."

"Brick," Steel suggested. *Fuck*, him and Brick were the only single ones left out of the crew.

"You turnin' down the job? Don't even answer that. You ain't turnin' down the job 'cause you're assigned to the fuckin' job. Don't like it? There's the fuckin' door."

Steel sat back and grinned, knowing D was just blowing smoke up his ass. His team was good and worked well together, he wasn't going to break it up just because someone turned down a job.

"Lucky for you, she's a fuckin' gym rat. You'll be able to work out while you watch her."

Steel's ears perked up.

"Figured you'd like that," D grumbled.

"Where's this job at?"

"Where you want it to be?"

Steel tilted his head. "Hawaii would be good."

"Well, fuck then, it's your lucky fuckin' day."

Steel's head popped up. "The job's in Hawaii?"

Diesel gave him a look. "Yeah. On the tropical island of Las Vegas. Lots of fuckin' sand for you out there. Can work on your fuckin' tan."

Steel lifted a shoulder, thinking about the possibilities. "Vegas ain't bad."

"I say Vegas? Sorry to get your fuckin' dick hard. Meant twenty-somethin' miles outside of it. Boulder City."

"So, what you're saying is, I'm gonna be sweating my balls off."

"You got balls?"

"Of steel," Steel reminded him. "Hence, my name."

Diesel grunted and shook his head.

"Is it twenty-four-seven? Or am I getting help?"

"You're it. Unless you don't think you can handle babysittin' one girl."

"I can handle it."

"Show up at a place called The Strike Zone an' ask for Peter Berger. He's her manager. He'll give you more details when you get there."

"And when am I getting there?"

D grunted, "Yesterday."

"Fuck."

"Goin' the fuck home now. Soon as Jewelee's up to feed Scarlet, gonna have her get you on the next available flight an' email you that shit, got me?"

Steel nodded. "Got you. Least I'll be close to the Strip."

"Don't be draggin' the girl to your underground fights, asshole. You'll leave her scarred for life. This is a payin' job, not a vacation. Need to stay on her twenty-four-seven."

The boss man knew him too well. "Twenty-four-seven. Roger that."

D shook his head and stood up from the chair, careful not to wake the sleeping baby. "Now, get gone. Gotta get home before she starts cryin' for Jewelee's tit."

Steel opened his mouth to make a joke, thought better of it and closed it instead. Beside Slade, he was one of the best fighters in the area. But he was sure fucking glad he never had to go against D in the ring. The man might not float like a butterfly, but he could sting like a fucking sledgehammer.

And joking about the boss man's ol' lady's tits might warrant a not-so-gentle *boop* from D's fist.

## Chapter Two

STEEL WALKED into The Strike Zone and sighed with relief when the cool air hit him. He swore his balls had sweated down to the size of peanuts. And his dick was permanently glued to what was left of them.

He wanted to rip off his cargo pants and stand in front of an A/C unit or at least toss some ice down his boxer briefs.

Whose stupid idea was it to build towns out in the desert?

The gym was in a warehouse-like building, a bit larger than Shadow Valley Fitness. His home away from home. Like Slade and Diamond's gym back home, this one had rolled rubber flooring, large screen TVs hanging above stationary bikes, treadmills and the normal cardio equipment. Across the large building he noticed a whole slew of free weights and weight-lifting equipment. To his right, large windows made up a wall and behind that wall were rooms where the gym probably held classes. Like Zumba or step aerobics or some such shit.

What caught his attention, though, was, while hardly anyone was using the gym since it was a workday and most nine-to-fivers came before or after work to get their sweat on, noises came from an open doorway to the left.

He stepped up to the front desk where a college-aged girl sat, busy on her cell phone. After standing in front of her for a good minute, he cleared his throat and she finally looked up.

"Hey."

"Well, hey! Busy fucking day?" he asked, making sure his heavy sarcasm was duly noted.

The girl cracked her gum and answered, "Not really."

There would be no way Slade or Diamond would tolerate a girl like this greeting their members.

The girl gave him a once over head to belt buckle, suddenly slapped a smile on her face and tossed her purple-tipped bleach blonde hair. "Can I help you with something?"

Yeah, no. Blondie was way too young for him. And would probably just lay in bed waiting for him to do all the work.

No fucking thanks.

"Looking for Peter Berger. He here?"

She lifted one shoulder and cracked her gum again. "Prolly in there." She pointed a finger toward the room to the left.

Steel gave her a chin lift and headed in that direction.

"Hey, are you a member?"

"Yep," he tossed over his shoulder and stepped up to the two propped open steel doors and instantly fell in love.

The "room" couldn't be considered a room at all, but an extension of the main warehouse. *Fuck*, this place was a lot larger than he originally thought. And it made his mouth water and his dick hard. It had an open floor plan with high ceilings and large industrial-type pendant lights hanging from the exposed metal beams.

An octagon-shaped cage sat in the middle of the space

with a full-sized boxing ring right next to it. Thicker mats covered a large area of one corner for what could be used for wrestling or MMA. A bag area took up another corner.

Slade needed to set up Shadow Valley Fitness like this so they could train for MMA and not just teach kickboxing and boxing, along with the rest of the normal fitness club stuff they offered.

It wasn't only the gym's setup giving him a hard-on. The noise he heard? It was a woman on the mats sparring with a man.

His brain rewound, then he pushed play again.

A *woman* sparring on the mats with a *man*.

*Hot fucking damn.*

A man at least fifty pounds heavier and six inches taller. But, *fuck*, she was going at him like a pro.

Amazingly enough, her larger partner was having a hard time blocking some of her blows. While they both wore protective head gear, she only wore a sports bra on her chiseled, muscular torso. A pair of black spats, that fit her like a second skin, covered her powerful thighs and ass. He was surprised to see both fighters wearing shin guards.

He found that curious. Normally boxers didn't wear shin guards while training. Mouthguards, yes. Sparring gloves, yes. Headgear and sometimes chest protectors for the women, yes.

But shin guards? Maybe she was a kickboxer.

"Anson Sterling?" a male voice said behind him.

Steel twisted his neck to size up the man approaching him. "Steel," he corrected him.

The blond-haired man, who looked pretty fucking buff himself, cocked an eyebrow at him as he stepped next to Steel. "You're not Anson Sterling?"

"That's what my daddy named me after my momma squeezed me out, but no one uses it." He turned back to watch the woman bounce around the mat on the balls of her bare feet.

"So, you want a check written to just 'Steel?' The bank will deposit it like that?"

Steel detected a bit of sarcasm in the man's words. "No checks. Wire the fees to my boss," he mumbled, distracted and unable to pull his eyes from the woman who continued to move efficiently around the mat, doling out punches like a champion boxer and skillfully dodging incoming hits.

She could move smoothly and quickly. She had power behind her strikes. And she knew how to anticipate her partner's next move.

She was no beginner in the ring.

The man moved from his side to block his view, holding out his hand. "I'm Pete Berger, Kat's manager and trainer."

With a hand to the guy's shoulder, Steel shoved him out of his line of vision. "Hold on, gotta watch this one. She's hot as fuck. She's giving me a—"

Berger cleared his throat loudly. "Maybe I made a mistake by contacting your organization. You won't be the best person to be Kat's bodyguard."

That statement drew Steel's attention to the man. "Why's that?"

"Because that 'hot as fuck' woman is Kat."

His whole body froze. *Hell*, time froze. Then he snapped out of it and closed his gaping mouth. "She's the girl who needs protection?"

Berger glanced over his shoulder toward the mat. "I'm not sure it's wise to call her a girl. Especially to her face."

"I was told it was a girl who was an athlete. I figured a gymnast, a tennis player, or... I don't know, a fucking swimmer. Not a fucking boxer."

"She's not a boxer."

Steel lifted his eyes from Berger back to the mat beyond him. "No? Sure as fuck looks like she's boxing."

"She's training."

"No shit."

It was then that this "Kat" threw a roundhouse kick and struck her partner's outer knee, making him collapse like a deck of cards to the mat. She fell on him and they began to grapple.

*Holy fuck.*

With her pinning the guy down, her ass up in the air, her tits shoved into his chest, Steel wished it was he who was on his back on that fucking mat.

*Damn.* Could he adjust himself without ol' Petey noticing?

From her position of pinning the other guy to the mat, after the guy tapped out, she jumped straight up and landed nimbly on her feet. *Fuck!* Just like a cat. He was right, she had to have some powerful thighs and calves to do that. Not to mention great balance and flexibility.

She offered a glove to her downed partner, who hooked it with his own, and she helped him stand. They pounded their gloves together, removed their headgear and mouth-guards before helping each other remove their sparring gloves.

Her tan skin was slick with sweat and her short dark brown hair was damp and plastered to her head.

Well, there went his half-chub. Women in shape could give him a raging hard-on, but the short hair was a no-fucking-go.

A hard pass.

"I thank you for flying all the way out here but if you can't treat Kat with respect, then we'll just find someone else."

Oh fuck no, he didn't fly the fuck out there for nothing. "I have no problem giving her respect. I'm a boxer myself. Also dabble in a little kickboxing and MMA." Steel jerked his chin up toward Kat and her partner, who were still standing center mat talking. "What I just saw her do gets my respect. But I gotta say... She probably doesn't need anyone protecting her."

If Berger couldn't see that, he was blind.

"That's what she thinks."

Steel shifted his gaze from Kat to Berger. "She's right."

"Until this person... this stalker is caught, I don't want her to be on her own. I have a wife and I can't stay with Kat twenty-four-seven since I'd like to keep my marriage in one piece. And I'm not a bodyguard, anyway. "

"Looks like you can hold your own, Berger."

Kat's manager tipped his head. "In a pinch, yes. But I prefer she was watched over by a trained professional. And I heard that In the Shadows Security was the best. Hopefully that wasn't wrong."

"It's not."

Berger nodded. "Then as long as you can conduct yourself in a professional manner, why don't I introduce you to Kat? I'll leave it up to her whether you stay or go."

*Great.* Leave the decision up to the woman who probably didn't want a babysitter. D would kill him if they lost this job. Berger was paying a hefty fee and all of Steel's expenses.

He needed to be on his best behavior until little Kitty Kat agreed with Steel keeping an eye on her.

Then after that...?

"Kat," Berger called out, catching her attention. "Come meet Mr. Sterling."

"Steel," Steel corrected him again, in a low growl this time.

"Anson, this is Katheryn Callahan."

Now the guy was just being a dick on purpose.

"Kat," she told him.

"Steel."

Her handshake was firm, and she gave his fingers a

strong squeeze. He wanted to chuckle at her attempt at trying to intimidate him. She was strong but she wasn't stronger than him.

"Steel?"

Her eyes were an interesting amber color and now she really reminded him of a kitty.

*Meow.*

"Yep. Prefer Steel just like you prefer Kat."

When her fingers loosened, his tightened on hers, keeping her there for a second longer. Then he let her loose. Those striking amber eyes narrowed on him and she gave him a good once over before stepping back, giving herself more space.

"Heard you have a persistent admirer," Steel said.

"Nothing I can't handle on my own."

Steel lifted his chin toward the now empty mat. "Pretty impressive."

"Now my life's complete," she responded dryly with an arched brow.

Oh, she was a fucking smart ass.

"He says he's an experienced boxer," Berger said.

Kat tilted her head and studied Steel. "Maybe we'll have to spar."

*Only if you take me down like you did your practice partner... and we're naked.*

"Unless you have a thing about fighting girls," she added.

Steel didn't miss the challenge in her voice. "I was told by Berger here that you're not a girl, you're a woman."

Her eyes slid to Berger and back to him. "And that's correct." She turned back to her manager. "He's the one that's supposed to stick to me like glue?"

"Yes, but only if you're okay with it. If you're not, we'll find someone else. Kat, I know you don't want this, but it's for the best. So, it's either *Steel* here or someone else."

Those tawny eyes, which easily distracted him from the too short hair, landed on him again. "So, I'm stuck with someone no matter what," she murmured. She ran her gaze from his feet up to the top of his head. "At least he's not hard to look at."

*Damn.* "I'll take that as a compliment," Steel said.

Kat lifted one shoulder. "I don't care how you take it." Then she just fucking *dismissed* him, giving him her back. "Anything new from the cops, Berg?"

Berger shook his head. "Nothing. I'll call the detective again tomorrow. For now, why don't you get showered and changed, and he can drive you home. Do you have a rental, Steel?"

Steel was still caught on the thought of Kitty Kat in the shower. He murmured a distracted, "Yeah."

"Good. We keep switching up cars as an extra precaution. I'll return her latest rental and you can use yours to get around for the next few days, then we'll switch it out again."

Now, *that* got his attention. Wasn't that his decision to make as her personal security? He'd let it go this time because he hadn't officially stepped into the position. But once he did, Berger was going to have to leave the decisions to him.

"How many days will he be sticking to me 'like glue?'" Kat asked Berger.

"As we already discussed, as long as it takes until the threat is handled."

*Threat.*

Steel's head spun toward Berger. "There have been threats, too? Not just some creepy stalker?"

Berger gave him a look Steel couldn't read. "Kat, head to the locker room. I'll catch Mr. Steel up to speed while you shower."

Kitty Kat took another hard look at him, then turned on her bare feet and wandered out into the main gym.

Steel did his best not to stare at her ass as she walked away since Berger was watching him carefully. He turned and gave Berger a big grin.

Berger sighed. "Please don't make me regret this."

"Don't worry, I got your girl."

"That's what I'm afraid of."

Steel got serious. "Now, hit me with some of the details so I know what the hell I'm in for."

"At this point, the info is limited. I can tell you it's a man. We've worked with several police departments because I've moved her twice already and he keeps finding her. Currently, we're dealing with a Las Vegas detective. However, I'm not sure how seriously he's taking it. Besides the correspondence, they have no fingerprints but plenty of DNA."

*DNA...* "Wasn't he in the system?"

"Not his DNA. That's why we keep hoping he'll mess up and they'll find prints. Unfortunately, he's been really good about leaving the scenes clean... in a way."

*Scenes.* Steel didn't like the sound of that, either.

Berger continued, "Whoever he is, he keeps finding her and delivering 'presents.'"

His gut twisted, starting to clue in with how big this problem might be. "Presents?"

"Not anything joyous, like Christmas presents. Let me give you some background first. It started with a letter, then it moved to phone calls and texts from a restricted number. Her phone number has been changed twice. So far, he hasn't gotten her latest one because we put her new account in her cousin's name. A cousin who lives in Indiana and doesn't have the same last name. Besides breaking into her apartment—"

"Was she home?"

He shook his head. "No, luckily. But maybe he plans it that way? So, besides that, we've found her car damaged twice. And equipment, like her gloves, have been stolen from locker rooms, from both previous gyms or venues. Personal items, like panties, sports bras, have also been stolen."

"This sounds personal and the conclusion is he's a sick fuck."

"I haven't told you about these gifts yet. His personal calling card."

He fucking couldn't wait to hear what the sicko's calling card was.

Chocolate? Hallmark cards? Hair? Teeth?

"It's semen."

"Semen as in cum? Not leaving body parts behind of Navy guys, right? 'Cause I know a SEAL who... Never mind." Steel reminded himself that he needed to behave professionally. "You don't think she knows him personally?"

"Because of what he leaves behind, the police called him a predatory stalker. And, no, I don't think she knows him at all. I can only assume they crossed paths at some point. But that's not hard to do with who she is."

"Who she is?" Steel repeated.

"Yes, her being a well-known athlete."

Steel wanted to correct him on that one, but he didn't. He had no fucking clue who Kat was. Still didn't. So, she was no "well-known athlete." Not like Serena Williams or Muhammad Ali.

"Some of the pictures he sent her were of him masturbating in her bedroom. She came home to find dried semen on her sheets."

Steel fought his cringe.

"He sent her a picture of a blow-up doll with a picture of her face glued to it. Semen all over the face. Those are just examples. Once he couldn't text or call anymore, he began to email through the contact page on her website. Plus, post letters on her door. Put them on her car. In her locker. He seems to be everywhere. Always watching."

"And she's not scared?" Because any woman in her right mind should be scared with what Berger had told him so far. And Steel was sure it wasn't everything.

"She says she's not. But if she is, she doesn't show it. Which makes me worry because I think she'd be more careful if she was. She sees him as annoying but not a physical threat. She thinks he would've gotten physical by now if he was."

Maybe, maybe not. "How long has this been going on?"

"Almost a year."

*What the fuck?* "And you're only now getting her some protection?"

He might have asked that a little too harshly, since Berger's expression turned annoyed. Well, fuck him. Steel was just as annoyed at Kat's manager for not getting her protection sooner.

"We thought the police would do their job. They haven't and I'm tired of waiting. I bug them constantly."

The detective assigned to Kat's case probably had a full caseload. Most detectives were overworked since police departments tended to be understaffed in most areas. "Who has these letters?"

"The police have most of the originals. I have a feeling she's thrown some away and not told me about them. I have copies of what the police have in a safe at home. But I also scanned them and kept them electronically."

Smart. "Email them to me. And forward any emails the guy sent through her website. I want to see everything you have."

"I didn't hire you to investigate this. I only want you to keep her safe."

"She'll be kept safe. But I also need to know what we're dealing with to do so." She'd be much safer if this stalker was found and arrested. Or taken out, so he didn't do the same thing to anyone else in the future. "You said she's got a cousin in Indiana. She have other family?"

"Yes, but... she hasn't gone home in a long time."

Again, she was smart not leading him home to her family. "Couldn't he find that shit out online?"

"Probably, but she's always kept her personal info online to a minimum. She stays as private as possible. She loves to compete, she loves to win, but she's not in it for fame."

"What's she in it for? The money?"

"The money pays the bills, but no, she's out to prove to herself and others she can do it."

"She doubted herself?"

"She doesn't talk about it, but no, I think others doubted her."

"Family?"

"She's never said."

Berger was lying. He knew something more about that but apparently wasn't willing to share.

Before he could dig deeper, Steel caught Kat standing in the open doorway before Berger did. He wondered if she heard the last part of the conversation. She didn't look happy, but then Steel wouldn't be happy, either, if someone was assigned to babysit him.

"Are you ready, Kat?" Berger called out.

"Sure," she said, her body language as tight as her answer.

As she turned to head back into the main gym area, Steel quickly asked Berger, "So, I'm on the job?"

Berger only hesitated for a second before saying, "You're on the job."

It might not have been said with a lot of enthusiasm but it was all he needed to hear.

"Kat!" Steel shouted.

After a few seconds, she stuck her head back into the doorway.

"You don't go anywhere without me. You don't ever walk away without me following you, understood?"

One dark eyebrow lifted, and she moved to stand in the doorway, her hands on her hips, dripping defiance.

"Don't need the attitude. Just need you to tell me you understand and agree."

Her gaze slid to Berger, who took an audible breath and said, "Kat, please."

Kat closed her eyes, said nothing, but remained where she stood.

"Need your email," Berger said.

Steel dug out his wallet and a business card. He handed it over to Berger. "That has the business email on it. Email everything there. Boss's woman will forward everything to me, this way the whole team can take a look at the letters. They might catch something I don't."

"Do you have investigative skills, Steel? Because I wasn't prepared to pay extra for that."

"I can tell you, if my team and I can solve the problem faster, it'll save you some scratch in the long run. It'll be less time you'll have to pay for her protection."

"Good point."

"I've got them occasionally."

Berger lowered his voice and turned away from the woman still impatiently waiting in the doorway. "Before you take Kat home, let me give you a piece of advice. She's smart, she's capable. Don't underestimate her. And definitely don't treat her like she's just a piece of ass. Life will be a lot easier if you don't piss her off."

"Know that from experience?"

"Fuck yes," Berger answered with a grimace.

"Roger that."

## Chapter Three

STEEL HAD PLUGGED the address Kat gave him into the Mustang GT's GPS. Not that he needed to. Her place was only a few minutes' drive from the gym. However, it didn't hurt to keep the address on hand since he wasn't familiar with the area.

Her eyes bore a hole into the side of his head as he drove, even though she wore dark sunglasses. "What's your background? What makes you capable of being my personal bodyguard?"

Steel bit back his grin. "Oh, I don't fucking know... this and that."

"Want to be more specific?"

"How about this... I can break a man's neck with one twist. Is that fucking specific enough?" He gave her a quick sideways glance to see her eyes go wide, but only for a split second.

"And that's your skill?"

He put his eyes back on the road. "If that alone isn't good enough, I got other skills." *With my tongue, my dick, my fingers...*

"Like boxing."

That, too. "Yeah, sure."

"Looks like you have dog tags hidden under your shirt."

She was observant. He liked that. And it was a good skill for a fighter to have. "Yep."

"Why do you hide them?"

"Because I'm not active duty. I'm retired."

"Then why wear them at all?"

He hooked a right into the entrance of an upscale gated community that had a big fancy sign. "Because they're a part of me."

"How so?"

"Got a code or an entry card or something?"

She leaned over to dig into the gym bag at her feet and when she sat up, she handed him a proximity card.

Steel powered down the driver's side window and held it in front of the card reader. The padded metal arm—which was a joke when it came to security—lifted. The Dirty Angels MC compound back in Shadow Valley had way better security than this, thank fuck.

He drove through and glanced at the GPS. He followed the map and took a road that went up an incline. As they drove, he also noticed the neighborhood was pretty fucking fancy just like the sign. That meant the homeowners' association could clearly afford better security.

"Third house on the right," she murmured when he took a right at a stop sign.

Steel's jaw flexed when he saw how big the house was. "You live here by yourself?"

She didn't answer him as he pulled into a curved driveway constructed of pavers. The front yard was stone with cactus and other plants that looked like they belonged in the desert. Not a blade of grass to be found. Made for easy maintenance, he guessed.

She pulled a garage door opener from her bag and hit the button. One of the doors lifted on the three-car garage.

The house was contemporary Southwest style, the exterior made of tan stucco and brown stone. Wasn't his taste, but whatever, since this was only temporary. And as long as it had a comfortable bed, electricity and running water, it was better than some of the tents he lived in out in the last desert he visited.

*Fuck*, he hated the desert. He hated sand unless it was on an island and he hated the goddamn heat.

He should've pushed this job off on Brick.

The spot he pulled into was the only empty one. Shutting the Ford down, he glanced to his left and saw two covered vehicles. Whatever was underneath the canvas covers looked expensive just by their shape.

How loaded was this chick?

Kat clicked the garage door opener again and the door automatically shut behind the vehicle as she climbed out, grabbing her bag.

He popped the trunk and unfolded himself from the vehicle, then saw her heading toward the interior house door. "Wait for me," he warned.

Her step stuttered slightly, but she kept moving.

"Kat. Wait for me. That's an order, not a suggestion."

This time her pace didn't stutter, it froze. He also didn't miss her fingers tightening on her gym bag.

Her head turned until she was looking at him over her shoulder. Since her shower, her dark hair was no longer plastered to her head. It was now fluffed up in short layers.

He still wasn't thrilled about super short hair on women, but, he had to admit, the cut fit her angular face perfectly. He wondered what that face looked like after a fight.

That was, if she even allowed contact from her opponent during a bout.

*Fuck*, he was getting a half-chub again.

"If you think I'm not going to move freely about this house, you're wrong."

Well, that half-chub was quickly moving into a full erection with her challenge.

Their gaze met and held. Oh, fuck yes, she was challenging him. Not only with her words, but her posture and the glare in her amber eyes.

Challenge accepted. "Let me clear something up for you. I'm not wrong, you are. When we get back here from wherever we have to go in the next few days or weeks, or however long the fuck I'm here, I'm going to sweep the fucking house first before you enter it. Once it's clear, you can *move freely about.*"

"You're an employee, don't forget that."

"No, Kat. I'm in charge during this job. It's my fucking duty to keep you safe and I'm going to do what I'm getting paid for."

"Do you always curse so much?"

"Fuck yes. Does cursing offend you?"

"Fuck no. Though, I'm sure you wouldn't care if it did."

Steel pinned his lips together to keep from grinning. "Now we got that cleared up, I'm going to grab my duffel and then sweep the house. Understood?"

She opened her mouth, only to shut it a second later. Even though she didn't look happy about it one bit.

Not that he gave a shit. She could get annoyed as fuck for all he cared, as long as she listened to his instructions.

He took his time grabbing his bag, closing the trunk and heading in her direction. When he passed her, he made sure his shoulder grazed her lightly. He wasn't surprised when she held her ground as he did so.

When he faced the door and she couldn't see him, he finally let that grin spread across his face. "Code?"

She rattled off four numbers, which he tucked into his memory and punched them into the top-notch security system. It was a relief to see no expense was spared with the brand and monitoring company.

However, that relief was short-lived once he walked in and swept the house. He let out a long, low whistle as he traveled through the open concept split-level home. The windows at the back were enormous and French doors opened to the outside in every room that faced the rear. Including the expansive master bedroom upstairs.

He opened both doors off that room and stepped out onto the private balcony overlooking, not only the pool, but Lake Mead in the distance.

The place had to be worth a cool two to three million dollars. Way out of his league, even with the good money he made working for Diesel.

He stepped back inside, happy to be out of the late afternoon ball-baking heat and secured the doors behind him. He stopped in the middle of the room to stare at the king-sized bed. It was a complete mess. No attempt had been made to even straighten the bed. At home and even on the road, he'd always squared the corners of his rack out of habit. Seeing that jumbled mess set his teeth on edge.

However, he noticed it just wasn't an unmade bed. By the way the bedding and sheets were tossed, whoever slept in it was restless.

Someone wasn't sleeping well.

Maybe she was more bothered by the stalker than she let on to her manager.

*Huh.*

If she didn't let someone she trusted know how worried she was by the fuckstick spying on her, that meant she'd do her damnedest to hide it from him, too.

"Aren't you done yet?" he heard her yell from downstairs.

He closed his eyes, gritted his teeth, and shook his head before heading toward the bedroom door. "Did I tell you the house was clear yet?" he yelled back, annoyed she couldn't follow simple fucking directions.

"It shouldn't take you that long to *clear* a house."

"This fucking *house* is probably four thousand square feet."

"And?"

He jogged down the steps to the front landing and down even more steps to the main floor.

He hated fucking split levels. But again, he wasn't moving in. He was only here to do a job. He didn't have to like the job, he just had to do it well.

He entered the kitchen where Kat leaned against the counter, her gym bag at her feet and her well-defined bare arms crossed defiantly over her chest. She wore another sports bra visible under a loose sleeveless tank that advertised the Mayweather Boxing Club in Vegas.

Steel jerked his chin up at her chest. "You train there?" Because if she did, he was going to be jealous as fuck.

"For a few months."

"They kick you out because you don't fucking listen?"

Her eyes narrowed on him.

He didn't give a shit if she was getting pissed because he was already there, so he might as well have company. "I told you to remain in the garage until I cleared the house. You disobeyed a direct order. Doing so not only puts you in danger but me as well."

"There was no danger."

"You didn't know that when you stepped through that door, did you?"

"I didn't hear you crying for help," she retorted.

"And if you did?"

"I would've come saved you."

Steel snorted and planted his hands on his hips. "What experience do you have in a real fight? Not one coordinated by your manager in a controlled environment with a referee making sure your pretty face doesn't get so fucking smashed in that you end up looking like a fucking bulldog?"

Her head snapped back.

"We're talking a real fucking fight with a man who wants to fucking kill you. Not like today on that mat where the guy is letting you have the upper hand because that's what he's paid to do. He's giving you false confidence. Teaching you to fight another woman in the ring with gloves, protective gear and mouthguards, not some mentally ill fucker who wants to hold you down and come on your face before he slices your fucking throat."

Steel watched the color drain out of her face, but she didn't break their locked gaze. Not even for a second.

"You don't know anything about me," she hissed.

Her panties were getting in a wad, but he continued anyway. "No? I know you live in a house that costs way too much scratch and is too big for one fucking *girl*." Even without dropping his gaze, he saw her fingers curl into fists and every muscle in her body tighten. "And before you tell me you're not a girl, you just proved you are by not fucking listening when I gave you a fucking order."

"I don't take orders from anyone."

Steel tilted his head. "Then why the fuck do you have a manager and trainer?"

"To make me a better fighter."

"And why the fuck do you think that manager hired me?" Steel lifted a hand before she could answer. "To keep you the fuck alive. And that means when I give you a fucking *order*, you fucking *listen*. Consider me your manager for the time I'm here. Not for kickboxing but for your safety."

"I'm not a fucking kickboxer."

"No?"

She dropped her chin but kept her eyes glued to his. "No."

"Then what are you?"

She pushed away from the counter, bent over and picked

up her gym bag. "Maybe you should have looked me up before you took the fucking job, *Steel*. A good bodyguard would've come prepared." She strode out of the kitchen without a backward glance.

Fuck him. She just pulled his pants down and gave him a direct kick in the fucking nuts.

Because she was right.

But she was still wrong about not listening to his order.

So, they were even.

*Damn it.*

He'd never heard of her, but then, he never followed any women's sports. Except beach volleyball. Now, *that* shit he watched. But not for the sport itself.

He pulled his cell phone out of his side pocket and pulled up Google. He typed Kat's full name into the search bar and waited the few seconds for the results to load.

As his eyes scanned all the links the search pulled up, he whispered, "Damn."

She was a fucking champion. With one of those big shiny belts and everything.

And it wasn't boxing. Nor kickboxing. It was fucking MMA.

The woman was a champion MMA fighter.

He'd read some of the articles later. Right then he went to the images tab and scrolled through some of those. Pictures of referees holding up her arm as she won fight after fight.

But she also lost a few. How her face wasn't fucked up after seeing some of those photos, he didn't know. Purple, swollen eyes. Bloody lips and mouthguards. Sliced cheeks. Bruises.

She fought some names he recognized and, even more impressive, she beat them.

And then there were the pictures of her title fights and, afterward, of her holding her championship belts. Last year.

The year before. The year before that. And even the one before that.

*Fuck.* She was the reigning women's bantamweight champion for the last four fucking years.

She'd even been challenged publicly by male MMA fighters, but he couldn't tell if she ever fought them. Again, he'd read those articles later when he was alone and could pull them up on his laptop.

Fucking Diesel! He had known what and who she was. He had to have. And all he mentioned was she was an athlete and "gym rat."

Steel went blindly into this whole thing thinking he had to protect some figure skater or dancer. Or, *fuck*, some girly sport competitor. A girl, or even a woman, who would be scared and, because of that, would listen and be easy to protect.

But fuck no.

He pulled up his text app and sent one to Diesel: *Fuckn asshole.*

The boss man texted back almost immediately. *Yeah, U R.*

————

Kat's stomach growled, but she refused to go back downstairs to make herself something to eat.

Not yet.

If she was lucky, the man who was tasked with "babysitting" her would simply disappear. At twenty-nine, as well as a champion MMA fighter, she didn't need his help since she was capable of taking care of herself.

Always had been. Always will be.

Berger was being paranoid. She'd had this stalker for months. While, yes, he'd done some criminal or obscene things to material objects, like her car, her apartment, her...

panties, he had plenty of opportunities to confront her in person and he hadn't.

Kat leaned her head back against the wicker chair, kicked her bare feet up on the matching ottoman, letting her gaze drift across the pool below to the lake in the distance.

This wasn't her dream home. Hell, this wasn't even her home. Even though it wasn't her style, she liked it. It was peaceful and the view soothed her nerves. Especially when she got up early to watch the sunrise.

Which was pretty much every morning since she was sleeping like shit.

She was tired of moving, changing phone numbers, wondering if someone would be hiding in the back seat of her car. Or now her rental car. She hadn't owned a car in months since she had to keep switching them out.

It was a pain in her fucking ass. And the detective needed a fire lit under him to get this solved.

It shouldn't have even gotten this far. If it wasn't for "the stalker" breaking into her last apartment and leaving his DNA all over her bed, along with a note on her pillow, then Berger never would have hired a bodyguard.

This house was her third place in a matter of nine months. And her third gym. It was wearing on Berger, too, since he kept having to relocate with her, and his wife wasn't thrilled about it.

Not only that, he was losing clients because he had to leave them behind to stick with her. That wasn't fair to him or his clients, and she hadn't asked that of him. However, they'd been a team for years. Berger began training her when he was still competing himself. He noticed her at an amateur match and approached her, telling Kat she possessed a natural ability and the classes she was taking weren't doing her a service. She needed real training with someone more experienced.

Next thing she knew, she was competing more often and,

once Berger retired from fighting and had more time to concentrate on her, he slipped easily into becoming her manager, too. He began arranging fights and sparring partners, courting sponsors and everything else needed to succeed in her career. Which was a lot.

She knew with the money she made, she was his main bread and butter. Because of that, Berger stuck with her and was also overly protective of her, which was why he hired a bossy babysitter.

A babysitter who was a complete dick.

She sighed. Dick or not, she couldn't avoid him forever by hiding in her room.

To make Berger happy, she would just deal with Steel being her shadow for the next few days. Hopefully, it wasn't longer than that. Otherwise, he was going to get on her nerves.

She tensed and kept her eyes on the lake in the distance when one of the French doors behind her opened and the subject of her thoughts stepped out.

She sucked in a breath, then tried to blow out her annoyance.

It failed.

"Think we need to set a rule," she murmured as she heard the door close.

"Think you forgot that I'm the boss of you until this is over."

She bit back her initial knee-jerk reaction and decided it was best to ignore his statement. "My bedroom's off limits. It'll be my sanctuary while you're here. You don't just walk in and do what you please."

"There's no part of this house—or your life, for that matter—that's off limits to me. That's the rule."

Her sport was full of men, some of them quite arrogant. She tried to avoid those who were. Unfortunately, it would be impossible to avoid the one behind her.

Unless she sent him packing.

Anson Sterling, aka "Steel," stepped in front of her chair and leaned back against the intricate wrought iron balcony railing.

She lifted her gaze from his bare feet and defined calves, his loose navy knee-length shorts and up his torso, pausing at the outline of his dog tags under his white "wife-beater" type tank top.

Apparently, he'd made himself at home and got comfortable.

With his hands braced behind him on the railing, she studied the way his muscles bulged in his bare arms and broad shoulders.

If the man had an ounce of fat on him, she'd be surprised.

His body looked intimidating and powerful, and she doubted he had a difficult time in the ring.

Maybe she'd get a chance to see him fight. She was sure he was impressive. But she suspected he was more power than grace.

Why were her thoughts leading her there? Why did she even care? That annoyed her more than him invading her personal space. "My bedroom is my private area. If you're going to stick to me like glue, I'll need some alone time."

"For what?"

She lifted her gaze higher, letting it slide along his tightly bearded jaw, over his lips and nose.

His nose had been broken at least once. Though, it wasn't badly crooked. Whoever set it, did it well and the average person probably couldn't tell at first it had been broken.

Kat could tell.

His eyes were a deep brown, his hair trimmed super short on the sides, just as short as his dark beard, but the top was longer. Long enough for a woman to run her fingers through it.

A woman who was not her.

His expression, which had been serious when he first stepped in front of her, now looked amused.

*Whatever.*

"I don't want to have to worry about you catching me undressed. I wouldn't want for you to embarrass yourself."

One side of his mouth lifted slightly. "There's no chance of that."

"Of seeing me naked?"

"Of me being embarrassed." He tilted his head. "The human body can be a beautiful thing."

"I take it you look at naked men a lot while in the locker room?"

The other side of his mouth curved up. "I appreciate a woman's body more."

Of course he did.

"How about respecting my privacy?"

"As soon as you give respect to me. Kat, let's get something else straight while we're setting boundaries. You don't need to like me. You just need to respect me."

"No, Steel, that's where you're wrong. I don't need to respect you. You need to earn it. And you don't earn it by encroaching on my personal space or dismissing my concerns."

"I have a job to do and I'm going to do it. Again, I don't give a shit if you don't like it... or me. But failure is not in my vocabulary, so I'm going to do what I have to do to make sure that doesn't happen. *Capisce?*"

She rolled her eyes before letting her gaze settle past him on a distant mountain. After minutes of silence, he shifted, but didn't move from where he leaned.

"Are you just going to stand there guarding me like I'm some breakable Ming vase? It's creepier than my stalker."

"I came in here to check on you and figured it couldn't hurt to get to know you a little bit since we're stuck with each other."

*Great.*

"You make enough scratch doing what you do to live here? Those cars, too?"

*Doing what you do...*

He continued, "And on that fucking note, this isn't the best place to be living with all these big windows. Anyone can be peeping in."

"I take it you finally did your research."

"Asked you a question."

"Technically you asked me two."

"Then I expect two answers."

Once again, she bit back her initial response. But it was a struggle. "I make good scratch, as you call it. But no, I can't afford this house or those cars."

"Then, is this your man's house?"

Her man? Was he the type who thought women couldn't survive without a man? Probably. Those were the type no matter what you did to prove them wrong, it didn't matter. You were always a helpless female.

"If you have to know, it's one of my sponsors. They were kind enough to let me borrow it since I can't stay anywhere for long. This is the third place I've moved into temporarily. And honestly, I'm fucking sick of moving. I'm tired of hiding and looking over my shoulder." *Fuck,* she didn't mean to let that last slip. She had done well at hiding her worry from Berger.

"Stalkers like to wear their victims down."

"No shit. I'm past worn down."

"After seeing you spar, I told Berger you could take care of yourself."

*Huh.* She didn't expect that from anyone, especially him. Maybe he'd decided to give her a little respect finally. "I can protect myself if the threat is face to face. Hard to do that when the man sticks to the shadows."

"Again, what do you know about real fighting? What you do isn't real."

So much for the split second of respect. "It's not, huh?" If he was trying to get to "know" her, insulting her was not the way to do it.

"No, and I can say that because I also do the same shit. What I do in the ring is not what I do in the field."

"The field?"

He jerked his chin up slightly, indicating her. "These assignments. Real life shit. Uncontrolled. The fight isn't stopped because of a bell or an injury. What happens out there?" He jerked his head toward beyond the balcony. "No cage. No bells. No time limits. No refs. No trainer. It's you fighting for your fucking life."

"I'm sure Google told you all about me and my skills."

He said nothing. She was right. He did exactly what she expected, some quick research when she had pointed out he hadn't prepared.

And he didn't seem the type to like being called out on it.

"I didn't dig that deep yet," he finally admitted.

"Be careful you don't fall into that hole while you're digging, it might be deeper than you think," she murmured.

Her attention was drawn back to him when he crossed his arms over his chest, making his thick biceps bunch. His skin was getting slick from sweat.

He wasn't used to this climate.

"You should go inside." *And get off my balcony and out of my room. And while you're at it, leave this house, the neighborhood and Nevada.*

He wiped a hand over his brow. "How can you stand this fucking heat?"

She lifted one shoulder like living in the devil's oven was

no big deal. "I'm used to it. It's bearable at this time of year, it's much worse in summer."

"Thank fuck this job will be over long before summer."

Yes, *thank fuck* for that.

"You grow up here in Nevada?"

How much should she give him? "Indiana." He could find that out easily enough on the internet once he started digging deeper, if he even took the time to do so.

"No deserts in Indiana," he said.

"No men just walking into my bedroom in Indiana, either. *Capisce*?"

"No men at all? You like pussy? 'Cause, just saying, you look like a dyke with that haircut."

He was purposely trying to get her riled up. Why? "You a dick? 'Cause, just saying, you act like a dick." She rose from the chair. "And now... since you won't leave my room, I will."

Before she could turn, he grabbed her. She stared at his fingers tightly circling her wrist, then lifted her eyes until they hit his. "Two things I won't tolerate you doing without permission. You walking into my room like you did and you touching me like you're currently doing." She jerked her arm, but he didn't release her.

"Women aren't born to be fighters. They're supposed to be the gentler sex. Women like you have a reason to fight. You got Daddy issues, Kitty Kat?"

*Women like you.*

It was her father all over again.

Women weren't supposed to be tough.

Women weren't supposed to be fighters.

They were supposed to be accommodating. Sweet and gentle. Obedient.

"Did your Daddy hurt you?"

A thick band tightened around Kat's chest. "Anyone else

ever tell you you're an asshole?" It was probably his middle name.

"Every damn day."

It was like he was proud of it. "Why's that? Do you have Mommy issues, *Anson*? Did she nurse you until you were ten? Do you still miss sucking on that tit?"

The fucker grinned.

None of this was funny. She wasn't finding it even the slightest bit entertaining and there was no way she could deal with him another minute. "You're fired."

His fingers squeezed even tighter around her wrist and his grin disappeared. "You didn't hire me, so you can't fire me."

"Bullshit. I'm paying you."

"Your manager is paying my boss. I don't want to be here, and you don't want me here, so it's mutual, Kat."

She jerked her arm again, harder this time, but his fingers were digging deep into her flesh. "I'm calling Berger."

"You fucking do that. But know this, you won't get someone better than me to protect your ass. I guarantee it. I've been protecting people for a long fucking time. Most men have a fucking conscience and will hesitate before doing the unthinkable, and that split second could mean your life or death."

*Life or death.*

He had said he could snap someone's neck in one twist. Now he was saying he would do that or whatever was necessary to protect her.

She was sure if she called Berger and had him fired, her manager would just hire someone else. And it was her guess that most alpha-male, Neanderthal-type bodyguards were dicks.

"You'd kill someone if my life was threatened?"

He deflected her question with a question. "Would you?"

"Your life? No. Mine? Yes," she answered truthfully.

"That's what makes us different and proves I'm capable for this job. For me, the answer to both of those questions is yes."

She wondered how honest that answer was. She also wondered if his nickname had anything to do with his ability to callously kill someone. Well, since they were getting to know each other... "Why Steel?"

His eyelids lowered just a tad and his face softened. "Got a set of them."

He thought he was such a fucking charmer. He probably had no problem talking women into his bed. But she was sure he had a problem with them staying. A woman could only deal with an asshole for so long, no matter how good the dick. "Do you want me to test that theory?"

His fingers flexed on her wrist. "How about you just take my word for it."

She lifted one shoulder. "Thought you might like a challenge since you think you've got a set of steel balls."

"I'll show you mine if you show me yours," Steel said. "I can guarantee mine are bigger."

"Why? Are they infected?"

Using her wrist, he pulled her closer and dropped his head until their faces were just inches apart. "If you want to challenge me at every turn, go ahead. I like a good challenge in and out of bed, Kitty Kat. But I can tell you any challenge you lay at my feet, I'm going to win. You think you're tough, but I can guarantee I'm tougher."

"You make a lot of guarantees, *Steel*."

"That's because I can."

"You're also very cocky."

"So are you, which again makes me think, especially with that short hair, you might like pussy."

"Because I'm not fawning all over you?" She jerked her arm again and this time he released her and she fell back a half-step. "And if I did, what would it matter? You keep saying you're here to do a job. So, Steel, do your fucking job. And by the way, who I fuck is none of your business."

She turned and shoved the door open, slamming it closed behind her before he could follow.

She picked up her pace when she heard the French door burst open, slam shut and his heavy footsteps following her. She moved as fast as she could without breaking into a jog, but he caught her out in the hall with a hand to the back of the neck.

With her heart racing, she spun on him, using her elbow to break his hold and took two steps back. He took two steps forward and she did not like the look in his dark eyes as he bumped her with his chest until her back was to the wall. Then he went toe to toe with her, not quite touching but close. Close enough she could feel his heat searing her and his warm breath on her parted lips.

"You're right, who you let lick your pussy doesn't affect my job one way or the other," he growled. "What I give a fuck about is you listening."

She did her best to steady her breathing, not wanting to give him any indication on how he affected her. "Are you done?"

"Are you going to listen?"

Kat pinned her lips together, avoided his eyes and then gave him a single nod. She'd agree just so he'd leave her the hell alone. "The sooner this is over, the better."

"Agreed." He stepped back and stared at her for a few moments, then said, "I'm starving. I Googled the closest Thai restaurant and they're delivering. Do we need to meet the driver at the gate?"

The sudden switch in topic made her head spin. This man was certainly going to keep her on her toes. "No, the guard will let them in." She also hated the fact that Thai food was one of her favorites. *Damn it.*

"Well, that's assuring. Any whack job just needs to say they're a pizza delivery driver and they're in."

"They could also just walk through the unguarded gate at the west entrance."

He dropped his head back and blew out a breath. "Great. So, this neighborhood isn't secure at all."

"Most aren't."

"No, but having a guard posted at any entrance is somewhat of a deterrent. Even if they're ninety years old." He stepped back. "At least the house has a decent security system. Don't go outside unless I'm with you."

"Even to use the pool?"

"Is the pool outside?"

Kat ground her teeth and shoved away from the wall. And like he did to her in the garage, she made sure to bump into him as she pushed past him.

## Chapter Four

STEEL SAT on the plush leather couch, his feet kicked up on the fancy schmancy coffee table, his Mac in his lap and the large overpriced TV hanging on the wall tuned to a sports channel. He had the volume turned low because the sports news was about a variety of sports—not just ones he was interested in—and some of those bored the fuck out of him.

Tapping a small white ball into a hole didn't get his blood pumping.

Though, right now, his veins were thumping but not over golf. His eyes scanned the emails that Jewel had forwarded to him and the rest of the team.

So far, no one else had responded. But then, it would take a while to sort through all the shit the boss lady had sent.

Steel downloaded all the attachments, which he assumed were the scanned copies of the notes left behind. He wanted to read them all in order to see if they escalated as they went. Luckily, Jewelee had marked the attachments and emails by chronological order.

He pulled up the first letter, which had been mailed with no return address to her condo outside of Los Angeles.

*My sweet Katheryn,*

*You don't know me yet, but you will. I have to confess, you've caught my eye. The moment I saw you I knew you were the one for me. My forever. My soulmate. I'm sure of it. And since you don't know me, I'll give us some time to get to know each other first. I'll continue to watch you and you can read my letters.*

*Then the day we meet face to face, we'll already know every-thing about each other.*

*It'll be perfect.*

*Until then...*

*All my love,*

*H.*

His sweet Katheryn.

*Sweet.* Steel snorted.

The letter wasn't dated, but the email indicated that it was received about a year ago.

A whole fucking year. This bastard had been stalking Kat a whole year. How she kept her shit together, he had no idea.

Physical and mental strength were two different things. Yeah, she was physically strong, but this had to wear on her mentally.

He was surprised she went as far as admitting it to him upstairs. Especially since Berger had given no indication that was true.

She was keeping it from her manager. That's why. She probably didn't want her life or career to be controlled by a stranger.

So, she continued forward like a good soldier and kept moving. However, the bastard managed to find her.

How?

She was in the public eye, but still... If he sent the letters to where she worked out or competed, that would be one thing, but he sent letters to her second apartment, too. An apartment with the rental agreement not even in her name. An address that certainly hadn't been publicized.

He read another letter "H" had left at her original condo in California.

*My sweet Katheryn,*

*I love watching you. You are so intelligent, beautiful and have the perfect figure. You would make a great mother for my children. When I think you're ready, I'll stop by when you're home and say hello. For now, I'll court you with gifts in hopes that when I come forward, you'll give me a chance to show you how much I love you.*

*I can't wait until the day we're together forever.*

*Until then...*

*All my love,*

*H.*

Steel wondered what the gift had been that accompanied the letter. Probably something with his cum on it.

He read one more. One that had been left in the apartment she'd rented outside of Las Vegas after she fled California.

*My sweet Katheryn,*

*I'm upset you moved so far away. It's such a long trip to come visit you, my love.*

*You probably think I'm crazy. I admit I am. I'm crazy in love with you.*

*Please don't move again. It makes my life much more difficult.*

*Until we're together forever, my sweet Katheryn...*

*All my love,*

*H.*

He skimmed through a few more, but there were so many, and like Berger said, "H" started emailing Kat through her website's contact page. Between emails and physical letters, there were dozens. He wondered how many Kat threw out from either frustration or anger. Or not taking this sick fuck seriously at first.

*My sweet Katheryn,*

*I am so in love with you. I hope you love the presents I leave you. I will give those to you in person soon. My hope is that those "gifts" will eventually give us the gift of life. We would make the perfect children together.*

*I only want what's best for you. And that's me. No one will ever love you like I do. No one will ever take care of you like I do. Please meet me at...*

"H" gave an address to a coffee shop somewhere in Vegas. Of course, she didn't meet him. Jewel's email stated the police had been sent instead, but they couldn't identify "H." And, of course, there was an emailed response from the man afterward.

*I waited four hours for you, my sweet Katheryn. You stood me up. Why are you ignoring me? Maybe I'll just come to your apartment. I only want to talk. I need to explain. I just want you to hear how much I love you.*

*Please just talk to me. Let me prove my love.*

That seemed to be the point where she came home to her apartment broken into and found cum all over her bed with a note left behind on the pillow which read, in part...

*You know by now just how much I love you, my sweet Katheryn. But after all these months, all my love letters and gifts, you continue to ignore me.*

And that's when she moved to her current location. This fucking monster house owned by a sponsor.

After the Thai had been delivered earlier, she'd taken a plateful and went back up to her room. He was tempted to force her to eat with him, but he figured it would just make everything worse.

She didn't want him there. He got it.

But she didn't have a choice.

And the more he read what the stalker wrote, Steel knew that "H" wasn't just going to go away. Eventually his stalking would come to a head and Kat could get hurt or killed. The man was unstable, as were all stalkers.

He heard a noise in the kitchen and twisted his neck to listen. She most likely brought her plate back down and he waited to see if she would join him.

After he heard nothing else from the kitchen after a few minutes, he figured she'd gone back upstairs.

Tomorrow would be a new day and hopefully a new attitude. He'd give her tonight since she needed time to get used to him being around and to face the fact he wasn't going anywhere until this was over and she was safe. Or until Diesel ordered him home.

And he didn't give a fuck if she liked it or not.

———

KAT SLID to a stop in the entryway to the kitchen, then quickly backed up so she wouldn't be seen.

The smell of coffee wafted over, and her eyes practically rolled in ecstasy. She slept like shit again last night. Even with her bulldog of a bodyguard a few doors down from her room.

That bulldog was now standing in front of the stove with his back to her, again in one of those white wife-beater type tanks.

She heard sizzling from the frying pan, and it smelled almost as good as the coffee.

She pressed a hand to her stomach when it protested loudly.

"Good time to tell you that I have eyes at the back of my head."

Kat cursed silently. They had a couple of hours before she was due to meet Berger at The Strike Zone, so she could conceivably go back upstairs until he was done with his breakfast.

"You can't keep avoiding me."

*Fuck*, it was like the man could read her thoughts, too.

"I can try" was on the tip of her tongue. But she bit it back and entered the kitchen instead, heading directly to the coffeemaker and grabbing a mug out of the cabinet above it.

"Help yourself," his deep voice rumbled.

"I will, since it's my coffee."

"Your sponsor didn't pay for that, too?"

"Are you jealous, Steel? You're not good enough in the ring for a sponsor?"

"I no longer fight in those types of venues."

"What types of venues do you fight in?"

He shut off the burner and turned, his eyes immediately raking down her body.

Kat did her best not to react. Instead, she stood there, preparing her coffee and ignoring his heated gaze.

"That's what you sleep in?"

She fought the urge to glance down at herself, instead she lifted the mug to her lips. She was wearing what she typically wore around the house. A sports bra and shorts. This morning she'd rolled the waistband of her gray fleece shorts down almost to her hip bones because they gapped too much at her waist.

"You don't know what I slept in last night? I figured you'd sneak into my bedroom and sit in the corner watching me."

"You would've known if I did because you were probably awake."

How did he know she wasn't sleeping?

"I have good instincts, Kat, it's why I'm good at what I do."

"You mean being a legal creepy stalker instead of a criminal one?"

He pursed his lips as he studied her, catching her off guard when he suddenly changed the subject. Again. Typical boxer, keeping her on her toes. "Do you only wear sports bras? Just so you know, they're not flattering for your tits."

She didn't wear them to be flattering. "They're comfortable. That's all that matters to me."

"The hair. The sports bras. No makeup. Not even lip gloss. Again, makes me think you like to eat pussy."

*Jesus.* This man must have constant fantasies of two women together. He probably thought he was man enough to handle two at once.

"Did you lie in bed imagining that last night?" When he didn't answer, she asked, "And anyway, what do you know about lip gloss?"

"More than you, apparently. I also know what it looks like when it leaves a ring around my cock."

"I bet you know what herpes looks like, too."

He unexpectedly jerked forward and she froze. But all he did was grab a plate sitting on the counter and turn back to the stove.

He was good at letting things roll off him. But then, so was she. And if pushed, she could out-asshole him.

She took another sip of coffee—at least he knew how to make it—and watched the muscles in his shoulders and arms flex as he scooped whatever he had in the pan onto his plate.

She dropped her gaze to the dish when he turned.

"That's what you're eating? Just an egg white omelet?" He had added veggies to it but no cheese. How boring.

"Yeah, my body is a temple. But I'm also having coffee and," he picked up a banana off the counter as he passed it, "this. You wanna banana?" He held it down low, almost at his crotch.

Kat didn't miss his intent. But she wasn't going to let him fluster her, either. So, she snagged it from his hand, peeled one end and lifted it.

His brown eyes followed every movement she made and he now stared at the tip of the banana held just a hairsbreadth from her lips.

His eyes narrowed and his own tongue flicked across his bottom lip, leaving moisture behind.

And he waited.

So did she.

Did she dare?

Yes, fuck him. If he wanted to be a jerk, two could play at that game.

She flicked the end of the banana with the tip of her tongue, tasting the slight sweetness. Then she touched it again, more intently this time.

And... one more time, sweeping her tongue across the end.

His nostrils flared and so did his eyes.

Dropping her eyelids low, she stuck her tongue out and ran the tip of the fruit down it, then closed her mouth, making sure he could see her swirling her tongue around the end of the banana.

An audible rush of air escaped him, but he didn't move.

He was watching her mouth so closely, she continued to work it, letting a small groan bubble up from the back of her throat.

She had him in her palm. Because of that, she smiled

around the banana, opened her mouth wider and bit the end off between her teeth.

She continued to chew as he winced, and his hips jerked back just the slightest bit.

"Fuck," he groaned.

"Was it as good for you as it was for me?" she asked after swallowing the mouthful of fruit.

"I figured you preferred a halved peach," he grumbled and moved over to the table, putting his plate down.

As he came closer, she stepped out of his way so he could grab a mug and fill it. He snagged two more bananas off the counter before settling in at the table.

"Seriously, is that all you're going to eat?"

"You have something else for me to eat?" he asked, his tone holding all kinds of suggestions.

She was glad he wasn't looking because heat had slipped into her cheeks. She hadn't blushed in a long damn time.

She couldn't let this man get to her.

She finished off the banana, went to the fridge, grabbed the eggs and an angus T-bone she had picked up at the butcher in town.

She turned on the gas under the built-in grill on the Viking stove and they ignored each other the twenty minutes it took for her to grill her steak to rare and cook her eggs just how she liked them. The whites firm, the yolks runny.

She took her breakfast over to the table and slapped half of her steak onto his now empty plate. "You're welcome."

He stared at the steak for a second, then lifted his head to watch her settle into the seat across from him. "How do you know I'm not a vegetarian?"

"Because there was chicken in your Thai last night."

"How do you know I'm not a chickatarian?"

Kat blinked. "You mean pollotarian?"

"Yeah, that. Something you're not because you like your meat. Preferably in a taco, right?"

"Jesus, Steel, we haven't even known each other twenty-four hours, can you give the sexual innuendos a break?"

"What sexual innuendos?" he asked with a grin, getting out of his seat and grabbing a steak knife from the wood knife block on the counter. He was still grinning when he dug into his steak.

"Good?" she asked around a mouthful.

"Fuck yes. Fuck those egg whites." He cut off a bite of steak and leaned across the table to dip it into one of her runny yokes.

"Hey!"

He popped the piece into his mouth and moaned. "You're on breakfast duty from now on."

"What about your temple?"

"I'll rebuild it when I get back to Pennsylvania."

She doubted eating steak was going to destroy his physique. Or that he'd even let it go to shit in the first place. Especially when she spent a minimum of two hours a day, five days a week at the gym. Sometimes up to four hours or more when a fight was coming up.

If the man was going to stick to her like "glue," he'd get in plenty of gym time while she did. And his body did nothing but scream that the man loved working out.

She had said yesterday he wasn't hard to look at. She hadn't been lying. He might be an asshole, but he was one hell of a hot one.

He sat back after scarfing down his steak and sucked at his teeth, drawing her out of her thoughts. "You don't have any toothpicks."

"I don't use toothpicks."

"We need to grab some when we go wherever we're going today."

"The gym."

"Okay, on our way to the gym, we need to stop."

54

"If you have shit stuck in your teeth, I'd suggest flossing them."

"Still need to pick some up."

She lifted and dropped one shoulder and concentrated on her plate. She didn't look up when he pushed away from the table.

Good. She'd get to finish eating in peace.

But no, just a few seconds later, he was back, putting a full mug of coffee in front of himself but also in front of her.

She hadn't even seen him swipe her mug.

*Son of a bitch.* He was making nice. He must want something.

Which was probably why he was staring at her while she tried to eat. She struggled to swallow a bite of steak.

"What time are we leaving?"

She poked at the egg on her plate with the fork. "We need to be there at ten."

"How long will we be there?"

Kat lifted her gaze to his. "You have a date?"

"Just trying to have conversation."

"Why?"

"Because we're going to be living together for who knows how long."

"Hopefully, not long," she said under her breath.

"You have a problem with men?"

"Just assholes," she said louder and shoved a piece of egg into her mouth.

"You don't think this stalker is anyone you know, right? Not some man you called an asshole?"

"I call it as I see it." She sucked in a breath to continue, but thought better of it and sighed instead. She was being an asshole, too, and she hated that he made her act that way. "No, I don't think it's anyone I know."

"An old boyfriend? Girlfriend? Someone whose heart you broke?"

"No."

"Anyone you've crossed paths with who seemed a little 'off?' Someone who stood out to you before this all began?"

She placed her fork on the plate and sat back. "I meet a lot of people. I've trained in many different gyms. I've traveled to competitions and bouts. I've done speeches at schools and martial arts schools, community centers. No one stood out to me."

"Do you have enemies?"

She shrugged one shoulder. "Maybe opponents who've lost to me? But it's rare I run across anyone who is pissed they've lost to the point of acting out like this. And we know it's not a woman."

"Because of the cum he's left."

"I mean, I guess it's possible a woman could collect it and... leave it in places."

"Like your bed."

"But I doubt it."

"Why?"

"Because I had photos texted to me."

He shifted in his chair, his attention going from casual to intense. "What kind of photos?"

"The time he broke into my apartment and left that bounty of creamy goodness? He also texted me a picture of him while he did the act itself. Of course, there was nothing identifiable in the photo." Just a gloved hand and a hard dick. Average sized and circumcised.

"How come I didn't see that photo?"

"Because I deleted it."

"The cops didn't even see it?"

"No. I didn't think, I just..." She pulled a long breath in through her nose and slowly released it. "I just got rid of it." She knew now that was stupid, but at the time she was too disturbed to keep it. It had been instinct to delete it immediately.

"It creeped you out."

"Of course."

"Did you tell the detective?"

"Yes. They said they were going to contact the cell phone company and see if they could retrieve it as evidence." She kept imagining a police lineup of men with erections so she could identify her stalker. She took a sip of her coffee, but this conversation and the memory was turning her stomach sour. "Whoever it is just wants me to be running scared."

"Why does he want you running scared?"

"Maybe so I have to back out of fights. It's probably just a bunch of bullshit to intimidate me."

"It's not bullshit if you're getting threats and had to fucking move."

"That was on Berg. Better be safe than sorry is his bull-shit mantra. I make him too much money for him to lose me."

"Your competition is women and you just said you didn't think it was a woman. We know it's not if you had the photo proof."

"But a lot of us have men trainers, managers, brothers, fathers... whatever. You know, people who have dicks."

"So, you *do* think it's someone you know."

*Jesus.* He was annoying her with all his questions. And making her head hurt. She pushed her plate away. "No. I don't know who the fuck it is."

"This bothers you more than you'd like."

"No shit."

"That's why you're not sleeping."

He was way too observant and if she lied, he'd most likely know. "I hate that it's controlling my life. I hate running scared."

"Kat, never underestimate a threat. You wouldn't in the ring, so why do it outside of it?"

"Because like I said, I hate that it's controlling my life."

"And you like control."

"Don't you?"

"Yeah, I like control," he murmured.

There was something about the way he said it that sent a shiver sliding down her spine. She quickly pushed away from the table and stood.

She did not want to explore how him saying that made her feel.

No fucking way.

If he knew her thoughts right now, he'd know she was definitely not a lesbian.

## Chapter Five

THE WHOLE TIME Kat was doing her thing with Berger in the other room, Steel did a bunch of cardio in between sets to work his back, arms and chest just to burn off some tension. Working up a good sweat would do that for him.

Usually.

He had his earbuds in as he listened to one of his numerous workout playlists. The current list was all '80s heavy metal. Even though he couldn't hear Kat sparring or doing whatever drills Berger was making her run through, he always made sure he could keep his eye on not only the entrance to the gym but the open doorway to the area where she was training.

But once again, the gym was dead, and any movement would catch his eye. Like the blonde college chick at the front desk pushing out her chest, flipping her hair around and chewing her gum like a fucking cow as she watched him work out.

She had even went as far as "accidentally" knocking something off the rear counter of the circular desk area and going out around to pick it up. Then bending over with excruciating slowness to make sure Steel did not miss that display.

While she had a nice ass, it wasn't Kat's ass. And even if it was, he wasn't touching a college girl with even the thought of going there.

Fuck no, his thoughts were on the woman—not girl—inside that room. Her shorts and sports bra this morning didn't leave much to the imagination. Even though the sports bra flattened her tits to her chest, her nipples pressing against the stretchy cotton were hard to miss. And while her slight V of muscle that ran inside her hip bones—what was called an Adonis Belt on a man—might not turn on men in general, it had flipped all kinds of switches within him. He found it hard to swallow steak when all he could think of was running his tongue along the ridge that led to something even better below it.

He almost fell off the treadmill when he tried to picture her naked in his bed. That gave his heart a better workout than his cardio routine.

It also sent the blood running south. And while he wore long shorts, they were silky and clingy enough to advertise the result of his fantasy. The last thing he wanted was the gum-snapping co-ed thinking it was for her.

Something was certainly snapping, and it wasn't gum when Kat exited the room, a sheen of sweat making her tan skin shine. Her hair was once again soaked, but rose in spikes, like she'd run her fingers through it to unstick it from her noggin.

Without a glance in his direction, she moved to the other side of the gym, threw her towel on the seat of a rowing machine and, after a few adjustments, began to row. She kept her attention forward and concentrated on her form.

Which looked good.

Steel was mesmerized by her smooth movements, her legs pushing powerfully as the seat slid back and forth on the track, her arms bending and flexing with each pull. She had to have set the tension high on the machine for her to be working that hard.

After watching her for a good ten minutes, she got off, wiped the machine down and then moved over to the free weights.

And fuck him, if she didn't pick up two ten-pound dumbbells and start doing squats. Not only that, she was doing it right in front of a mirror. He got an almost three-sixty view of her going down low and pushing back up.

Going down low...

Pushing back up.

*Fuck.* Going down...

He closed his eyes and pictured her squatting over his cock.

The clearing of a throat had him lurching so hard he had to catch the treadmill's handrails to keep from falling backwards and landing on the floor on his ass.

He frowned at Berger for interrupting his live-action fantasy. He also hoped his compass wasn't pointing north.

He shut the machine down and stepped off. Though maybe he should've stayed on since Kat's manager was a good inch taller than him. Staying on the treadmill would've given Steel the upper hand.

"She done soon?" Steel asked as if he hadn't just imagined the man's client naked and riding his cock.

"I'm done with her for the day. I'm sure she'll let you know when she's ready to go. But that's not why I need to talk to you."

Steel's attention flipped from Kat's ass of steel...

*Fuck*, he liked that. His name on her ass.

Berger cleared his throat again.

*Damn it.*

"Let's hear it," Steel muttered, preparing for Berger to

rip him a new one, figuring Kat aired her grievances about him to her manager.

What Berger said next surprised him, even though it shouldn't have. "The website got another email last night from our friend, H."

*Fuck.* Persistent motherfucker, wasn't he? "You have it on your phone?"

"No."

"Is it bad?"

"No worse than the rest. Though, he's frustrated he has no idea where she is."

Well, that was good to know. That bought the detective a little more time to find the bastard.

"But he also made it clear he was determined to find her again. And soon."

Of course. "Forward it to the detective and me ASAP."

"Right." Berger mumbled, then turned to walk away.

"Hey, Berger."

Kat's manager stopped and glanced back over his shoulder.

"Does she have any fights coming up soon?"

"One. A big one."

"How soon?"

"In two weeks."

"Where?"

"Luckily, Vegas. That's why I moved her in this direction. Close but not too close."

And, of course, a big sponsor happened to have a house locally. Steel was sure that helped influence Berger's decision.

"Is it a championship fight?"

Berger turned around and shook his blond head. "No. But she's fighting Jayne Edwards."

*Hell*, even Steel had heard of her. "Calamity Jayne."

"Yes."

"Isn't she undefeated?"

"She is. That's why Kat wants to fight her."

Steel's eyebrows pinned together. "Are they in the same class?"

"No, and not even in the same organization. Jayne's a featherweight in the UFC, but she challenged Kat publicly and Kat accepted it, even though she's a weight class lower."

Why would Kat want to fight a woman who was bigger than her *and* undefeated in her own class? What did she have to prove? "Do you think she can win?"

"It's possible, but win or lose, she's going to make a lot money on this fight. It's not only in Vegas, it's pay-per-view."

*Win or lose, she's going to make a lot money on this fight.*

Kat didn't seem to be all about the prize money, but maybe Berger was. He'd make a good chunk of change either way. What bugged Steel was that Berger wasn't positive she could win the fight. "And this is only two weeks away?"

"Yes."

"Are you doing anything different with her training?"

"As you saw yesterday and today, she's sparring with men."

"Are these men she's sparring with holding back?" Of course, they were. If he said otherwise, he was lying.

"I told them not to."

Which meant they were. "I'm going to be her partner starting tomorrow until the fight."

Berger frowned. "That's unnecessary."

"That wasn't a suggestion."

"It sure sounded like a suggestion, since I'm not only her manager but her trainer."

"And I'm her bodyguard. I'm capable of being a good sparring partner and I won't baby her."

"What's your weight?"

"Two-oh-two."

"Steel, she's a buck thirty."

"And I'll take that into consideration when we spar."

"I don't want her risking injury with full contact sparring."

"You'd rather have her ass kicked in the cage? In front of millions of people? What's she gonna make if she wins?"

"They're the main event so she's not only getting paid to enter the cage, but she's getting a 'fight of the night' bonus."

"And if she wins?"

"Add another fifty on top of that."

Steel whistled. Kat could walk away with a hundred and fifty big ones in one night. *If* she won.

"Is it normally that much?" Maybe he was in the wrong line of work and he needed to fight professionally.

"No. Again, this is a special event. Though, with her championship fights, she rakes in that and sometimes more if she wins. Plus, winning the belt ensures her endorsements and good sponsors."

"Which means you're making good scratch off her."

Berger tilted his head and studied Steel before answering, "I earn my salary."

"I'm sure you do, Berger," he muttered.

"I'll forward you that email," Berger threw over his shoulder as he turned and strode away.

"You do that."

Steel barely heard, "And you keep her safe," as Berger pushed out of the door into the Nevada afternoon heat.

"And that's why you pay me the big bucks," Steel muttered under his breath. He turned to see where Kat was. She was standing in the same spot but was no longer doing squats.

No, she was standing there and had most likely watched the whole exchange between her manager and her bodyguard in the mirror. She might have even overheard some of the conversation.

Kat jerked into motion when their eyes met in the mirror and she beelined toward the women's locker room.

Steel moved to stand guard outside of it until she was done. Because that was why he was getting paid the big bucks.

———

HE HADN'T SHOWERED at the gym because he didn't want to leave Kat alone and he doubted she wanted to accompany him into the men's locker room. Or have him join her in the women's.

So, he waited.

Now it was late afternoon and after spending an extraordinary long time in the shower—for reasons no one else needed to know—he headed downstairs to see where she was. He had checked her room on his way down, thinking she'd be holed up in there, but she wasn't. Both her room and balcony—her so-called "sanctuary" away from him—were empty.

Maybe she was making him a late afternoon snack.

He snorted as he jogged down the curved stairway, thinking she'd be the perfect woman if she was not only a master in the kitchen but one in bed.

And she grew out her hair.

Though, he had to admit, two days in and her short hair was growing on him. He still preferred long hair so he could fist it while he was taking a woman from behind. Or while she was sucking his cock.

He adjusted himself before he hit the landing and headed straight for the kitchen, disappointed he didn't smell anything cooking.

The kitchen was empty, too.

He cruised through the living room, the library and the

entertainment room, which were all deserted. Now his temper was rising and his feet were moving faster. "Kat!"

He paused, turned his head slightly and listened.

Nothing.

His heart began to thump, and he mentally took a tour through the large home to figure out what room she might be apt to hang out in. If not her bedroom or the entertainment room where the TV was, then where?

Had she left in the rental? Or one of the expensive sports cars?

He rushed to the garage and was relieved to see all three vehicles still tucked in their spots where they belonged.

Kat was the only occupant not where she belonged.

Which was in the house.

Especially after he instructed her not to go outside without him. His fingers twitched with the urge to teach her a lesson about disobeying his direct orders. Though, he'd probably enjoy that "lesson" more than she'd learn anything by it.

He headed to the French doors that led out to the pool. Not even the slightest disturbance could be seen in the water. Not a splash, not a ripple, nothing.

Did that fucker find her and snag her right from under his fucking nose?

If so, he'd not only kill the guy, he'd never be able to live it down.

He saw how Mercy reacted after Rissa had been taken from their "safe house." He also witnessed Hunter beat himself up when Leo was kidnapped by his abusive biological father. And recently, Ellie being snagged by a drug cartel had almost pushed Walker over the edge.

He was determined not to let that happen in this case. He whipped open the door and, as he strode out into the waning heat of the day, he yelled, "Kat!"

Heading toward the insanely large pool house as fast as

his legs could take him without breaking into a run, he stutter-stepped when he heard it.

A bubbling of water, like a pot of soup on the stove coming to a boil. Or like his blood.

Oh yes.

Someone was fucking cooked all right.

His head twisted toward the sound, and, fuck him, she was in the in-ground hot tub. Her head was leaned back against the flagstone edge and her eyes were closed, beads of sweat or water beaded on her forehead.

She looked so relaxed. Oh, fuck yes, she did.

That would change in a split second.

He moved to the tub, leaned over and pushed the button to shut off the noisy jets.

Kat reacted so quickly; she almost went completely under the water. She sputtered, stood and faced him.

"If you had fucking long hair like a fucking woman, I'd drag your ass inside and teach you a fucking lesson about listening."

She planted her hands on her hips, her face hard. "Then it's a good thing my hair is 'dyke' short. But I don't need long hair, asshole, for you to try it. You think you're such a big badass. You don't intimidate me."

Steel unclenched his jaws. "Get the fuck out of the hot tub."

"I'm not done. I still have another five minutes."

"You're done." He sucked in a breath because his boiling pot's lid was dancing dangerously. "I told you not to go outside without me, Kat. And you disobeyed. You put yourself at risk."

"I can handle that risk."

"You *think* you can."

Her chin came up even higher. "I *know* I can."

"And you call me cocky." He reached for her. "Get out of the fucking hot tub."

She knocked his arm away from her, leaned over and turned the jets back on. Before she could settle back into the water, he kicked his Nike slides off his feet and jumped down into the tub.

She shifted to the other side but was still within reach.

"Kat, I said get out of the tub or I'll carry you out."

"Go fuck yourself."

"Already did," he muttered, grabbing her arm. When he stooped low enough to throw her over his shoulder, she twisted from his wet grasp.

She fell back and the water splashed up around them and over the side. She could've cracked her fucking head open by fighting him. He snagged her upper arm and hauled her to the steps and onto the concrete patio that surrounded the tub.

At the same time, he tried to ignore the fact that she not only wore a bikini, it was a yellow string bikini that hardly covered anything. The top was plastered to her tits. Though not huge, they were bigger than he expected because, for once, they weren't bound to her chest in one of those fucking ugly-ass sports bras.

Yep, he tried to ignore all of that because as she fought him, those tits bounced freely.

But as he began to drag her toward the French doors, she did a maneuver that helped her break free again.

"Asshole!" she screamed and slammed both palms into his chest, making him grunt from the force.

"Right! I'm an asshole. I told you not to go outside by yourself and you didn't listen. But I'm the fucking asshole!"

"You don't manhandle women."

"You're a goddamn fighter, woman!"

"You have no right to touch me without my permission."

"I don't, do I?"

Instead of backing away and heading inside since she

had her freedom, she stepped forward, going chest to chest with him. *Fuck*, she was a piece of work.

"No."

*Fucking Christ*, he loved a damn challenge and her going toe to toe with him, staring him directly in the eye with the fucking attitude she had, was better than porn. It fucking got his blood pumping, his heart thumping and his dick hard as fuck.

"You're my responsibility and I'll touch you when I need to."

There was nothing he wanted more than to shove her against one of the large windows that lined the patio, rip her bathing suit off and fuck her hard and fast from behind to take off that sharp edge.

He had thought he'd done so when he whacked off in the shower, but, fuck no, seeing her in her little wet string bikini had set him right back on edge again. He was crawling out of his skin with it.

Her chin was angled up, amber eyes narrowed, and she panted.

His eyes flicked to her heaving breasts and there was one thing he couldn't miss. Or two, to be exact. "Do I make your nipples hard, Kitty Kat? Maybe I'm wrong and you swing both ways."

"It doesn't matter how I swing. But no matter what, it won't be in your direction."

He leaned in and asked the same question she had when it came to his steel balls. "Do you want me to test that theory?"

"How about you just take my word for it," she echoed his response.

Their eyes held and neither of them moved. But their gaze broke when she swallowed, and he watched her throat lift and fall.

"I see your pulse trying to escape your neck, Kitty Kat. Does this excite you?"

"Nothing about you excites me."

"Do you know when people lie, they have tells? Little habits that give away that they're lying. Like their pulse quickening. Or their eyes shifting. Or even the slightest muscle twitch."

"Your dick is hard, Steel. That's a tell, and I bet that's twitching, too. Does it get you excited when you try to intimidate women?"

He leaned in even closer, so close her ragged breath washed over his lips when he said, "No, Kitty Kat, it's when they're not intimidated that gets me excited. I like a woman who can give as good as she gets."

"Give as good as she gets? So, you like to take dick, then? You like a woman who knows how to work a strap-on?"

"Figures you'd know about strap-ons."

"I like the real thing, Steel. But I prefer a dick on a man who isn't one."

Steel grinned and Kat narrowed her eyes at that grin. When she moved to step back, he snagged her wrist and held her in place, still toe to toe. Faces inches from each other. Their bodies a hairsbreadth apart.

He watched a bead of water roll down her temple from her hair. Her eyelashes were still spiky from being wet. Her eyes held fire.

Oh, fuck yes. He was getting to her.

She didn't try to pull from his grip, instead she demanded, "Let go of me."

"You expect me to listen to your demands, when you don't listen to mine? Here's a little lesson for you, Kat. I'm not here to make your life miserable. I'm not here to make you like me. I'm only here to keep you safe."

"Then why are you touching me?"

"Because you're making my job difficult by going against my orders."

"That's not why you're touching me."

"No, it's not," he murmured, dropping her wrist. Before she could get a chance to step away, he grabbed the sides of her face and took her mouth.

Or tried to.

Her hands came up and grasped both his wrists, her fingers flexing against him but not pushing him away. However, she also wasn't opening her mouth to let him in.

He was getting mixed signals.

Without much effort, he broke one of his wrists free, and slid his hand from her jawline to the back of her neck, where his fingers curled, holding her tightly. His other hand slipped down her neck, across her chest, barely brushed over one of her pebbled nipples, down her ribs, along the curve of her waist until he dug his fingers in at her hip.

But she still had her lips pinned closed.

She wasn't fighting him; she wasn't trying to break free.

But he could feel her battling with herself.

Her breathing still came quickly and he swore he detected a tremble run through her.

*Fuck yes*, she wasn't immune to him. She was trying to deny it and she might be strong enough to do it, but she still lingered. Hesitated.

Keeping their lips connected, he turned and pushed her backwards with his chest against hers until she was pinned against one of the posts that supported the upper deck. He slid the tip of his tongue along the seam of her mouth, asking her to let him in.

*Fuck*, he wanted to taste her. There. And other places.

He hadn't met a woman like her in a long time. If ever.

And he knew he was playing with fire. But he was pretty fucking sure it would be worth getting burned.

He tilted his head slightly and licked along her lips

again, hoping she'd open them this time. He wasn't forcing his tongue inside, because he was pretty fucking sure he'd lose it.

And that would be a damn fucking shame.

She wasn't melting against him; she wasn't stiff, either.

She was driving him nuts.

Suddenly her mouth was open and he was in.

Her tongue clashed with his in a fight they could both enjoy. She'd give an inch and then take it back. The struggle continued, turning it into the hottest fucking kiss he ever had.

His cock was throbbing between them, her diamond hard nipples pressing into his chest through his damp tank top.

But she still hadn't melted against him. She wasn't clinging to him, weak in the knees. Fuck no. The only thing she was giving him was her mouth. That was it.

He wanted more.

So, he took more.

He slid the hand at her hip back up until he was brushing his thumb back and forth over the hard nub beneath her damp bikini top. He deepened the kiss, digging his fingers harder into the flesh at the back of her neck.

And he finally got it. A reaction.

A noise bubbled up her throat and he took that as a sign she wanted more, just like he did.

Capturing that nipple between his fingers, he tweaked it, causing her to jerk. She shoved his tongue out of her mouth and before he could stop it, she chomped down on his bottom lip, grabbing hold.

He grunted and tried to pull away but that only made the pain worse, so he stayed perfectly still.

After a few seconds, she finally released him and pulled her head back. "Let me go."

He released her neck and took a step back, wiping the back of his hand along his mouth and seeing bright red.

She fucking bit him.

He studied her, with her back still against the post. Her chest was rising and falling rapidly, her face flushed, but her eyes a little wider than normal.

She was surprised by her own reaction to him. That was clear.

"If you think biting me will discourage me, you're wrong. I eat that shit up, Kitty Kat. And I didn't do anything you didn't want. So, if you don't want to do something you'll regret later, go inside. Because you might be warring with yourself, but you want this as much as me."

"No, I don't."

He shook his head, though that didn't help his throbbing lip. "Get inside now. Before I prove you're lying."

She quickly moved to the French doors off the kitchen.

"Kat," he called, staring at the blood on the back of his fingers. He didn't bother to look up, but he knew she hesitated. "You like to get rough? You'll get that chance. I already talked with Berger. I'm your sparring partner tomorrow."

The only answer he got from her was the door being slammed shut.

"Fuck," he muttered, gingerly testing his lip with his fingers.

Then he smiled. Even though it hurt like fuck.

———

KAT'S HEART was racing as she paused just inside the kitchen and glanced over her shoulder through the multiple panes of glass that made up the fancy double door.

Lifting her shaking fingers, she wiped away some blood that clung to her lip.

She needed a shower and a few minutes with the hand-held shower head. Hopefully that would wash away her thoughts because they had turned dark and dirty when he kissed her.

Steel now had his back to her and was standing out in the sun at the edge of the pool.

In a powerful surge of motion, he ripped his soaked tank over his head and whipped it to the concrete where it landed in a wet splat. Then he ran a hand through the longer hair at the top as his head dropped forward.

Kat held her breath when he hooked his thumbs into the waistband of his just-as-damp shorts and shoved them down until they dropped to his ankles.

The man wore nothing underneath them.

Kat closed her eyes for a split moment in her fight to keep from checking him out, but she lost that battle.

She let her gaze roam from the top of his head to his broad, muscular back. She had gotten peeks of the large tattoo there because he wore tanks often since regular T-shirts were probably tight for him in the shoulders and arms. She could pretty much figure out it was a military insignia that took up all that landscape. But she was too far away to get a good look at the detail.

His hips were lean, of course, but his ass...

*Fuck.* They were two perfect globes of smooth skin over muscle. And before she could rip her eyes from it, those muscles flexed as he pushed off his toes and did a perfect dive into the pool, hardly making a splash.

He disappeared below the surface a few times, each time coming up and shaking the water from his face and hair. Most likely trying to clear the same thoughts filling her own head.

She needed to go upstairs and get away from the door and stop gawking at him. But before she could make her feet move, he was pulling himself back out of the pool. Not using the ladder or steps. Hell no. He used his powerful arms to easily haul himself out of the water and onto the concrete.

The afternoon sun caught the gleam of his wet skin and the two metal dog tags that hung on a chain around his neck.

Just below that was what was left of his earlier erection, because there was no way he was that large when he was completely soft.

She had felt how big he was when he had her pinned to the post. She guessed he might be above average but not by much. The size of his cock was as perfect as his ass.

However, she would not be experiencing it. Not anytime soon.

*Hell*, not ever.

She was not getting involved with her bodyguard just like in the movie with Kevin Costner and Whitney Houston.

Especially when he proved himself to be an asshole time and time again.

No, she needed to keep him at arm's length and keep things between them to business only. Because when her stalker was finally caught, he'd head back to Pennsylvania.

With her stalker and him gone, she'd finally be able to breathe again.

# Chapter Six

STEEL KEPT his hands up and concentrated on both her right leg and fist. He finally figured out Kat's pattern when it came to punches and kicks. What she was most comfortable with and what she was most effective with, too. He was now successfully blocking both, but a few had slipped through in the beginning and, for a woman, she packed a fucking wallop. Just like yesterday's bite.

The faster his heart beat while they sparred, the faster his lip throbbed.

He had also taken her to the mat twice in the last twenty minutes. And they were soon going to have to break for the day. He'd been going hard at her that whole time, keeping her on her toes and while he held back some force when it came to his punches and kicks, he still gave about eighty percent. Enough to injure her, which he wanted to avoid.

But he also wanted Kat to expect Calamity Jayne going full out to take her down. Jayne was bigger and stronger and wouldn't give Kat any mercy. In fact, the videos he watched on YouTube last night showed she could be totally vicious. She liked to make her opponents bleed. She liked to hurt them, but she somehow pulled it off without any penalties.

She toyed with them, even when she had the ability to take them out quickly. In all the fights he watched, Jayne reminded him of a cat playing with her captive mouse. She didn't want to eat her catch, she just wanted to torture it. For fun.

She was a sneaky bitch. Even so, Steel was impressed with how the woman won her fights because everything she did in the cage was legal, but he worried for Kat.

Kat needed to get the upper hand with her in the first round. Otherwise, he was afraid that Jayne would wear her down and easily win the fight.

But now, here on the mats at The Strike Zone, neither Kat nor Steel wore any protective gear except for MMA gloves with the open fingers. That had been her choice, not his, and he wondered why she decided that since she'd worn shin guards the past two days with her other partners.

Maybe she needed to prove her toughness with him. Why? He didn't know.

But what he did know, it was soon time to take her down one last time and get some time in grappling. He wasn't used to ground fighting since he preferred boxing and kick-boxing. That was what he did in the ring with Slade when they sparred and what he did in his underground fights.

Most of his opponents never made it past the first few punches and kicks, or even some of his choke holds, for the fight to go to ground. He didn't know a lot of wrestling moves, but since he outweighed Kat by about seventy pounds, he was pretty fucking sure he could figure out how to get her to tap out.

However, getting her down to the mat was proving to be difficult. Every time he tried to grab her, she ducked and moved quickly. Much quicker than him since she was much lighter on her feet in comparison. He normally liked to keep two feet solidly planted to keep his balance and use the power of a twist behind his punch to knock someone the fuck out. And if that didn't work, a good kick to the head would.

But he had an idea. Kat's kicking skills were fucking impressive and he had to snap himself out of it more than once as he watched how flexible and powerful her leg movements were.

He kept reminding himself to pay attention and not get caught up in any fantasies. Otherwise, he was going to catch a foot alongside the head, and then have to worry about more than just a cut lip.

She probably heard what he was about to say many times, but he would say it anyway to drive it home. "The reach with your leg is longer than your arm, so use that to your advantage. Jayne likes to punch and then follow up with a choke hold to get her opponents to the ground. You need to stay out of the range of her fist and keep her from grabbing you. If she puts you in a clinch and gets you down, it's over, Kat."

Kat continued to bounce around the mat on the balls of her feet, sweat sliding down her skin and soaking her hair and sports bra. She had her fists raised to about chest height and her eyes attentively followed every move he made.

"If you only kick low, she's going to learn that pattern. I'm thinking for every low kick, you do a quick spin with a high kick to follow. Got it?"

Kat didn't answer him around her mouthguard, instead she just nodded sharply once, drops of sweat dripping off the spiky ends of her hair and dotting the mat around them.

"Let's practice that. Fake a punch, kick low, then high. Aim for her temple. Make her head spin. Once you rattle her brain, follow up with a direct punch, elbow strike or knee strike to the head. Got it?"

Kat nodded again.

And miracle of all miracles, the woman was actually

listening. At least she listened to his instructions when they were on the mat.

Somewhat.

He wondered why. And if something had changed after their kiss.

Because, fuck him, it wasn't like she talked to him about it afterward. Last night, he ate his dinner by himself and, again this morning, he went solo for breakfast.

He heard Kat only go downstairs once he went to bed last night to watch the YouTube videos. After a couple of hours of analyzing Calamity Jayne, he got in a little girl-on-girl porn before crashing.

The car ride this morning was almost completely silent, too.

But her whole demeanor changed once she came out of the locker room ready to spar with him. Even though she only wore a sports bra and tight black compression shorts, she wore it like a suit of armor and was prepared to slay some dragons.

Or slay his ass.

Every once in a while, he'd run his tongue over the cut on his lip, and the metallic taste would remind him of that kiss. She had been holding back yesterday, and he was dying to find out what would happen when she didn't.

But now was not the time to be distracted by that, not when a shin was headed toward his ribs.

He turned and knocked it away. "That's center. Go low, then high. One, two. Bam, bam."

She jabbed at him and he easily deflected it, then she kicked him low enough to make his knee buckle. He caught himself and braced for her higher kick. When it came it still wasn't high enough for what he needed.

"Kick higher, Kat," he yelled at her. "Go for my head."

Yes, he was taller than Kat and even taller than Calamity Jayne. But, *fuck*, he'd seen Kat get some impressive height. He knew what she was capable of when she combined her kick with a spin.

She could be getting too tired.

She took two more jabs at him, connecting once in the solar plexus, but he quickly regained his breath as he dodged the lower kick and, as her body began to swing, he knew what was coming next.

As she twisted mid-air, her heel aimed at the side of his head, he ducked, snagged her ankle and yanked.

She fell hard to the mat with a grunt, landing on one hand, her elbow and a hip while air whooshed from her lungs.

He didn't give her a chance to recover before he dropped almost all his weight on her, pinning her to the mat, and got her into a guillotine choke hold.

He squeezed enough to restrict her air but not choke her out.

"Escape, Kat," he urged her.

"Kat," Berger yelled. "Tap out if you need to."

When the fuck did he come back in? Steel had told Kat's manager and trainer to take a walk while they sparred because in the beginning, he stood on the edge of the mat yelling instructions at Steel. And he wasn't having any part of that bullshit.

Luckily Berger gave in, even though reluctantly. Otherwise, it might have ended up being the two of them on the mat instead of him and Kat.

Now he was about to bust Berger in the fucking mouth' if he didn't let Steel do what he needed to do.

Which was get Kat prepared for the fight of her career.

Berger might only be seeing dollar signs, but Steel knew deep down Kat needed and wanted this win. He saw it. He understood that hunger. For that reason, he would do everything he could to help her get what she wanted. With or without Berger's help.

If Berger kept stepping in, Steel would train her back at the house. But, unfortunately, there weren't any mats there.

His attention was drawn back to Kat as she attempted to escape not only his choke hold but his weight. "Don't you fucking tap out. You get the fuck out of this hold."

Her face was red from exertion, but her eyes held a focused determination. And all kinds of sounds—sounds of exertion he could imagine coming from her when she had sex—escaped around her mouthguard. There might have been a few curses peppered in there. Though, he knew she couldn't curse in the ring during a legal fight according to the rules.

Illegal ones? Everyone let the F-bomb drop. *Hell*, the opponents brutally taunted each other non-stop. Steel had heard every insult known to man during an underground fight. It got both the fighters—and the betting audience— pumped and ready to pound each other into the dirt, concrete or pavement.

But back on the mat, Kat was currently doing her best to wedge her feet and hands between them, using any method possible to break his hold.

She wasn't allowed to pinch, bite or head butt him. Or, *thank fuck*, knee him in the nuts. He sure as fuck hoped she followed those rules since he wasn't wearing a cup.

"C'mon, Kat. Jayne's bigger than you, better than you. She's going to kick your ass in front of millions of people. Show them you can win. Or at least go down hard trying."

He knew throwing the possibility of losing at her would get her working harder to escape.

"Tap out, Kat," Berger said. "Sterling, let her go."

Steel ignored the deliberate use of his last name. "Do it, Kat. Tap out and I'll make it worse next time. Get the fuck out of this hold. Hurt me if you have to."

*Just don't knee me in the nuts.*

Kat grimaced around her mouthguard and elbowed

him in the ribs before slamming her heel into his shin. That had to have hurt her more than him. But she didn't give up.

She didn't tap out.

"Good girl," he murmured close to her ear, knowing that would piss her the fuck off.

And it did.

Even though the growl was muffled by the mouthguard, he heard it and fought his grin as she began using her fists, elbows and feet as much as possible. She turned into a wildcat, her body bowing, flexing and twisting as if she was fighting for her life.

As he took the blows, he winced and knew he'd be sporting bruises later. But he'd wear every fucking one of those with honor.

Kat was not a quitter and he respected the fuck out of that.

However, he wasn't, either.

He tightened his choke hold, now completely cutting off her oxygen. Her face began to turn purple, but she didn't panic and also didn't tap out.

She was stubborn as fuck. She would actually pass out before giving up.

He needed to make a decision.

That decision was made by her manager, who was now standing over the both of them, his face also almost purple but not from a lack of oxygen.

"Kat, tap out!" Berger yelled. "Fucking let her go, Steel!"

Steel put his mouth to Kat's ear and whispered, "You ready to tap out, Kitty Kat?"

She had stopped fighting and her nails, even though short, now dug into his forearms.

"You've gone too far!" Berger screamed at him, getting closer and about to jump in to interfere.

If he did, it was on. And Steel wasn't going to keep it at eighty percent with Berger.

He released his hold and Kat took a big gasp of air before rolling away from him and onto her knees, hands to her throat.

Her voice was rough, and her breathing ragged when she said, "I didn't tap out."

"And you have to know when to quit," Steel reminded her as he got to his feet.

"Kat." Berger reached out to help her stand, but she lifted a hand to ward him off, her chest still heaving, her face red, still slightly bent over trying to catch her breath.

"I'm fine," she told him.

Berger spun toward Steel and bellowed, "You're fired!"

*Fuck.* "I'll let her decide that." He slid his eyes to Kat, who had finally made it to her feet and had her gloves planted on her hips as she sucked in oxygen. Sweat dripped down the sides of her face as she stared at him.

Something behind those amber eyes got him right in the gut.

Was it respect?

*Nah*, couldn't be.

"Berger, why don't you give us a minute?" Steel murmured, not looking in the fuming man's direction.

"No."

Without breaking Steel's gaze, Kat said, "Berg, just give us a few."

"Kat..."

"Please." That single word Kat uttered was firm and wasn't a request. Steel knew it and, luckily, so did Berger.

But it still took a good thirty seconds before Berger urged, "Yell if you need me," in a tight voice. The static-filled air around them moved when Berger strode out of the training room and into the main gym, muttering under his breath the whole time.

Steel waited until the man was clear of the room, taking some of the tension with him. "Am I fired, Kitty Kat?"

If she really wanted him gone, now would be the perfect time to push it. He would have no choice if Berger and her both agreed.

Steel watched as her throat undulated. The throat which still bore a red mark from how tightly he'd held her there. "Not if you can work with me to get me ready for this fight."

"Like what I just did?"

"Yes. Don't give me any quarter."

"Kat, it's sparring, not a fight. You don't go one hundred percent. In fact, you shouldn't."

"Then, like today, go as far as you think I need. The male partners he's been getting me are handling me with kid gloves. I'm not going to win like that."

He then stated something they both knew. "You want to win."

Kat simply shot him a look.

Steel grinned. "Fuck yes, you want to win," he repeated more firmly. "I get it. But Berger's not going to like it."

But, *hot damn*, he loved that tenacity.

"I'm his boss. In turn, I'm yours," she finally said.

And, *hot damn*, those words made his dick twitch. "Think we had that discussion."

"Then maybe you should just listen."

Steel pointed a finger at her. "Pot." He jerked his thumb at his chest. "Kettle."

"No shit," she muttered.

When he took a step toward her, her spine snapped straight and her eyes became wary, but he ignored it and approached her anyway.

When he was so close he could feel the heat radiating off her and inhale the metallic scent of her sweat, he reached out.

He could see her struggle not to step out of range and remain where she was.

His fingers curved around the front of her throat and his thumb slid back and forth over the discolored skin he had caused. "You should've tapped out. Don't let your pride affect your decisions. Especially in the ring. It's stupid and dangerous, Kat. You don't win if you die trying."

"You let me go before I blacked out."

"Only because I thought I would have to beat Berger's ass." Which wasn't entirely true. He'd been about to let her go anyway, but he didn't want her to know that.

"Next time don't let me go before I tap out."

He shifted even closer. "Kat..."

Her chin lifted slightly. "I can't lose that fight."

"Berger said you'll be raking it in win or lose."

"It's not about the money."

And there it was. "Yeah, I get that, Kitty Kat."

Her chin lifted even higher. "You know I hate that."

"No, you don't," he whispered, dropping his head until he was looking directly down into her eyes, their lips barely a few inches apart. "You haven't told me once to stop using it."

He stopped the motion of his thumb over the pulse trying to escape her throat. He ran his tongue over his bottom lip, then whispered, "You gonna make me bleed this time?"

"Yes," she whispered back.

He grinned. "I was never into soft, amenable women."

"Why do you think I care who you're into?"

"Because I saw the fear in your eyes by your own reaction to our kiss, Kat. It scared you. Just imagine how good it could be if you let yourself enjoy it."

"Sex with you would be a power play. And a mistake."

"Only if you make it that."

"I guess we'll never find out for sure."

"A fucking pity if that's true," Steel murmured.

Out of the corner of his eye, he saw a body beelining toward them. He sighed, released her throat and took a step back just in case Berger tried to get physical with him.

"Kat, you okay?" Berger's narrowed blue eyes slid from her to Steel and back.

Steel watched Kat mentally shake herself before answering her manager. "Yes, I'm okay."

"What did you two discuss?" It wasn't a question but a demand.

Steel was about to tell him to fuck off when Kat turned to Berger and stated, "Steel will be my sparring partner until the fight," surprising the fuck out of them both.

"I'm not sure that's a good idea. I don't want you hurt."

"I'm not going to hurt her," Steel grumbled.

Berger's eyes met his and his eyebrows rose. "No?"

"No." Steel hoped to fuck that would be true.

And if it wasn't, he'd kick his own ass.

———

"Pool in ten," Steel had yelled at her as she headed into the house earlier from the garage. "No bikini. Something you can swim laps in."

She hadn't answered him, instead had gone directly upstairs and put on the only bathing suit she had packed during her last move which could withstand doing laps.

Now she stood by the pool, mesmerized by the way the sun was reflecting off the still water, as she waited for Steel to come out and bark more orders at her.

He sure was a bossy fuck.

If Berger hadn't interrupted them at the gym, she had a feeling Steel would've kissed her again.

Would she have let him?

She closed her eyes, taking herself back to that moment, and imagined what would've happened if she had.

Not only did that replay make her nipples ache, but heat slide through her that wasn't the result of the Nevada late afternoon sun.

*Dumb, dumb, dumb.*

It was stupid of her to even consider having sex with him.

It would be one of the biggest mistakes in her life.

Maybe not the biggest, but close.

Even so...

She had a hard time ignoring how his kiss yesterday affected her. More than she wanted to admit.

And that was the exact reason why she bit him. Because he could have easily convinced her to take it further.

She shouldn't.

He was her bodyguard. She was his client.

She needed to convince herself it was a bad idea.

So bad.

So, so, so bad.

*Damn it.* He was such an alpha-hole. Unfortunately, such a freaking hot one.

And he was strong enough personality-wise not to be turned off by her strength and determination. Which was a problem with most of the men she'd dated in the past.

Like Steel calling her a "dyke," the few men she dated would stick around only for one or two dates before they thought she was "butch" or a lesbian when she didn't immediately sleep with them. Or drop to her knees in gratitude when they bought her dinner. Or because they found out what she did for a living.

Despite what they thought, she wasn't a lesbian. She wasn't even bi.

However, strong women intimidated many men.

But, fuck them. It wasn't her problem if they had a

complex about it. If they wanted a meek and mild woman who was ready to settle down, get married and pop out babies, it wasn't her.

It might never be her.

She still had so many more things she wanted to do in life before being tied to a husband or children. She had a long bucket list and planned on checking off every one of those things once she had enough money tucked away from her fights. *And* she retired.

She was not going to turn into her mother, who did nothing but serve her father like a "good wife" was supposed to do, according to her parents.

*Fuck that.*

Her mother was nobody but "Mrs. Callahan" anymore. She was Kat's father's wife. She was Kat and Annabelle's mother.

The day she got married to Pat Callahan, her mother ceased being Lana Mueller.

If that made her happy, then fine. But Kat didn't want that for her future. She decided at a young age, she would never let that happen to her. She would never lose her own identity because she became a wife and mother.

She would always be Kat Callahan.

And if a man couldn't accept that? Then fuck him, too.

An easy way to avoid that problem was to never get married or have children.

Simple.

Even now, she answered to herself and, in a way, to Berger. But that was it.

She made her own money. She wrote her own destiny.

And she hated that this stalker had any control over her life. Even a sliver.

Her head snapped up and her heart began to pound when one of the French doors opened and shut behind her.

She forced herself to remain where she was and not turn to watch him approach.

"Didn't have you do extra cardio at the gym because after our intense sparring, swimming will be better."

He was right behind her and she was reluctant to turn around to see what he was wearing. Or not wearing.

She pursed her lips. Had the Nevada heat just kicked up a notch?

He stepped into the narrow space between her and the pool. "D'you hear me?" He tilted his dark head and squinted at her since the sun was still high in the sky.

"Are those your swim trunks?" she asked as if in a trance, suddenly having a hard time swallowing.

"I didn't bring swim trunks," he said, his brow going low. "I didn't plan on going swimming. This isn't a vacation."

She pushed, "Then what are you wearing?" past her dry throat as she struggled not to stare at his bulging thighs—and other things—that the silky olive-green short shorts he wore did not cover sufficiently. She was also trying to avoid staring at his hairless bare chest.

In fact, she wasn't sure where the hell to look besides her feet or the sky.

"Silkies. We run in them."

"We?" she squeaked. How the hell did anything important stay in those shorts when men ran? Impossible.

"We, as in us Marines."

With the way he said "us Marines" with pride, she expected him to add an *oorah* to the end of it. "You were a Marine," she murmured like she had a loss of oxygen to her brain and could only repeat things mindlessly.

His brow dropped lower. "Yeah. Is the fucking sun getting to you, or what?"

"No," she forced past her lips.

"Well, you're all fucking flushed like you're overheating."

Yes, because she was wondering what those shorts would

look like once they were wet. Which was stupid because she had seen him naked when he jumped into the pool yesterday. So, if she tried hard enough, she could picture what they'd look like.

The problem was, picturing that was making her even hotter and she'd rather see the real thing.

What the hell was wrong with her?

She needed to get into the pool and let the water cool off not only her heated skin but her thoughts.

When he snapped his fingers in front of her face and barked, "Kat! Snap out of it!" she startled and instinctively reacted, putting her hands up and shoving him away from her.

However, with him standing at the edge of the pool and not expecting quite that reaction, he lost his balance and snagged her wrist as he fell backward.

Kat gasped as he pulled her with him over the edge and they both hit the water. Well, Steel hit the water first. She hit Steel before hitting the water.

Her gasp caused her to suck in a lungful of water as they both went under in a tangle of arms and legs. Before she could get her head above the water, he broke the surface pulling her with him with a few strong kicks.

She coughed, trying to empty her lungs of the chlorinated water and fill them with air.

"What the fuck, Kat!"

He hauled her to the edge where she held on until she could breathe somewhat freely again. Only Steel's arm remained around her middle like a steel band, as if he was worried she'd go back under since they were in the deep end.

"I'm fine. You can let me go," she managed. Sort of. She coughed once more to clear her air passage.

However, now she was having trouble breathing, not because of inhaling water, but because he had his body pressing hers against the side of the pool. His massive naked and wet chest was glued to her almost naked back.

"Let me go."

"Not until you explain why the fuck you pushed me into the pool."

She told him the truth. "You startled me when you snapped your fingers in front of my face."

"You were out of it."

"I was not."

"Your eyes were glazed over."

Maybe that was true. A little drool might have been accumulated at the corner of her mouth, too. Hopefully, he hadn't noticed.

"I'm just tired."

"Bullshit. We sparred for less than a half hour."

"It was the hardest I've sparred in a long time."

"Again, bullshit."

He forced her to turn until her back was pressed against the side of the pool and they were now chest to chest. Literally *chest to chest*. He was lower in the water and she could feel the silky fabric of those shorts swirling against her thighs as he clung to the side against her.

"When are you going to admit it?" He was eye to eye with her and he grabbed her chin when she tried to look away.

"Admit what?" She shoved at his chest, but she didn't have good leverage since they were too close, so he didn't even budge. "Give me some space."

"Why, Kat? Why do you need space? Is being this close affecting you?"

"No."

"Once again, bullshit."

"You're so fucking cocky."

"And you're so fucking stubborn."

"You think I'm stubborn because I won't fall to your feet

and suck your cock, just like every other man has expected from me? Give a woman a little bit of attention and then expect her to spread her legs out of gratitude?"

His brows slid together. "What?"

"And then get pissed when she doesn't."

"What the fuck are you talking about?"

"You. Men! All of you."

"I'm not asking you to do shit out of gratitude. What's wrong with you?"

Kat closed her eyes to avoid his intense gaze. She could see his anger bubbling up and she was throwing out every excuse she could think of to get him to back off.

But in truth, she didn't want him to back off.

She wanted him to push forward.

She wanted to be able to let go. To accept anything he was willing to give her.

Because, also in truth, she needed it.

She'd been wound so tight for so long, she needed a release.

She needed an escape. To forget, even for a little while, all the weight that had been placed on her shoulders since she started competing.

And, for shit's sake, she was the one who put it there. She was the one to blame.

Not Berger, not her competitors. Nobody but her.

She was the one who continued to push herself hard, sometimes to the point of breaking. Because she had to prove everyone wrong. Every fucking person who had ever doubted her.

But not once in the last few days he'd been in Boulder City, had Steel doubted her. Not once.

And she kept being a bitch to him. Even though he was willing to step in and help her when he didn't need to.

Even so, she couldn't let him see her crumble. To weaken. Because that would be a mistake.

It would also make her vulnerable. And she couldn't allow that.

Because if he found that loose string inside her and pulled it, everything might just unravel.

And then what would be left? Nothing but a tangled mess.

# Chapter Seven

STEEL WATCHED KAT CAREFULLY. Even though she had her eyes closed and her head turned away, her body had tensed against him and her face showed her internal struggle.

He had no idea what she was fighting.

But he could understand it.

He'd done it. And he'd seen the men around him do it, too.

She was fighting some sort of demon, but he didn't know what and he was pretty fucking sure she'd never tell him.

And that was fine. Everyone had their secrets. Things that might never see the light of day.

But, for fuck's sake, he had this crazy urge to dig that shit out from deep within her and make it right.

He had this feeling that it was her against the world. She was dealing with shit alone. Yeah, family in Indiana had been mentioned but not once since that first day he walked into The Strike Zone had she taken a call or received one from family.

She'd talked to no one that he'd been aware of.

Yeah, she had Berger, but he was paid.

Just like Steel was being paid.

The two people closest to her right now were on her payroll.

And then, of course, there was the fuckstick stalker. The whole reason Steel was there in the first place.

Her face was still turned away, her eyes squeezed shut, her jaw tight, when he leaned in even closer, putting his mouth just to her ear. He asked in a low whisper, "What's wrong, Kitty Kat?"

A shudder swept through her, one that rippled the water around them. And as her head whipped back to face him and her eyes opened, he backed off just enough to give her a little space but not enough to let her escape.

"What's wrong?" She. Was. Pissed. "It's you, all right? You're what's wrong with me." Her hand flew up out of the water, splashing them both as she circled it in front of him. "It's all this. It's you. What you're wearing. Everything about you."

No, not pissed. Frustrated. And maybe a little pissed, too. He didn't even bother to fight the slow grin that crept over his face. "Yeah?"

So, she wasn't immune to him.

"Yeah! And now you're going to ride that pony to death, aren't you? You're going to whip it until it stumbles and falls and you're going to have to shoot it to put it out of its misery, aren't you?"

"Are you the pony I'm riding?"

She rolled her eyes. "That's what you got out of all of that?"

"No, but I'm kind of liking that scenario."

"Of course you would. You think you're irresistible."

"And that's where you're wrong, Kitty Kat."

Her eyes narrowed. "Stop calling me that."

"It fits you. Light on your feet. Powerful. Beautiful. Smart. Also, at times aloof but definitely independent. I bet you like to play when you're in the mood and when you do, you do it hard. And I bet with the right attention, you purr, too. Do you purr, Kitty Kat?"

"You forget the part where I bite when provoked."

"You say that like it's a bad thing." He lifted his fingers to his mouth, drawing her eyes there. "But I didn't forget."

Even when he dropped his fingers, her gaze remained on his lips. He let them curve upward and she slowly raised her eyes to his.

"What do you need, Kitty Kat?"

He held his breath waiting for her answer when her mouth opened. Then it snapped shut and her eyes became guarded.

"Are you going to deny yourself something you want?"

"You think what I want is you?"

"You can use me, Kat, however you'd like. I won't judge."

"Everybody judges."

"Not me. Not in this case. You want to use me to get something you need? I volunteer. You can use me hard and I won't break. You want to bite me, scratch me, hit me, hold me down and dominate me, I'll allow it. This one time only."

Her eyes had widened slightly as he made his offer. "Why would you let someone hurt you?"

"Not someone, you."

"Why me?"

He ignored that question. "If you want me to take control, be rough with you, be gentle with you, any way you want it, you just say the word, Kat. I'm up for anything."

"Again, why?"

"Because I want it, too."

"I'm sure you can find somebody else to—"

He cut her off. "I don't want somebody else. I want you."

"You shouldn't."

"And you think you shouldn't want me, either. But you do."

Her lips parted and a shuddered breath escape. "I don't want to."

"But you do." He smothered his grin. He was working way too hard for this and if he grinned now, she was going to shut down and say no.

He wrapped his fingers around her waist and lifted her out of the pool to sit her on the edge. She didn't fight him, but she didn't help, either.

He watched the water sluice down her body. She had ditched the bikini like he'd asked and wore a two piece that covered her the same as a one-piece. This one was black and basic and designed for serious swimming.

She was supposed to be doing laps right now.

She should be doing laps.

But, no, instead Steel stood in the pool between her knees as she sat on the edge. Not moving away.

But still, like a bird waiting to take flight.

In one way, this woman had strength and determination, but in another she was unsure of herself. Of the people around her.

Which sucked.

If you didn't have people you trusted at your back, you had nothing.

His team and Diesel had his six. Kat might have Berger, but not completely. Steel didn't trust him one hundred percent and he was good at reading people. That was one reason he came home in one piece from the Middle East and not in a box covered in an American flag.

"One time offer to do what you want to me, Kat." *Fuck,* he was so fucking hard hoping she'd take the offer.

She avoided his eyes when she said, "I can't."

"Didn't realize 'can't' was in your vocabulary." With

disappointment, he pushed away from the pool's edge and moved to a spot where he could pull himself out of the water.

After he did so, he walked closer to Kat, who still sat there, now staring at the pool. When she didn't look up at him, he said, "Half hour of laps. Start now, I'll be back out when your time is up."

Then he went inside to give her space.

He turned to make sure she followed his instructions and it surprised the fuck out of him when she did. She slipped back into the water and with an easy pace, began to swim freestyle from one end to the other.

From where he stood, he could see she was a good swimmer. And because of the stalker, he wasn't going to leave her unattended long. Just long enough to change out of his wet Silkies and into dry clothes.

If he stayed in the pool with her, he would keep pushing her to admit what she wanted. He didn't have a condom on him anyway, even if she said yes. Fucking her without one would be stupid. She tempted him too much, and he needed to keep his head on straight.

Plus, if she gave in and then had second thoughts afterward, she might run to Berger and his ass would be on the next flight back to Pittsburgh. Then Diesel would rip off his head and shit down his neck at that loss of money.

He wanted her but he could wait until she was ready. Because he had no doubt that time was coming.

———

He was watching her. She just didn't know from where inside the house. After his shit-fit at her going outside without him the other day, there was no way he'd leave her outside and not be watching.

He in no way reminded her of someone who was careless. He took his job seriously. And he could be intense.

She had almost taken him up on his offer earlier. She'd been so close.

But she didn't want to do anything she'd regret later.

She kept having to tell herself that having sex with him would be a mistake. How could they keep a professional relationship after that? How could she stay in the house with him afterward? It could—no, *would*—get uncomfortable.

She didn't want Berger to have to hire another bodyguard when they had a perfectly good one already. One who was also willing to get her ready for her upcoming bout with Calamity Jayne.

And right now, that's where her concentration should be. Not on the damn stalker. Not on the man who was making her feel things she'd never felt before.

The whole half hour she swam, she couldn't get her mind off what "using him" would entail.

*Hell*, in truth, she wouldn't even know where to start. Even so, she felt that deep-seated need to do it anyway.

However, she'd probably fumble through it and he'd laugh at her.

*If you want me to take control, be rough with you, be gentle with you, any way you want it, you just say the word, Kat. I'm up for anything.*

She pulled herself over the edge of the pool to find the lounge chairs empty. He never did come back out, even though she swore she did laps for more than a half hour. In fact, after the first few warm-up laps, she had pushed herself until both her muscles and lungs burned. But she continued until she had nothing left. Until the frustration, not only from the situation the stalker had forced her into, but also at wanting Steel had dissipated.

But had it really?

She was disappointed he hadn't come back out, because

she would not go to him. He would have to be the one to take what he wanted.

What they both wanted.

Because she had no idea what she wanted when it came to sex.

None.

Especially with a man like Steel.

She grabbed the towel from where she'd thrown it on one of the chairs earlier and wiped down her hair and face, then dried off the rest of her body. She threw the towel over her shoulder and went inside.

When the cool air conditioning hit her damp skin, she shivered. The kitchen was empty, only the hum of the over-sized stainless-steel built-in refrigerator greeting her.

She worked her way through the house and up the steps, looking forward to removing the wet suit that clung to her skin.

She closed her bedroom door behind her and was about to peel off the damp suit when she spotted him. Lounging in one of the wicker chairs on her balcony.

*Son of a bitch.* He *had* been watching her the whole time. But where he relaxed with his feet up, she hadn't been able to see him from the pool.

Instead of changing, she headed outside. "You have one of these in your own room."

"Not with the unfettered view yours has."

He would've gotten another *unfettered* view if she had ripped off her bathing suit without realizing he was out there. She only noticed him because his arms and shoulders were wider than the chair. "We had this discussion about you just coming into my room."

"You weren't in here."

"But I am now. You need to leave so I can change."

She stood in the doorway behind his chair and he hadn't turned to look at her.

He could have just as easily come downstairs and sat by the pool to watch her while she swam, but instead, he waited for her in her room. And if she asked for a reason why, he'd probably give her some bullshit story.

"What if the stalker had shown up while I was in the pool and you were up here? Would you have jumped off the balcony to save me?"

"No. I would have shot his ass."

She had not seen him carry a gun yet. In fact, she had found that curious for a bodyguard. "You have a gun?"

"I have a couple guns."

"And you're a good shot?"

"I do all right."

A former Marine probably did more than all right.

The air between them suddenly turned thick. Now that she was done swimming, he had no reason to remain on her balcony, but he wasn't moving.

But then, neither was she.

She should go take a shower, close and lock the bathroom door, and maybe when she was done, he'd be gone.

"Kat." Just her name and the way he said it in his deep, rough voice had her clutching the door frame. Her name on his lips held promises of what he could and would do to her.

If she let him.

Her heart began to thump.

"Kat," he repeated, still in a low voice, but more firmly.

"Yeah?" she breathed.

"Go to the railing, grab it with both hands and face the pool."

He still hadn't looked at her, still hadn't moved.

"Kat."

She closed her eyes at the way he said her name again. "Yes?" barely came out of her mouth because she'd stopped breathing.

"Do what I said or tell me to leave."

It was on the tip of her tongue to say, "Leave." Her brain was telling her to demand he leave, for her not to obey.

But it was the heat that swirled through her, the excitement of the unknown, the power behind his voice that propelled her forward. Like her feet had a mind of their own. She rounded his chair, not looking at him.

Afraid to look at him.

And she was not afraid of men.

She stopped in front of the rail, staring down at it and the pool just beyond.

She expected for him to give her the order again, but he didn't.

The balcony remained silent except for the pounding of her heart, which had moved from her chest into her ears.

She lifted her hands slowly until she held them right above the top wrought iron rail. She spread her fingers out, seeing them shake.

She could still walk away. Tell him to leave. She didn't have to do anything he said.

When she finally curled them around the warm metal, the breath rushed out of her.

The tremble from her hands worked its way up her arms and soon her whole body was buzzing. Her pussy clenched involuntarily, her breasts ached, her nipples drew tight.

She jerked as she heard him surge from the chair. She closed her eyes and waited.

Her whole body was a mess of nerves, each one crackling and popping as he approached. She was the prey tied to a trap like a lure, awaiting the predator.

His much bigger hands curled around the railing alongside hers. Close but not touching. Then the heat of his body against hers sent a blaze swirling through her own, which landed in her core as it clenched.

He wasn't even touching her yet and it was the most erotic thing ever.

Or it was until his warm breath hit her skin at the edge of her damp hair when he whispered, "Kat."

She jumped as his nose slid up the side of her neck slowly. His one hand leaving the railing and planting firmly against her stomach, fingers wide, holding her there.

Goosebumps exploded over her body as he ran his nose back down, the touch so light. And then his tongue replaced it as he took another trip up and back down.

Then his lips.

And, *holy shit*, she might just orgasm with what he was doing.

The hand spread over her belly slid lower, the tips of a couple long fingers worming their way past the elastic band of the swimsuit bottoms. But he didn't press further.

No, instead he continued his onslaught of his mouth along her neck. And now shoulders. Occasionally scraping his teeth against her skin, nipping her. Nothing painful. Light touches, teasing bites.

She rocked back against him.

"Keep your hands on the railing," his order came out rough, sending another shockwave through her.

She curled her fingers tighter around the metal to keep herself there.

The fingers on her belly slid lower. But not low enough.

She bit back a groan.

He removed his left hand from the railing and planted it on her belly above his right hand. But unlike the other one which went lower, this one slid upward. His fingers traced the bottom curves of her breasts covered in the Lycra bathing suit. He slid his hand higher, avoiding her nipples that ached for his touch and curled around the front of her throat, tipping her head back against his chest.

His right hand moved even lower, almost to the edge of the small patch of hair she kept there.

"Steel." She barely got the whisper out.

"Yeah, baby?" he asked in her ear. "What do you need?"

He knew what she needed. He just wanted her to ask for it.

No. Beg for it.

She refused to beg.

Warm breath slid over the shell of her ear when he encouraged her to, "Purr for me, Kitty Kat."

When a little growl slid up her throat, she swallowed it back down. She closed her eyes, fighting every reaction her body betrayed her with. Every reaction that proved to him that he had been right. She wanted this, too. The wetness between her legs, the pebbling of her nipples, her breathing becoming more shallow and rapid.

But she couldn't contain it. She couldn't hold it back. The noise that finally slid up her throat, the noise he could feel under his palm held there. The noise he could hear because his cheek was pressed to the side of her head. The noise she let go because his finger—one single finger—moved down far enough to part that patch of hair and dip into her wetness.

One finger. That was all it took for her to fall apart. To lose her mind. To abandon all control.

To experience what she never had before.

"Kat, relax. You're wound tight."

Yes, she was tightly wound because she was trying not to shatter, to let go of that rail, to turn to him and demand that he fuck her. To just hand him the control and let him do to her what he will.

To trust him completely.

To show her everything she'd never had for all these years. Everything she denied herself because she didn't think it was necessary.

He was proving *her* wrong.

With a single finger.

A finger that stroked her gently but had done nothing further than that.

She twisted her head until her face was hidden against his neck. "Please."

"Please what, Kitty Kat?"

She didn't know what. She didn't know what she needed from him. He was the one who needed to know. He was the one who had to show her what she needed.

He was the one...

He was the one who finally slid his finger inside her, quickly followed by a second one.

Her back arched, her mouth opened, and she panted against the skin of his neck. His erection pressed into her back, but his breathing remained steady as he worked his fingers in and out of her.

When he added his thumb to her clit, she struggled to capture the whimper before it escaped, but she failed.

She was so slick. She could not only feel it but hear how wet she was as he continued to play with her.

She released a little gasp when he rolled her nipple through the damp fabric.

His words rumbled from deep within his chest as he murmured, "That's it, Kitty Kat, show me how much you want this."

She did. She wanted this. She never wanted this from anyone before. But then...

"You're so fucking wet," he said into her ear. "Tell me what you want, Kat. I need to hear it."

He expected her to not only know, but to talk? Now?

"Do you want to come?"

She tried to push out a "yes," but her throat convulsed instead.

And then *everything* began to convulse. Her inner muscles

clenched tightly around his fingers and her orgasm exploded from her center and radiated out.

She had no idea it could be that intense. That powerful.

Her hips were no longer her own as they moved with his fingers, riding those waves.

He was talking low, his voice tense as her climax was the longest she'd ever experienced, but she had no idea what those words were.

His thumb brushing one last time against her clit made her jerk, because now it was too sensitive.

She'd never felt this weak before, like all her bones had disintegrated within her body. But Steel held her up and against him.

She realized she still held the top rail in a death grip. "Can I let go?"

"You already did," came his rumble.

She pried her stiff fingers from the metal and began to pull away from him, but he held her tighter.

"Are you going to leave me hanging, Kat?" He shifted his hips just enough to make his point.

Was she?

STEEL WASN'T sure what to think. The woman ran cold one minute, hot the next. And she was blazing when he brought her to orgasm.

But now he had a problem. What he would consider a *big* problem.

And if Kat decided his problem wasn't hers, then he'd have no choice but to accept that. But, for fuck's sake, he hoped she really didn't just leave him hanging.

The whole time he had watched her swim had been like foreplay. Watching her smoothly move through the water, her muscles defined but still feminine. Her arm and back muscles flexing with each stroke. Her thighs and calves working with each kick.

He had been tempted to go down to her. Instead, he'd stayed upstairs and moved to her balcony where he'd have a good view.

And now, she stood within his arms, tense once again.

When he had told her to go to the rail and grab it, it had been a test. If she had told him to fuck off, then he knew she either wasn't interested at all or simply wasn't ready. But when she moved to the rail and wrapped her fingers around it until her knuckles turned white, he knew she did want it. She was interested, but something was holding her back.

She was either denying herself for some reason or was... afraid?

Was it possible?

Was she scared of sex, or him? Or maybe it was sex *with* him.

Or did she have a man already? Was he trying to get in somewhere where he shouldn't?

He hadn't gotten any indication of it, but Kat hadn't been the most open. "Is someone already in there, Kat?"

"What?"

"Am I trying to get in where someone already is? Do you belong to someone? Am I stepping on someone's territory?"

"If all that misogynistic bullshit means you're asking if I have a boyfriend, I don't."

*Well, thank fuck for that.* "Is it me, then? Because right now, I want to toss you over my fucking shoulder, take you inside and make you come harder than you just did out here on the balcony. So, is it me?" Her delayed answer had him releasing her and stepping back. "It's me."

*Fuck.* He'd been pushing her and—

"No," she sighed and shook her head, "it's me."

He frowned. "Yeah, you don't want me."

"It's not you," she said.

Then it hit him. "You don't like sex." But that couldn't be true, her response to him touching her in no way proved that. The woman, once she relaxed, had totally let go. And who the fuck didn't like sex?

Was that even a thing?

She opened her mouth and avoided his eyes. "I'm not good at it."

"Not good at what?" What wasn't she good at? Not being able to separate her feelings from sex? Not being able just to have a one-night stand or just a sexual relationship with someone?

"Sex."

He pinned his lips together and schooled his face. She wasn't fucking with him. No, she was being genuine and thought she wasn't good at sex. But from what he'd just saw, heard and felt from her was someone who was responsive. And being responsive was a huge part of being good at sex.

"Hold up. Did someone tell you that?"

"Yes."

"Who?"

It took her a long time to answer. Too long. "A guy in high school."

"A guy in high school told you you sucked at sex." He tried not to snort because she was being totally fucking serious. A guy in high school had no clue what good sex was. At that age, there was only one reason to fuck. To get off. And they usually didn't care if the girl did. So, if someone told her that...

"Yes. I think he was pretending to like me just so..."

Just so he could get down her pants. Steel knew that trick. He knew plenty of guys who "liked" a girl only to get laid and then once he got the girl, he moved on.

It was an asshole move.

And he *might* have been one of those assholes.

"It was one asshole. What about the rest?"

Did the woman just blush? Did Kat, the fighter, just fucking blush?

*Oh fuck.* "He was your first?"

She spun away from him. "I don't want to talk about this." But as she pushed past him to go inside, he grabbed her bicep to stop her and moved to stand in front of her.

Tucking a finger under her chin, he lifted it. She still wouldn't look at him, but the heat was now gone from her cheeks. In fact, she looked pissed.

"Kat—"

She jerked her arm out of his grip and he let her go. But she didn't move away. Instead, she finally met his eyes and with a stubborn tilt of her head, she stated, "He wasn't my first. He was my only."

Steel blinked. Then his eyes slid to the side as he ran those words once more through his brain. He had to have heard her wrong.

There was no way this woman standing before him—who might not be thirty yet, but close enough—only had sex with some asshole teenage boy once and never had it again.

*No. Fucking. Way.*

That just did not compute in his head.

"He was the only one you ever had sex with?"

She didn't answer.

He tried again. "He took your virginity and then didn't want anything to do with you?"

"It doesn't matter."

Oh yes the fuck it did. It bothered her. He could hear it in her voice no matter how hard she tried to hide it. And not only that, it mattered enough for her not to try having it with anyone else.

He hoped the motherfucker who did that to Kat eventually had come down with a bad case of the crabs.

"He told the rest of the seniors I was easy, so I spent the rest of my high school years fighting them off."

"Fighting," he repeated in a whisper.

"Yes, *fighting* them off. They thought I was easy and would put out. They didn't care that he told them I was a 'horrible lay.'"

Of course, they fucking didn't. They were just looking for a warm hole to bust a nut into.

"How old were you?"

Her jaw got even tighter. "Does it matter?"

"Yes." Yes, it fucking did. Because he needed to know how many years she had to fight off those assholes. How many years she had to protect herself against them probably getting handsy and not taking no for an answer.

*Jesus fuck.* He'd pushed her, too.

No wonder she bit his lip.

"I was a freshman."

Steel's brain went back in time to figure out how old she had been as a freshman. He couldn't even remember how old he'd been. Fourteen? Fifteen?

Too fucking young.

"But you've dated, right?" It still blew his mind she hadn't found anyone else to attempt it with again.

"I've tried."

"And no one..."

"No one."

*Damn.* "He was a boy; you need a man."

"And you think you'll convince me I'll be good at sex or enjoy it because you're a man?"

"I've gotten no complaints."

She threw her hands up and went inside. He followed her in, closing the door behind him.

His eyes slid to the condoms he had thrown on her nightstand earlier. However, right now, he needed the patience of a saint.

Unfortunately, he didn't have the patience of a saint. But he would do his goddamn best.

"Are you telling me you didn't enjoy what happened on that balcony? Because if you say no, you're lying. You just need someone to show you how good sex can be. And by the way you responded out there, Kat..."

Even though her back was to him, he knew the exact moment she spotted the handful of condoms next to the bed. She went over to them and once there, turned, holding one up between her fingers.

He shrugged. "Like you said, I'm an asshole. I had plans. I thought you'd be interested. I didn't know the reasons for your mixed signals, now I do. So, I was wrong..." *Fuck*, he hoped he wasn't wrong.

She tossed the condom back on the nightstand. "You weren't wrong. And yes, whatever you did to me out there," her eyes slid to the balcony doors and held there for a long moment, then slid back to him. "I liked it."

*No shit.* He wanted to point out that she more than "liked" it. But he also wasn't stupid.

"And... I want you to do it again."

"Now?" He winced when his voice cracked in the middle of that question. He cleared his throat with a low cough.

"I'm not... I don't know..."

This strong woman was once again unsure of herself. He fucking hated that. He went over to her and, as he approached, her face tilted up until they were toe to toe. He ran his thumb along her jawline.

"All that means, Kat, is we go slow."

He might fucking die doing it, but for fuck's sake, he was going to enjoy whatever time he had with Kat before he did.

————

HE WAS GOING to fucking die. Just drop over dead.

Having Kat sleeping pinned against him when he hadn't even had a chance to fuck her yet was just going to kill him.

He'd had a perpetual erection since earlier and he hadn't been able to do anything about it.

He wanted to. But he was the stupid ass who suggested they take it slow.

Just like his death.

Maybe he needed to go back to his own room and take care of his issue. And of course, unlike him, Kat was sleeping soundly.

He had made her come about four times.

Four.

Kat – 4. Steel – 0.

*Fuck.*

His tongue and his fingers had gotten a great workout while his cock whimpered in suffering. And worse, his balls were ready to pack up and leave him.

He turned his head to read the clock next to the bed. Midnight.

It was time for his rounds anyway. Maybe he could take a quick pit stop on the way around the house and relieve some of his frustration.

He smoothly rolled toward the edge of the bed, trying not to wake her.

Apparently, he failed. He was halfway across the room when she asked sleepily, "What's the matter?"

"Nothing. Go back to sleep."

Even in the limited light he could see her push up onto her elbows and a dark chunk of her short hair fall across her forehead. "Where are you going?"

He couldn't believe how much he liked short hair right now. "On my rounds."

"Rounds? Have you been doing that since you came here?"

"Yes."

"Are you coming back here then?"

"Do you want me to?"

"Yes."

Even though she probably couldn't see it in the dark, he turned his head away and smiled. "Give me ten."

And as tempted as he was to turn that ten into twenty, he didn't. He walked both the outside and inside of the house, made sure everything was secure and headed back to Kat.

Who was still awake, waiting for him.

He was glad he hadn't taken a detour, because not five minutes later, he got to see if it was possible to grip her short hair while she learned to give him head.

The short answer was, fuck yes.

## Chapter Eight

THE ROOM SEEMED SMALL. Most likely because it was packed with a variety of male bodies. Or mostly male from what she could see. And the smell—like a men's locker room gone horribly wrong—was also enough to make her gag.

Like last night, when she'd taken Steel's cock in her mouth and accidentally took it too deep.

He had laid back in the bed, letting her experiment. Sometimes a little noise—possibly a whimper, but she didn't point that out to him—would escape him and when that happened, she'd concentrate on whatever caused it.

Eventually his relaxed demeanor changed just about the same time his breathing did. And when his muscles clenched beneath her fingers, which she was letting explore his body as she licked, sucked and nibbled down his length, he barked out a warning.

But she didn't heed it because she was enjoying watching him lose his shit.

Then he really lost his shit. Right into her mouth.

His hot wad of cum had sat on her tongue for a few seconds while she decided whether to get up and go spit it out, or just swallow it.

During her dilemma, Steel said her choice either way wouldn't insult him, he was just happy to finally relieve himself of his load.

After she came back from the bathroom, she had asked him what men preferred and he'd answered, "They prefer you suck their cock. What you do with it afterwards, they don't give a shit. They might say they do, but spit or swallow, we really don't care."

Which she told him was very enlightening and he gave her a sexy grin until she told him next time she'd try swallowing, which got her a response of, "fuck," on a low groan and him planting a fat, noisy kiss on her mouth before falling into a coma.

She wiped away her current smile caused by that memory, and let her gaze sweep the room again.

Steel's hand was planted solidly at the small of her back. She had a feeling it was to "claim" her since, upon closer inspection, she *was* the only woman there and a lot of the men's eyes had turned toward her when she'd walked in.

She also figured out it wasn't just the smell of piss and sweat that permeated the room. It was beer and booze.

And plenty of it.

Since drunks would try things they normally wouldn't while they were sober, Steel kept her close, which she appreciated. She could hold her own, but not against a roomful of possibly drunk men with a mob mentality, especially in tight quarters.

Some places in Vegas could be seedy. This was definitely one of those spots.

But then, it wasn't a permanent place for fights since it was rare that an underground fight would happen at the same location. Tonight, it was in this room in some run-down brick building. Next week, it would be in some other hole.

At least that's what Bobby, one of her sparring partners, told her. This morning, as she made Steel breakfast, he had asked if she knew where any underground fights were.

He quickly followed that question with, "And don't pretend you don't fucking know what I'm talking about."

Of course she knew about underground fights, she'd just never went to one. She had no reason to and she doubted Berger, or her sponsors would approve.

"I know what you're talking about, but I never had a reason to go to one."

"You don't. Doesn't mean I don't."

She had turned from the stove where she was making them omelets—*with* the yolks—and sausage, while he got the coffee brewing.

"Do you know what you're getting into?"

Steel smiled at the coffeemaker. "Just want to go spar a little bit."

Which was a bullshit answer. Underground fights weren't for "sparring." They were for beating the fuck out of an opponent and taking home cash winnings.

"You can spar at The Strike Zone," she reminded him.

"Can't make bank at The Strike Zone."

"So, you've done this before."

"Kitty Kat, this ain't my first rodeo."

"Is this something you do on the regular?"

"When I'm in the mood. Or have some frustration to work out."

She had pursed her lips and studied him before stating, "Frustration from me."

"Told you we're going to go slow. Whatever you need, whatever you want, you're going to get. When you're ready. Not before."

A man coming the opposite direction bumped into Kat, bringing her back to the present. "Sorry, honey," the drunk slurred. Then he stopped and let his gaze rake up and down her body. "*Sweeeeeet.* Are you here to be a ring girl? Where's your bikini?"

"It's going to be in your dreams, when I knock you the fuck out. Get lost, asshole," Steel growled in his face, his arm now thrown heavily over her shoulders.

Definitely staking his claim to anyone watching.

Normally, she wouldn't tolerate that. She glanced around the room of men in various states of undress and drunkenness. She also wasn't stupid.

She assumed the guys in only a pair of jeans or shorts were either waiting their turn to get into the makeshift ring or had already fought.

The crowd cheered and the yells became even louder as Steel worked their way closer to the center of the room, his hand tightening on her shoulder as he guided her.

"This was a bad idea bringing you," he muttered just loud enough for her to catch.

"But you need this."

"Fuck yeah. I need this," he answered, his eyes continually assessing the room and the groups of men. "And I'm not leaving you anywhere alone until that stalker gets caught."

She lifted an eyebrow. "You think it's safer here?"

He brought her to an abrupt halt and tipped his face down to hers. "You're always safer with me."

She rolled her lips inward to keep from grinning and rolling her eyes. "So damn cocky."

He snorted and shook his head before steering her to a guy standing by the ring watching the current fight closely.

The organizer was the epitome of sleaze. He fit the bill when it came to someone who ran illegal underground fights. He also had a big brute of a man standing behind him. Kat assumed the big guy was a bodyguard or maybe the person who held the cash.

She wasn't sure. And she certainly didn't care enough to ask. She just wanted Steel to do what he came for, to get what he needed, so they could get the hell out of there.

She might need another shower after his fight. A long one while using a scrub brush.

Kat turned her eyes to the current fight in the "ring" while Steel talked to Mr. Sleazy. The two men going at it were definitely amateurs. They had no form, no plan, they were just trying to beat the snot out of each other. And while doing so, they were both losing a lot of blood.

Kat was sure that blood wasn't cleaned up after each fight, either.

"I sure hope you're vaccinated against Hepatitis," she muttered when Steel was done with Sammy Sleazebag.

"I don't plan on touching the floor," he told her. "Two more bouts and I'm in the ring."

"Against who?"

He shrugged and at the same time dropped his arm around her shoulders again, pulling her against his side. "Don't care. I just told the guy the bigger the better."

Kat leaned away enough to stare up at him. "Seriously?"

He dropped his gaze from the activity in the ring to her. "Yeah. Why?"

"You just want to fight the biggest, baddest mother-fucker in the joint?"

A grin spread over his face and his toothpick flicked from one corner of his mouth to the other. "Yeah. I want a challenge."

"I'm certainly not that," she muttered.

"Not in the ring, no."

That comment made her believe she was a challenge to him in other ways.

"Kitty Kat, I don't go a hundred percent with you when we spar. You know that."

"Because I'm a woman."

"Because it's sparring," he countered.

"And I'm a woman."

"There's no reason to go full bore with you, Kat, just so you can prove yourself. That would be stupid. You don't need to beat a man; you need to beat Calamity Jayne."

"I can beat a man."

He took a deep inhale and she realized he was beginning to get annoyed. "You can't beat me."

*Damn.* "That sounds like a challenge."

His dark eyes landed on hers. "It's not. Get it out of your fucking head. I will not fight you. You want to spar, I'm good with it. I will not knock you out, because, Kat, no matter how tough you think you are, you cannot go even one round with me in a real fight. And that's not a challenge, it's the fucking truth. You might not like to hear it, but you have to accept it."

"Okay, fine. But I can beat a man."

"Jesus fuck," he muttered and shook his head. "If you're trying to work me the fuck up for my fight, you're doing a good job at it."

A loud cheer went up around the room and a few seconds later, one of the men fell to the floor out cold. A floor, Kat noted, that was concrete and not a mat.

A few more seconds later, someone was dragging the knocked-out guy out of the center of the "ring" by his feet, leaving a bloody trail behind.

After a shout and a fist pump into the air, the winner left the ring wearing a bloody grin and collected a wad of cash from Sammy McSleazebag.

Not even a minute later, two more guys entered. One looked like he weighed about a buck ten and had just smoked meth, the other a good two-twenty and looked like he'd just ate two whole large pizzas.

"Well, you'd better get ready, this won't last long," she murmured to Steel.

And she was right. It was over before it even started.

The lightweight screamed at the top of his lungs as he charged the bigger guy and launched himself at him, while the big guy clobbered the guy upside the head mid-flight. The meth-head dropped instantly to the ground at the bigger guy's feet. It was then that Kat had to wince when the skinny one got a good kick in the head for good measure.

Sammy Sleazemaster yelled to Steel, "You're up."

Steel dropped his arm from around her shoulders, spit his toothpick out and ripped his tank top over his head. He pressed it into her hands as he leaned in and planted a big, fat kiss on her lips, surprising her. "For luck."

"You need luck?"

"Fuck no." He stepped up to the ring, then said over his broad shoulder, "Stay close where I can see you, got me?"

She wasn't planning on taking a stroll through the room to socialize. Instead, she moved closer to the ring or whatever it was supposed to be. Basically, it was some length of rope hooked to some poles that were set up in a sort of square.

Steel entered the ring, jogged in place for a few seconds, jerked his head to the left and to the right, swung his arms around a few times and then his eyes sliced through the crowd surrounding the ring.

Probably wondering who his opponent was.

A group of rowdy, noisy men parted opposite from where Steel stood and a man who had to be at least three hundred pounds and an NFL linebacker made his way into the ring.

*Holy fuck.*

"Steel," she called out, her heart in her throat.

His eyes flicked to her but only for a second before they landed on the huge guy. Steel didn't look worried. In fact, his eyes narrowed, and his fingers curled into fists.

Bare knuckled fighting. That's what they were doing. No

protection. Nothing. Not even a mouthguard. One good punch from that guy and Steel could lose every one of his straight, white teeth.

Basically, this was street fighting with money being tossed around. And from what she could see so far, a lot of it.

A deep voice yelled, "Fight!" and the two men approached each other flat-footed. The huge guy had to be three inches taller than Steel, which became obvious as they closed in on one another.

A big meaty fist headed toward Steel's face and he leaned back in time for the guy to miss. Steel recovered quickly and moved to the side, cracking the guy in his ribs with his shin.

The big man didn't even flinch.

Kat was bouncing on her toes, her muscles working as if she was in the ring with Steel. She moved the same as he moved around the ring, dodging and ducking punches, kicking and punching, but basically not trying to take the guy out, only trying to tire him out.

Which didn't take long.

There were no rules here. No bell. No timed rounds. Someone simply yelled "Fight!" and the action started and didn't end until it was over in one way or another.

In a way, she liked that. Watching Steel in the ring got her heart pumping and her blood flowing. Watching his body as he moved, watching his strength as he kicked and punched, turned her on more than she wanted to admit.

The tattoo on his back rippled and moved as he did. He said he was a Marine, but his tattoo was not the typical symbol for the Marines. She knew what that looked like. She made a mental note to ask him about it later.

The two men currently circled each other, their fists up, but the big guy had slowed down a lot. Even so, there was still power behind his punch, which was evident when Steel missed a block and took one to the face. Good thing it glanced off his cheek and didn't connect with his teeth or nose.

He might have a black eye or a bruise after that but that should be all. He wasn't bleeding and he hadn't slowed down.

Steel let him get in two more hits. One to the gut and a kick to the thigh. But that last kick was the big guy's downfall. He was so tired, he lost his balance before he could plant his foot back on the ground. Steel saw his opportunity and went in for the kill. He swept the weight-bearing leg out from under the guy and as the big man tumbled to the ground, Steel got in a good kick to the temple and a punch square in the guy's face.

The guy's head flopped backward as he landed heavily to his knees onto the concrete and then slowly toppled over like a huge felled tree.

Even after all that, he wasn't knocked out. He was still conscious and was attempting to get to his feet.

Steel solved that problem by squatting down, grabbing the guy's head and introducing it to his knee. Once, twice and...

Goodnight.

It was over.

A roar went up around the room since the big guy was probably a local favorite. That meant a lot of people lost money.

Which didn't make them happy.

Steel would probably want to grab his winnings and leave quickly, but she wasn't ready to leave yet.

She watched him leave the ring, approach Sleazemeister and grab a handful of cash, tucking it into a zippered pocket of the nylon running pants he wore. He came back over to her, sweat dripping off his face as he pulled on his sneakers and put his hand out for his tank top.

Before he pulled it on, he used it to wipe off his face, leaving blood smears and sweat stains on it.

"Maybe we should've brought a towel," she muttered, her nose wrinkling up.

He didn't answer. He was obviously still too pumped up. Kat didn't miss the veins popping out of his shoulder and arm muscles.

And, *holy shit*, that was hot as fuck.

If they weren't in a disgusting room full of smelly strangers, she'd tackle him right there.

He tipped his head toward her, his eyes still jacked, his blood probably still humming through his veins. She knew how she felt after a fight, especially after a win and it was a complete high.

Invincible. That's how she felt after they held her fist up declaring her the winner.

"Let's go."

Because he was jacked, she knew he wouldn't like what she said next, "I want in."

"No."

"I want in," she stated louder and headed toward Sammy McSleaze.

Steel grabbed her arm none too gently, stopping her. "And I said no. There are no females here to fight."

"I can beat these guys. It'll be good practice for my fight with Jayne."

"No, you can't. They fight dirty."

"I can fight dirty."

"You saw the size of the guy I just fought. You could pull someone like that."

"I'll ask for someone smaller."

"You don't get a choice."

"I thought you asked Sammy for the biggest guy?"

"Sammy?"

"The organizer."

"His name is Sammy? I thought it was Tommy."

"Tommy. Sammy. Who cares?" She tugged at her arm, but he didn't let her go. "I want to fight."

A growl escaped his lips and continued throughout his next words, "No, Kat. Let's go."

If it was possible, she would have shot daggers from her eyes at his hand holding her back. Since that wasn't possible, she lifted her narrowed ones to his. "I'm staying. I want in on this action. Wasn't it you who said that I can't protect myself and can only fight in a controlled environment? Let me prove you wrong."

"You have nothing to prove."

"What about you?"

His head jerked back, and his frown turned into a menacing scowl. "What about me?"

"Why are you here? You don't need the money. I know what Berg is paying you. Or, really, what I'm paying you. What do *you* have to prove?"

"Nothing. I like a good fight without limitations. And to relieve my... frustration."

Ah, yes, his frustration excuse. "You could relieve frustration with a good run." She set her jaw. "Come on, I want this."

"Kat," he growled.

"Steel, I need to do this."

"You're going to get hurt."

She shrugged. "Then I get hurt. I've been hurt before."

"You don't have a mouthguard, no gloves, nothing. It would be bare fists. And, for fuck's sake, their fists are bigger than yours."

"I don't care."

"You get off on getting hurt?"

*What?* "No. Do you?"

He leaned close and growled in her ear. "Yeah, sometimes I do, Kat. Sometimes I fucking lose to punish myself for all the shit I've done. Sometimes I purposely lose to remember what the fuck it feels like to feel something. I have a feeling it's the same for you."

"No."

"Bullshit," he grunted. "I saw it those two days you sparred with someone other than me. I've seen you take a hit when you could have avoided it. But you won't try that bullshit with me because you know I won't tolerate it."

"You're imagining things."

His fingers on her arm tightened to the point of pain.

He suddenly let her go and jerked his chin up toward the organizer. "Go. But don't expect me to watch."

# Chapter Nine

*GO. BUT DON'T EXPECT me to watch.*

As soon as that came out of his mouth, he knew that was a big fucking lie. He was her paid bodyguard, he had no choice but to watch.

But the fuck if he wanted to.

He did not want to see a man beating the shit out of Kat. In fact, if that happened, nobody could stop him from entering the ring to save her.

And if he did that, she would hate his guts.

Then he'd be kicked out of her bed and the opportunity to take her where he wanted to take her would just disappear.

*Poof.* Gone.

No more giving her explosive orgasms, no more feeling her hot little mouth around his cock, no chance at getting in where he was dying to go.

But even so, there was no fucking way he could watch her get fucked up.

After talking with the organizer, she came back to him, bouncing on her toes, and grabbed his tank, shaking it. Her eyes were lit up when she said, "Next fight."

*Great.* "Kat, you can back out."

The light in her eyes extinguished and she planted her feet. "I'm not backing out. I just got in."

He closed his eyes and sucked in a long breath in an attempt not to grab her and drag her ass out of there.

*Patience.*

*Fucking patience.*

Just like he needed when it came to wanting to have sex with her.

*Jesus fuck.* Right now, he had zero patience. But he dug deep. "Remember, there's no ref, no rounds, no breaks. It goes until someone taps out, gets knocked out or *dies.*"

She responded with more snark than he had patience for. "Are you saying I shouldn't die if I want to win?"

He ground his teeth, then muttered, "That would be ideal."

She smiled, rose up on her toes and pressed her mouth to his. "For luck," she said when it was over.

He cocked an eyebrow. "You need luck?"

"Fuck no," she echoed his earlier response, her smile even wider now.

*Jesus,* he never saw someone so excited to get their ass kicked. Because in this room, with these fighters, that was going to happen. Then he was going to totally lose his shit.

Another roar went up and Steel knew exactly why. When he looked over her shoulder toward the ring, he was right. The current fight was over.

The visibly stunned, but still conscious, loser was being helped away by two other men as he shook his head, probably trying to get rid of the stars he was seeing.

*Fuck,* it was time. "Kat..."

"I'll be fine," she said, her eyes on the ring as she patted his stomach.

*Patted his fucking stomach.* Like that was going to make it all better. "Most of these guys are not professional."

"I've seen that."

"They're not going to care you're a woman."

"Good."

*Good!* He didn't know if he should laugh or cry at that answer.

Then she was kicking off her flip-flops and was about to rip her T-shirt up and over her head when he grabbed her wrist.

"Uh, no. Shirt on."

"I'm wearing a sports bra."

*No shit.* Her tits were flattened out like fucking lumpy pancakes.

"Shirt stays on," he growled. "This is not The Strike Zone. This is not a controlled environment, Kat. I'm one fucking man." He hoped the way he said that last part made his meaning clear. He could fend off a few of them but not a whole roomful of horny, drunk and violent men.

Though, he would die trying.

It surprised the shit out of him when she dropped the hem of her shirt and gave him a quick nod.

*Thank fuck.*

But then she was gone, working her way through the ropes into the makeshift ring.

Immediately the shouts, whistles and cat calls turned deafening. Just that alone made him want to throw her over his shoulder and carry her out of that ring and out of that building. He'd rather fight Kat than a whole crowd of men.

His eyes scanned that crowd as he reached into his pocket for his wallet and pulled out another toothpick.

After tucking it between his lips, he pushed past a couple of men to get closer to the ring, in case he needed to grab her and make a quick exit.

He kept scanning the mob surrounding the ring until the man slated to fight Kat stepped inside.

He was about six foot to her five foot nothing and had

about sixty pounds on her, if not more, by the looks of the beer gut hanging over the waistline of his dirty and stained gray sweatpants. He wore no shirt and his hairy chest and belly was already slick with sweat.

The good news was, he appeared out of shape, so that was one thing Kat had on him. She had endurance, smarts and skill. Steel hoped the guy lacked all three of those.

While he should feel relieved with her opponent, he didn't. The fighter she drew might not be in the best shape, but he also might be a mean son of a bitch and did outweigh her. If he got her to the ground, she could be fucked.

And not in the way Steel wanted to fuck her.

He shoved another guy, who tried to worm his way in front of him, out of his line of sight. When the guy began to bitch, Steel just gave him a look.

It was enough.

He turned his attention back to the ring. That was where he needed to keep it, that was where it needed to be. No one in that building, in that room, gave a fuck what happened to Kat. Only him. That meant it was his duty to make sure nothing happened to her. During the fight or afterward.

Someone yelled, "Fight!" and the man just stood there, waiting for Kat to make a move.

She did. Bouncing barefoot in her cat-like way up to him, she gave him a Cheshire cat smile, which caught the guy off guard, and then popped him a good one right in the nose.

Unfortunately, it didn't even faze the guy. He returned her smile and then took a wild swing. Kat ducked and dodged before popping the guy again.

Once again, it didn't affect him.

Steel knew the power behind her punches. For her size, she was strong. But for him to just shake off those hits? He started to worry. "Slow it down, Kat. Don't tire yourself out."

"Hey, no coaching from the peanut gallery," came from the drunk asshole next to him.

Kat probably couldn't hear him anyway since the room was so loud. *Hell*, Steel could hardly hear himself think.

Her opponent did a roundhouse kick that surprised both Steel and Kat. *What the fuck?*

He must know martial arts. Or at least took martial arts when he was a kid. Because he sure didn't look like he'd kept up with it.

But the sloppy kick, if it had made contact, could've done some damage.

He took a couple more jabs at Kat, missing each time as she kept on her toes.

*Thatta girl. You watch his moves; I'll watch the rest of the crowd.*

But he wasn't watching the crowd when the guy did another roundhouse kick.

*What the fuck!* Was that the only martial art move he knew?

Kat skirted it, but then bounced right back in front of the guy. She wasn't kicking at all and she wasn't quick on the punches, either. Steel was glad to see that she was biding her time like he did during his own fight.

She'd lob a few punches just to keep the man moving but then she'd make sure she was out of the strike zone of his kicks.

The man was getting tired. Steel spotted it the second the man was about to launch into his third roundhouse. He wasn't the only one who saw it coming, so did Kat.

Steel held his breath as she stopped dead, planted both feet and waited for the kick. And when the man kicked high, she ducked low, and as she quickly rose, she kneed him right in the nuts, dropping him instantly to his ass on the concrete.

The whole room collectively groaned, including Steel, who had to fight from covering his own crotch at that point and wincing.

*Damn.*

Steel spit out the toothpick that had snapped in two during the nut-busting move Kat did.

With the guy sitting on the ground unable to move, Kat did her own roundhouse kick, nailing him upside the head. That took him the rest of the way down, flat on his back.

Then she moved to his head and got him into an anaconda choke hold.

Steel could barely hear Kat demanding the guy to "tap out" over the yelling crowd as she tightened the hold around his neck, cutting off his air supply completely and slowly squeezing the life out of him.

With a purple face and, Steel was sure, purple as fuck balls, a few more seconds later the guy finally tapped out.

Kat released him and quickly moved out of his range, heading toward Steel, but keeping alert. She was wearing a big smile and once again her eyes were lit up. Her whole body noticeably wired.

As soon as she was within arm's length, he grabbed her, helped her through the ropes and said, "Shoes on. Get your money. We're getting the fuck out of here."

He was relieved she didn't argue, and kept a hand on her as she got her money from Tommy. As soon as she tucked it into the pocket of her track pants, he was steering her right back out of the crowd, pushing men out of the way when needed.

"Keep walking and don't stop until we get to the car, got me?"

"Yes."

Even though she agreed, he kept talking just loud enough for her to hear. "Both of us just took a lot of dough from these guys. We came in as underdogs and everyone was betting against us. They won't be happy to lose that much scratch, so we need to split ASAP."

She walked faster to keep up with him. "You have a gun?"

"In the car."

That response got her jogging back to where Steel had parked the rental. He kept one eye on her and another over his shoulder to make sure they weren't being followed.

Luckily, they weren't, but he was still relieved when the Mustang came into view. He popped the locks as he approached, and Kat quickly climbed in. As soon as he got in the driver's seat, he hit the start button and locked the doors.

He turned his head to look at her profile in the dark. "You don't say a word of this to Berger, otherwise my ass is going to get fired from this job. Then I'm never going to hear the end of it."

He wasn't even sure she heard him when she turned to face him and yelled, "I did it."

The excitement in her voice was hard to miss. In fact, it smacked him upside the head.

"Yeah," he grumbled and shoved the gear shifter into drive.

"I did it, Steel. I fucking did it."

"Yeah. I saw, Kat."

"You didn't think I could."

He wasn't going to argue that.

"But I did."

"Yeah, Kat, I know."

Suddenly she launched herself out of her seat and at him, grabbed his face and kissed him hard. He let off the gas since he couldn't see shit and didn't want to wreck. He pulled out of her grip. "Hey! I'm trying to drive."

"I did it, Steel," she whispered as she sank back into the

passenger seat and pulled the seatbelt across her body, latching herself in.

Steel grinned at the windshield. "Yeah, baby, you did it. You did good."

———

SHE WAS BUZZING. What had happened in that room gave her a high like no other.

She had done it. And proved Steel wrong.

Proved that whole damn room wrong.

Her. Kat Callahan had won her first underground fight.

Against a man.

She could hardly sit still in the passenger seat as Steel pointed the Ford back toward Boulder City.

They needed to get back to the house because she needed to burn off some of her energy and she knew just how she wanted to do it.

"Starving. Going to hit an all-night diner."

"No!" burst out of her before she could stop it.

His head twisted toward her. "Why not?"

"Because..." *I need to jump your fucking bones. Like now.* "Because we're gross. We need a shower first. I don't want to sit in a diner and eat as dirty as we are."

"No one's going to care. It's like two o'clock in the morning. Nobody smells or looks good at two."

"I can't think of eating while I'm this disgusting." Lie. She could, but that didn't matter. What mattered was making the trip back to Boulder City as quickly as possible, otherwise she was going to have him pull over somewhere. And she didn't want the first time she had sex with Steel to be in a rental car.

She also didn't want to have sex for the second time in her life in a car, either.

She was sure with Steel it would be better than her first time, but still...

No.

And they *were* disgustingly filthy. Both of them.

"I'm hungry," he grumbled.

"So am I," she snapped, then reined in her impatience. "But we need to get back."

His head twisted toward her again and she could feel him studying her. She faced front and ignored him, trying to keep her knee from bouncing a mile a minute. Ignoring her raw knuckles, she wrung her hands in her lap instead.

"What's wrong with you?"

"Nothing. I'm just wound up."

"No shit."

Good thing the fight had been south of the city so the trip back to the house was only twenty minutes. Even so, she was climbing out of her skin that whole time. And it got worse as the garage door opened and he pulled the Mustang into its spot.

She was out of the car before he even had it in park.

"Kat!" he barked as she rushed from the car. "You don't go inside without me."

She wasn't running to get inside. She was running around the front of the car and, as soon as he unfolded all six feet of him out of it and closed the door, she hit him full force with her body, slamming him against the Mustang.

His arms automatically went around her as she climbed up his body, her arms circling his neck and her legs his waist.

She took his mouth just as it opened. His surprised response was muffled and quickly turned to a groan as she swept her tongue between his lips and kissed him hard and long. His fingers ran up her spine until he grasped the back of her head, holding on as he began to kiss her back.

Yes, that's what she wanted. Needed. But tonight she wanted more than last night.

Tonight, she wanted everything.

Her heart pounded and her blood rushed as he kissed her fiercely, the fingers on his other hand digging into her ass to keep her anchored at his waist.

It wasn't long until she discovered how "okay" he was with her attacking him. His cock was hard and hot through his nylon pants as it pressed against her. And thinking about him being inside her made everything on her clench in anticipation.

She broke off the kiss. "We need to go upstairs." Her voice was husky and breathy. Nothing like it was normally.

Her nipples ached for his touch, his mouth. And so did her pussy.

"We were supposed to go slow," he reminded her.

She shook her head. "Fuck slow. I've wasted too much time."

He pulled his head back and his dark eyes hit hers. "Is this all because of the fight?"

"Do you want to question it? Or just do it?"

He didn't even hesitate. "Door number two."

"Then why are we still in the garage?"

"Good fucking question." He carried her through the garage with her still wrapped around his chest and waist. With one hand he held her tightly, with the other he opened and shut the door, reset the alarm and then strode through the dark house and up the stairs, not even breathing heavily under her weight.

The whole time, she was kissing, sucking and biting along his neck, and he almost stumbled on the stairs once. But he didn't tell her to stop. No, he moved even faster.

He kicked the partially open door to her bedroom, and she expected him to throw her on the bed and ravish her, but he didn't. Instead, he let her slide slowly down his body, making sure her pussy slid over the evidence of his approval of her actions.

"Shower," she whispered.

"You want your first time in the shower?"

*Your first time.*

She needed to look at it like that. That this was her first time, because the time when she was a freshman no longer counted. She needed a do-over.

"No, the bed. But we need to wash off the filth first."

"Go. I can wait."

She raised her eyebrows at him. "Go? You don't want to join me?"

"I'll ask again, Kitty Kat, do you want your first time in the shower?"

She grinned. "Can't control yourself?"

"You're wired as fuck right now, are you sure you can control *yourself*? I'm pretty fucking irresistible." The last was said with a cocky grin.

Kat snorted. "You were until that comment."

Her flip-flops flew across the room when she kicked them off. She tugged her T-shirt off and threw it at Steel, then shucked her track pants and panties in one swoop.

Steel's nostrils were flaring, and his eyes held a lot of heat as he let his gaze rake down her body. She lifted her hands to the sports bra, which was still damp from sweat. "Hate these, do you?"

"Sometimes there's a need for them, but not all the time. You've got great tits, Kitty Kat."

"Are you saying I should flaunt them?"

His eyes narrowed a bit and he pursed his lips. "Didn't say that."

She slowly wiggled the damp elastic fabric up over her breasts and head, then threw it in his face with a laugh.

Steel wasn't laughing, he was looking way too intense. "We're tag teaming this shower, Kat. Get your ass in there quick."

"Impatient?"

"Your enthusiasm is rubbing off on me. Get your ass in the shower double time. Because remember when I said I was hungry? I need to eat. And it's going to be you."

Kat's thighs quivered as she rushed past him into the master bathroom, quickly turning on the lights, starting the shower and getting in.

She was in and out in two minutes flat.

"Damn," Steel whispered when she came out of the bathroom to find he had stripped down, as well. And his cock was in his hand, hard as... *steel.* "That was quick."

She passed him and gave his delectable muscular bare ass a stinging slap. "Double time, soldier."

"I was never a soldier," he grumbled.

"You said you were a Marine."

"Marines aren't soldiers."

Kat shrugged. "Semantics."

"Not even. Right now I don't have time to explain it to you, because some sassy-mouthed woman needs to be fucked good and hard for the first time in her life."

"Oh yeah?"

"Yeah."

"Well, then double time, Marine! *Hoorah!*"

"Jesus fuck," Steel grumbled as he went, leaving the door open. She heard from inside the bathroom, "It's *oorah!*"

"*Oorah* fucking cares?" she yelled back, unable to contain her "sassy mouth." She was a mixture of nerves and excitement.

She ran to the nightstand where she had stashed the pile of condoms in the drawer and dug them all back out, tossing them onto the bed. She stood beside it staring at the mattress and all the condoms, unsure what to do with herself in the meantime.

"Jesus fuck," she heard muttered again, this time behind her. How did he sneak up on her? "Are we going to use all of them?"

She turned. "Are we?"

He grinned. "We can try."

Kat grinned. She lost that grin as her gaze roamed down his body. His dark hair was wet, a few drops of water clung to his pecs and face and rolled down his six-pack abs. And one particular drop of water took the path of dark hair that went from his navel to the thicker patch around his erection. Which also had a bead on the tip, but not from water. "How did you take a shower that quickly?"

"In boot camp, you learn to shower *really* quick. Enough chit chat."

"I agree." Then she launched herself at him just like in the garage. He caught her as she clung to his chest and licked a drop of water from his neck. "Too much talking, not enough action, Marine."

"Fuck, Kat," he grumbled.

"Yes, please."

She went for his mouth, but he pulled back to ask, "You sure you're ready?"

"I am so fucking ready," she whispered and kissed him.

They were both panting when they broke that kiss.

"Kat," he whispered.

"Yes?"

"Just reminding you, you thought I was an asshole."

"*Was?*"

He snorted, took a couple steps toward the bed and toppled them both to it. Kat lost her breath when his weight hit her, then she lost it again when he stole it in a kiss that was so hot, so intense, she swore the sheets would catch on fire.

Not that she had a lot to compare it to, but the man could kiss. He could suck the soul right out of her, stealing it forever.

He couldn't have it forever, but he could have it tonight.

She rolled her head back as he moved from her mouth,

down her throat, then down farther to suck one of her nipples deep into his mouth. She didn't even stifle her groan, instead, she wanted him to hear just how good that felt. And by digging her fingertips into the back of his head, she wanted to keep him right there.

His teeth scraped the very tip of her nipple and her back arched in response, then he moved to the other one while his fingers twisted and tweaked the one he just abandoned with his mouth.

*Good grief*, she never had this. None of this. She had missed *all* of this. All because she let one immature teenager fuck with her head. She denied herself this pleasure because of some *man-child*.

She'd love to go some rounds in the ring with that asshole.

Steel nipping her nipple hard enough to make it hurt drew her out of her thoughts.

He lifted his head. "Are you with me?"

"Yes."

"Your whole body tensed. Do you need me to stop?"

She closed her eyes and pushed her thoughts of the past out of her head. "No, I need you to keep going." She shoved at his shoulders. "You said you were hungry, so shut up and eat."

He growled and his tongue left a wet trail down her stomach as he moved lower. But before he got to what she had considered the good part last night, he slipped off the bed onto his knees, yanked her roughly to the edge of the mattress and threw her legs over his shoulders. Her hips surged upward as his mouth sucked hard on her clit and he rolled her aching nipples between his fingers at the same time.

*Holy shit... fuck... fuck... fuckity shit. Yes... Oh... fuck yes!*

Then she realized his shoulders were shaking. Did she say all that out loud? Was he laughing at her?

She pounded the heel of her foot against his back and lifted her head. "Are you laughing at me?"

His eyes tipped up to hers and he lifted his head. That was not the reaction she wanted, either.

"Kitty Kat, you respond however you want. The louder the better."

Her head flopped back down as he scraped his beard along her inner thigh and got back to work.

She ignored everything other than what his mouth and fingers were doing. Which was wreaking havoc on her sanity.

One hand still worked her nipples, while the other joined his mouth. Touching and stroking and dipping inside her. Taking her close to orgasm but not quite reaching it.

He was teasing her.

Torturing her.

Driving her to crazy town.

His tongue circled and flicked, his lips plucked and sucked. And finally when his fingers plunged inside of her, she might have started to speak in tongues.

And she didn't care. Nope. Not one bit.

Because the orgasm that ripped through her, which she thought would be like the angels singing, was instead like the devil ripping out her soul.

And, *hell yes*, it was even better than last night. Last night she didn't know what to expect, tonight she did. And the man could deliver.

She didn't even realize her eyes were squeezed shut until she heard her name rumbling from deep within his chest.

She opened them and rose onto her elbows. His face looked pained, his muscles tight as he remained on his knees on the floor, watching her.

"You okay?" she asked.

"I will be. Just say the word."

"How about two?" she asked. "Fuck me." As relief

crossed his face, she threw up a hand and yelled, "No! I want to fuck you."

"Normally, I'd say 'hell yes' to that, but Kat..."

"I want to fuck you. Let me."

Steel blew out a breath. "Kat—"

"Let me," she said more firmly. She could do this. She wasn't exactly a virgin and also wasn't sheltered. She had a general knowledge about sex, she just never gave herself the opportunity to enjoy it.

"You can't wait until the second time?"

When she shot him a look, he threw up his hands and rose to his feet. Then he leaned over the bed, swept the condoms to the side and climbed onto the bed.

Kat got to her knees and pointed to his cock. "That looks painful."

"You're fucking killing me here, Kat."

"For you, not for me. Though..." The first time had been rough and painful, and that guy's cock hadn't been quite as large as Steel's.

"Kat," he growled. "Do what you're going to do or I'm taking over." He snagged the closest condom, ripped it open and rolled it on. "Okay," he announced.

"Okay?"

"Do your thing."

*Do your thing.* "Will you tell me if I do something wrong?"

"Holy fuck," he groaned and rolled his eyes toward the ceiling. His eyes hit hers again. "I can't tell you if you're doing something wrong unless you're doing it."

Point taken.

But before she could move, he surged up with a muttered, "Fuck this," tackled her and she found herself pinned beneath him, with his thick thighs spreading hers and his cock pressed hard against her. He planted his forearms on either side of her head and dropped his mouth to hers. "Let me do it this time. Otherwise, there isn't going to be a next time, yeah? Kitty Kat, I don't want to be laughed at during my funeral because some hot piece of ass killed me with her indecision, especially after I've survived a fucking war."

"Hot piece of ass?"

"Sorry, I meant *smoking* hot piece of ass."

As she opened her mouth, he smothered her response by taking it roughly, plunging his tongue in and totally taking control.

For the moment, she figured she could let that comment go.

His knees worked her thighs wider and he shifted as he kissed her. Then his hand was between them, sliding the head of his cock back and forth through her slickness.

She groaned into his mouth and tilted her hips, encouraging him. Not that he needed encouragement.

She thought she was jumping out of her skin in the car, now it was worse. He wasn't entering her, just sliding his cock between her folds. Slow damn torture.

Was this revenge?

"Steel," she groaned, digging her fingers into his back, for once wishing she had nails. Their mouths were now just a breath apart, his coming steady but quickly as it swept over her lips.

"Kat," he murmured, sliding his cock down one more time until it caught *right there*. Right where it needed to be.

This was happening.

It was happening.

She made a bad decision last time. She hoped this time wasn't the same.

She didn't want to live with another mistake.

*Please don't be a mistake.*

She tensed when she expected him to take her hard and fast like he said. But he didn't. He was going excruciatingly slow. Sliding in little by little, letting her body adjust to his.

Once completely inside her, he stilled, filling her, stretching her, connecting the two of them. His mouth dropped to her ear and he breathed, "Kat."

The way he said her name shot fireworks through her, then goosebumps exploded along her skin. She tightened her legs around his hips, spreading her fingers along the back of his head, and the fingertips of her other hand digging into the hard muscles of his back, holding him closer.

Neither moved for the longest time.

Her heart began to thump more intensely the longer it went. She wasn't sure what to do. She wasn't sure what was going on.

She had no idea what to expect, but she knew it wasn't him simply lying still while buried deep inside her.

This was something more than just them having sex. But she didn't know what, she didn't know why.

She had no fucking clue what was normal and what wasn't.

She shouldn't have been so stupid; she shouldn't have waited all these years. No man wanted a woman who was so damn inexperienced.

An unfamiliar sting filled her eyes and, *damn it*, she was not going to cry. She never cried.

And who the hell cried during sex when it was consensual?

She was not an emotional female who fell apart easily. That wasn't her.

It wasn't.

Fear began to claw at her gut. Fear that he could pull emotions out of her, emotions she had tucked away a long time ago.

She couldn't let that happen. She couldn't.

Finally, his mouth was against hers again. Lightly. She tried to calm her panicked breathing.

Then he began to move.

His hips moved smoothly like a rocking boat. And all the tension that had been building up and those crazy thoughts in her head were suddenly swept away.

All that remained in that bed was her and him.

And suddenly that scared the shit out of her, too.

## Chapter Ten

STEEL WAS STRUGGLING. He'd never taken his time or been so careful while having sex before.

He had no reason to. Sex was just that. Sex. A necessary function for a man like him.

He'd had sex more times than he could remember since he lost his virginity at the early age of fourteen. But no one... Not one of those females had he ever cared about. They'd all been a means to an end.

Did that make him an asshole?

Sure.

Had he ever cared?

Fuck no.

But everything about Kat was different. Her strength. Her vulnerability. Her determination. Her inexperience.

There were so many layers to this woman and he wanted to peel back every fucking one. He never wanted to do that before and it should scare the fuck out of him.

But it didn't.

To him, it was a challenge.

To open her up. To have her give him everything.

He wanted to discover every one of her weaknesses just

the same as he wanted to discover every one of her strengths.

And, *fuck him*, he said he'd never get caught as he watched four of his five teammates go down hard. He thought it would make them weak. It didn't. Their women only made them stronger. If he hadn't seen it with his own eyes, he wouldn't have believed it.

Not that he was looking for the same thing from Kat. He wasn't. But if he was...

*Christ*, he needed to get out of his own head and concentrate on the woman who was giving him what he wanted from the exact moment he saw her at The Strike Zone.

He never thought it would happen, but it was and he needed to give her all of his attention. Especially now. He needed to show her how good sex could be. He needed to wipe away the memories she had of her shitty-ass first and only time.

Little rotten bastard. He'd love to meet that asshole in a dark alley. He stole something from her and it wasn't just her virginity.

"Hey... Are you with me?"

The question he'd asked her earlier was now being asked of him. And it drew him out of his thoughts and back into the room, into the bed, into Kat.

"Yeah," he murmured. "I'm with you, Kitty Kat."

Then he noticed it. The shine of tears in her eyes. He couldn't tell if it was worry or sadness that wrinkled the corners. Or fear that caused the tight press of her lips.

*I'm not good at it.*

*He told them I was a 'horrible lay.'*

That motherfucker had fucked with her head and he needed to correct that.

He ran his nose along her jawline, then paused over her mouth, which parted, and he inhaled every breath she took.

And he gave his to her.

Then he kicked his own ass for getting distracted, for planting that seed of doubt in her head.

Even the strongest person had weaknesses.

But if it was up to him, he'd make sure Kat became confident during sex. Just as confident as she was in the cage.

He gripped her bottom lip between his teeth and tugged gently. When he let go, he said softly, "Kitty Kat, you don't know how good you feel. You're fucking hot, and wet, and tight. So fucking responsive. Never hold back, none of your reactions are wrong. I want to hear every single one. Don't hold back on telling me what you want. Anything you want, I'll give it to you. Anything you need, I'll do my best to give you that, too."

"Steel—"

"No. Let me show you how fucking lucky I am. How lucky I am you invited me into your bed. How lucky you made me by choosing *me* to show you how good it can be. This might sound crazy, but it's an honor and I need to show you how much I appreciate what you're giving me."

"Steel," she breathed.

He dropped his mouth to her ear. "You've got a fire in you, Kat, and I want to feel that heat. I want it to scorch me."

She turned her head until her mouth was against his ear. "Then show me how to burn."

Even if he wanted to, he couldn't beat back his grin.

She wanted to burn.

It was time to stoke that fire. Time to touch those flames.

As he took her mouth, he worked one arm under her ass, tilting her hips. He brushed his thumb back and forth over the tight bead of her nipple.

Being inside her was like a tight, wet fist which squeezed and rippled as he began to move in earnest, planting his knees into the mattress and rocking his hips. Keeping it gentle but driving deep.

Tonight was to simply show her what two people could share.

Next time they could experiment. Show her what he liked, figure out what she liked, too.

But tonight was solely about her.

When her thighs tightened against his hips, he made it a point to pay attention to each response. Just like she did when she gave him head last night. Being a fierce competitor, she knew how to read movements and reactions.

So did he.

As he drove deep into her wet heat, her hips moved with the same rhythm and she squeezed him tightly, making him work harder to keep from losing his shit.

Her fingers dug into his back, and little whimpers escaped with each ragged breath.

*Fuck.* That shit tightened his balls and made him more determined than ever to make this a night she'd never forget.

And, admittedly, a night he might never forget, either.

He'd never had a virgin and though, technically, while Kat wasn't one, to him she was. Being her "first" was a huge responsibility. One that laid heavily on his conscience.

Again, he didn't know why. He didn't know why doing this with Kat was different from what he'd done with numerous other women.

Why Kat?

"Steel," she whimpered, her hips lifting to meet each thrust.

Her eyes were closed, and he felt a pull to connect with her, more than just physically.

That *boy* had fucked with her head, now Kat was fucking with his.

"Kitty Kat, look at me."

She didn't.

"Kat," he said more firmly. "Look at me."

Nothing. Her body was still moving with his, rocking smoothly like the push and pull of the ocean's waves. So, he had that. But that was all.

He drew his nose along hers again and whispered, "Kat."

Finally, her eyes opened and again there were tears gathered, but not yet spilled.

His eyebrows pinned together and he slowed.

Her hands slid down his back and gripped his ass. "Don't stop."

"I'm not hurting you, right?" For fuck's sake, not hurting her was why he was taking it slow and careful, why he was holding himself back, keeping himself from doing what he really wanted to do.

"No..."

*Then, what the fuck?* "You look like you're about to cry."

"I'm... I... I'm upset I let one asshole cripple me like that. That I never had this."

"I'm not upset about that, Kitty Kat. You know why?"

She lifted an eyebrow. "Because you've been having sex forever?"

"No. Because of that asshole, I'm the one who gets to give you this."

She blinked, then he watched as her mind processed what he'd just said. "Well, keep giving it to me."

His rhythm stuttered when he laughed and she smiled while slapping him hard on the ass.

That made him jerk and thrust deeper. Her eyelids became heavy and he was afraid she'd close them again.

"Keep your eyes on me, Kat. Stick with me."

"I'm with you."

He brushed his lips lightly over hers, then said, "Hang

on, baby. Time for me to give you a taste of what I really want to give you."

Her eyes locked with his and he swore she gave him a little nod as if letting him know she was ready.

He pulled his arm from under her hips, released the nipple he'd been toying with and said, "Put your arms like a goalpost."

"Soccer or football?"

"Kat," he growled.

Her lips twitched as she did as told, putting her hands on both sides of her head, her elbows bent.

Instead of capturing her wrists and stretching her arms above her head, he interlaced his fingers with hers and pressed their interlocked hands into the mattress.

He put his mouth to hers. "From the second I saw you, Kat, I wanted to take you like this. But this is only one of many ways."

Her warm breath merged with his as she asked, "Are you going to show me them all?"

"I sure as fuck hope so." He crushed his mouth to hers and no longer took her gently. He took her as if this was the one and only chance he'd have with her. As if it was all or nothing.

With her hands pinned to the bed, her body bowed beneath him, she gasped into his mouth but didn't pull away and her heels dug into the back of his thighs as she met him thrust for thrust.

He fucked her hard and fast, capturing each one of her cries. Until finally, he ended the kiss and stared down at her.

Those amber eyes remained open and on him, holding a little bit of surprise but what he saw also encouraged him.

She was no delicate fucking flower. And he liked that.

He powered as deep and hard as he could and she stayed with him, her fingers flexing and tightening around his with each pound.

But she didn't tell him to stop or slow down, she whispered, "Yessss. Oh fuck yes."

*Oh fuck yes* was right.

He wanted her to come just as explosively as she did when his mouth was on her. This time he'd get to feel it. To experience it firsthand. Even though he knew it would be his downfall, he still wanted it. "Come for me, Kitty Kat."

"Make me." Even though it was breathless, he couldn't miss that stubbornness.

He smothered another chuckle and worked on doing just that.

When her back bowed off the bed, he drove deep one more time, staying there and grinding hard, feeling the waves of her orgasm ripple around him. Watching her face twist as she came hard. Her eyes finally left his as they rolled back, her fingers squeezing his so hard, he might have lost feeling in them.

But he didn't care.

Watching her fall apart, knowing it was him that finally gave her that, it was worth it if she crippled him.

And when he was done watching her, when her body melted back into the bed, when her fingers loosened just slightly...

He began again. This time slow and steady until his balls drew tight. Until he felt the pressure. He wasn't sure he could hold off until she came a second time, so he didn't.

He let himself chase after what she'd had, and with their damp cheeks plastered together, he came as hard as she did, unable to hold back his grunt.

After the last throb of his cock, the very last twitch, he remained inside her until he was forced to move, to get rid of the condom.

When he came back out of the bathroom, seeing her in the bed, her short hair a mess, her eyelids heavy but her eyes on him as he walked naked across the room, for a moment, just a moment, he hoped the cops never found that fucking stalker.

Because when they did, this was over.

And, fuck him, he was not ready for that.

Not now and he wasn't sure if he'd ever be.

———

STEEL ROLLED out of bed and tugged on a pair of long shorts. His ass was dragging and he had struggled to wake up. They had gotten in around two-thirty in the morning and then had sex. He'd hoped to fuck Kat again before they had to leave for the gym. But he hadn't checked the house last night like he normally did.

He needed to do that before he got distracted with losing himself again in Kat's amazing body.

Plus, he wanted to set the timer on the coffeemaker. Because by the time he was done with her this morning, they might be running a bit behind. It was a given that they'd both need a dose of caffeine.

He jogged barefooted down the stairs and headed toward the kitchen to do that first.

Once there, he automatically went through the motions of getting the coffeemaker set up. But as he stood staring at it, all those thoughts he had when he was fucking Kat came back to him like a tsunami.

He shook his head. Crazy.

Maybe he hadn't been thinking straight because he'd been exhausted. He never had thoughts like that before in his life. Not about a woman. Not about anyone.

He had bought a cock cage as a joke for Ryder when he tied his ass to Kelsea. He certainly wasn't going to buy one for himself. Fuck no. That was not on his wish list on Adam & Eve's website.

He was not getting caught. No fucking way.

This was a good time to remind himself that Kat was a job. He was her bodyguard. If she wanted him to be a bodyguard with bennies, he was okay with that.

But his other thoughts?

No. Just fucking no. He was not going to be taken to his knees by pussy.

He closed his eyes. Then why the fuck did he want to rush upstairs and climb back in bed with her?

*Damn it.*

He needed to get his rounds done before he could do just that.

He spun on his heels and headed to check out back first. As he approached the long line of large windows that faced the pool, his heart seized, and his pace stuttered.

His pulse began to pound at his temples as he tried to make sense of what he was seeing.

He unlocked the French doors and rushed outside, spinning to look again at the windows. From the outside, he could clearly read what was written.

In what seemed to be spray paint, bright red messages were written at angles across three windows.

## SLUT
## WHORE
## CHEATER

*Holy fuck.*

*Fucking motherfucker.*

Kat's stalker had found her.

He fucking found her *again*.

He looked around for any other evidence and his gaze landed on a pair of black panties tacked to one of the posts that supported the balconies above.

And those panties, which he could only assume were

Kat's, had a thick, whitish substance crusted on the crotch area.

Steel slowly blinked as he inhaled oxygen into his lungs, held it for a second, then released it just as slowly.

The cum wasn't fresh, so the message hadn't been left recently. It could've been after they'd left for the fight yesterday or sometime last night.

The fucker was good at finding Kat.

And that bugged the hell out of Steel.

A piece of white paper was sticking out from under the panties.

He took two long strides over to the wood post, jerked out the nail that held both items and let his eyes scan the note. As he read, his jaw became so tight it began to seize.

CHEATER! WHORE! BITCH! YOU'VE DONE NOTHING BUT LEAD ME ON!

I HOPE YOU FALL THROUGH ONE OF THOSE WINDOWS AND THE BROKEN GLASS SLICES YOUR THROAT AND YOUR WRISTS.

I WILL FUCKING KILL YOU AFTER SEEING WHAT YOU DID WITH HIM. I TOLD YOU I WAS THE MAN FOR YOU. I GAVE YOU ALL OF THOSE PRECIOUS GIFTS AND YOU DIDN'T CARE ABOUT ANY OF THEM. YOU JUST WANTED TO BE A FUCKING SLUT.

WHO IS HE? I HATE THAT HE CALLS YOU KITTY KAT!

YOU GAVE HIM WHAT WAS MINE, KATH-ERYN. YOU LET HIM LIE BETWEEN YOUR THIGHS. YOU LET HIM INSIDE OF YOU. HE GAVE YOU HIS SEED! YOU'RE SUPPOSED TO HAVE MY CHILDREN, NOT HIS! NOW YOU ARE RUINED!

## YOU'VE BECOME SO UGLY AND DESERVE TO BE PUNISHED!

Steel's chest compressed. He not only found Kat, he saw them. He fucking saw them.

He heard them.

He knew Steel called her Kitty Kat.

He had gotten that fucking close to them.

And that meant Steel failed.

He fucking failed to protect Kat.

They were leaving. He was getting Kat the fuck out of there. But first, he needed to clear the property. Because if that fucker was still hiding somewhere, watching and waiting...

If he was, his last breath was about to be taken.

Steel found the back gate still locked, so he had to assume "H" scaled the six-foot privacy fence.

After he cleared the pool house, the garage and the lower level of the house, he took the steps two at a time, calling for Kat. "Kat, get up and get dressed."

No response.

His heart began to pound harder.

"Kat!" he yelled as he hit the top of the stairs and rushed down the hallway to the master bedroom. The door was still open, and he breathed a sigh of relief when he noticed Kat still in bed, her eyes turned toward him sleepily. "We need to go."

"We have time," she answered, starting to roll over and burrow deeper under the covers.

"Kat, get the fuck out of bed. Now. Pack your shit. We're leaving."

She shot up in bed and the sheet fell away from her, annoying the fuck out of him. He wasn't going to enjoy her naked body this morning like he'd planned because of that fucking motherfucker!

He ground his teeth. "Get dressed. Get packed. Now. No shower. Nothing. We don't have time to waste."

Her eyes went wide. "What's wrong?"

"We had a visitor. He knows where you are. So, we're moving."

"Steel..."

"Don't give me lip right now, Kat, yeah? Do what I say. After you're dressed, get Berger on the phone. We're cancelling all of your upcoming fights."

That got her out of bed in a hurry. And it wasn't because she was scared. Hell no. She was pissed. "Steel."

He lifted a palm to her and shook his head. He didn't need an argument right now. "No, Kat."

"You can't just cancel my fights. This is my fucking career!"

"And it's my job to do what's necessary to protect you, Kat. Do it. If you don't, I will. You know what? Fuck it. I'll handle it."

"Steel!"

"This is more than just about your career, Kat, it's your life. You have no career if you're dead."

"That's what the hell I'm paying you for. To keep me from being dead! And he doesn't want to kill me, anyway. He just wants to fuck me."

"No, woman, he doesn't want to fuck you. He wants to crawl inside you and own your fucking soul. It has nothing to do with sex. It has to do with control. It's a sick obsession."

She sucked in a sharp breath at his words, but she didn't argue them, instead she said, "I'm not going to let him control my life."

"Too late. Pack up. I'm done talking about this."

He stalked out of the bedroom, not waiting to see if she would listen, and into the spare one where his duffel was. Digging through it he found what he needed, pulling on a pair of cargo pants, a tank top and socks. Yanking up the pant legs, he strapped a buck knife to one calf and his .38 to the other, then tugged on his boots.

He pulled his leather holster from his bag and shrugged that on, too. After securing his Glock .45 at his side, he pulled out a plain black windbreaker which would fucking kill him in the heat of day. But wearing it would only be temporary, just until he got Kat somewhere more secure.

He went to grab his cell phone to call Berger, but it lit up, beating him to it. He swiped the screen and put the man on speaker phone, throwing the it back on the bed, so he could finish packing while he gave Kat's manager the rundown.

But before he could catch Berger up to speed, the manager's pissed-off voice filled the room. "The website got a really interesting email, Steel."

Steel closed his eyes. He could only imagine it said the same shit as the note outside. Someone was super torqued and wanted to make sure his message was received loud and clear.

"What the fuck did you do? Certainly not your fucking job. Because a professional wouldn't get involved with the person he was hired to protect. That proves to me you're not a professional but a fucking meathead without a lick of common sense."

Steel shoved a pile of dirty clothes into his bag and growled, "Back off, Berger."

But the man didn't back off. Fuck no, he continued making Steel's blood boil. "I hired you to protect her, to be her bodyguard. That's it. Not her trainer, not her manager. Not her hired dick."

"By 'hired dick' you better fucking mean investigator."

"You know what I fucking mean."

A muscle popped in his jaw. "Who she fucks is none of your fucking business."

"The hell it isn't. She needs to concentrate on her career while she's in her prime, while she's on top. Once it collapses and she's washed up, then she can concentrate on the rest. Not before."

"You're afraid you're going to lose your meal ticket."

"She's got skills, Steel. Don't act like you don't see them. I helped her develop them. Me. Not any of her former trainers or instructors. They gave her the basics, the foundation, but I took that to the next level. I took that chunk of coal and honed it to diamond. They didn't do that. And you certainly didn't, either."

This conversation was getting them nowhere.

He didn't have time to argue with the asshole on the other end of the phone. Instead he told Berger what he found outside, and before he let the man interrupt, he added, "Cancel all her fights. Public appearances. Hell, just cancel everything until this fucker is found."

"No!" Kat yelled.

He glanced over his shoulder to see her standing in the doorway of the spare bedroom. How much she'd heard, he had no fucking clue.

At least she was dressed, and he hoped to fuck she'd packed. If not, they were leaving her shit behind and she would just have to deal with it.

He grabbed the phone off the bed and took it off speaker, turning his back and ignoring her. Two people pissed at him was nothing new.

With one hand, he kept packing.

"I can't cancel the fight with Calamity Jayne. It's only a week away."

"Do it."

"Steel!" she yelled from the doorway. He again ignored her and concentrated on the voice in his ear.

"Is that what Kat wants?" Berger asked.

"It's what I want."

"I can't cancel the fight. If she backs out now this will destroy her career. Everything she's worked for will be for nothing. And she'll never forgive you for that."

Steel didn't give a shit about that. His priority was keeping her safe, not happy. If she stayed pissed at him until the end of the job, so be it.

However, he also couldn't ignore everything Kat had done to build her career. He had watched her in that ring last night and knew she was born to be a fighter.

It was in her blood, just like it was in his.

He told himself he wouldn't care if Kat was pissed at him, but he was lying to himself.

*For fuck's sake.*

He scraped a hand through the top of his hair and glanced over his shoulder, as Berger continued to talk.

"Do your fucking job. Go to Vegas. I'll set you up in a hotel there. She only has one other small venue fight coming up next month. I can cancel that without any repercussions. But she needs to fight Jayne."

Steel rolled his eyes to the ceiling, holding his phone so tightly his fingers fused to it. This whole thing made him want to scream. "Fine. This is on you, though, Berger. I have a safe place for her and as soon as that fight's over, if that fucker isn't caught yet, we're headed there."

"Where?"

"Not information I'm sharing at this time. And I'm also picking the hotel. I'll let you know where we are after we're settled, not before."

He was keeping Berger on a need-to-know basis. He could be the weak link in this whole situation.

He could be the fucking weak link.

*Fucking motherfucker.*

His eyes lifted to Kat's, who still stood in the doorway, her hands on her hips, not looking any kind of happy.

*Jesus fuck.*

"Listen up, Berger, and listen good. I've changed my mind. I won't be telling you what hotel we're at."

"Steel—"

"Shut it and listen. I don't want you around Kat at all." Berger tried to interrupt again but Steel kept talking. "Not at the hotel. Not at the gym. Nowhere. I'll keep working with her to get her ready for the fight—"

"Steel—"

"And I'll get her into a secure hotel. The next time you see her will be at the venue and then we're leaving Vegas right after. No press conferences before or after the fight. I don't care what excuses you have to make. In your down-time, ride that detective's ass. Send him that email. I'll text you a pic of the note I found and shots of the windows. Make sure the detective gets those, too. You might want to get them out here to dust for prints, but I doubt he left any. I'll be in touch. And don't you fucking contact Kat, either. I'll get her to the fight. You take care of the rest."

"Steel—" Berger began again.

"Just do it," Steel barked into the phone and cut the call off.

He stared at Kat for a minute, feeling about as annoyed as she looked. "You got your fucking fight. But after that we're heading home."

"Home, where? To LA?"

He shoved the last of his clothes into his duffel and zippered it shut. "Fuck no."

"Indiana?"

"Shadow Valley."

Her dark eyebrows pinned together. "Where?"

"Exactly. Just let that fucker try to follow you there." He threw the strap of his duffel over his shoulder. "Your shit better be packed. We're heading out in T-minus two minutes."

"I'm packed."

"Then start moving."

She turned, gathered her bags that had been waiting in the hallway, and he followed her down the stairs toward the garage.

Once there, he figured "H" might recognize the Mustang if he was watching them. And Steel had no doubt he was.

"What's under the car covers?"

"I don't know."

He uncovered one and found a new white Corvette with dark tinted windows. Perfect.

"Got a hat?" he asked Kat as he searched the car for the hidden keys.

"Yes."

"Hat and sunglasses on. Don't remove them until I tell you." His fingers found the keys under the driver's seat. Stupid for Kat's sponsor, but lucky for him. He straightened and looked over the roof of the car to Kat. "Get in."

"We can't steal their car!"

"We're only borrowing it to get where we need to go. I'll get Berger to return it and the rental."

Borrow. Steal. He didn't give a fuck. Whatever it was would get them to Vegas in record time.

And that was all that mattered.

## Chapter Eleven

WITH HER ARMS crossed at her waist, Kat stared out of the large wall of windows from the top floor of a tall, fancy casino hotel. A floor usually reserved for high rollers.

From what she understood, the owner owed someone Steel knew named Mercy a favor.

A keycard was necessary for the elevator to get up to what was called the Royal Suite. Not only that, there were two large men stationed outside their door.

Steel informed her they were hunkering down until the fight, so he had the hotel manager fill the suite with food, drinks and other items. Along with access to room service, Steel said they'd want for nothing.

Even more surprising, the owner of the hotel had sparring equipment brought up to the room. Not only that, but a huge mat for them to practice.

A fucking wrestling mat was set up in the center of the large, open living space of a luxury suite. Unbelievable.

Kat shook her head. She bet the management got some pretty crazy requests, but never one like that before.

"How much is this costing?" she whispered to the

evening sky lit up by all the colorful lights along the Vegas Strip.

In the window's reflection, she watched Steel's head turn from where he studied the mat.

"Nothing. It's being comped."

"The owner... This Michael must owe your friend Mercy a lot."

"Paranzino owes Mercy's woman a lot. Mercy's just collecting on the debt."

The stalker was now affecting so many more people than just her.

They had only been in the suite for an hour now and despite the floor-to-ceiling wall of windows overlooking the Strip, she was already feeling trapped.

"He's getting what he wants. He's caging me in."

Kat watched Steel's reflection approach and he stepped into her, pressing his chest to her back. His hands slid from her shoulders down to her forearms in a sort of embrace.

His voice rumbled low and deep when he said, "This is your choice, Kat. You could cancel the fight and we could go home."

"Home," she murmured, not letting herself lean back against him. "Your home, not mine."

"Somewhere safe until he's caught."

"We don't know if he'll ever be caught. I can't do this forever."

"Once I get you back to Shadow Valley, get you in a secure location, I will handle finding him."

He would do that for her? He wasn't getting paid to track down some masturbating whack-job. "Just you?"

"My team."

"Do you think you and your team can do more than what the detective and *his* team are doing?"

"Fuck yeah."

She tilted her head back and turned it enough so see his face. "How?"

"We all have special skills."

"All. As in your team?"

"Yep."

"Like?"

When he didn't answer, she prodded, "Tell me about your tattoo. I know what the Marines' emblem looks like and your tattoo doesn't look like that."

"No."

That was his answer? Just a simple no? "What does it stand for?"

"MARSOC."

Kat frowned. "What?"

"Marines' special operations. I was a Marine Raider. On our uniform we wore a pin and I had that emblem tatted onto my back."

"What does *Spiritus Invictus* mean?"

He dropped his chin to the top of her head. "Unconquerable spirit."

She finally let herself rest back against him and when she did, his arms tightened around her. She didn't want to think about how good that felt.

She had always taken care of herself, but now... Now, it was nice to have someone else to rely on. For the moment, at least.

She just couldn't let herself get used to it.

"Is your whole team special forces?"

"Yes. Except our boss."

"But your boss leads a team of military badasses?"

Steel's chuckle rumbled against her back. "He's a badass in his own right."

She stewed on that for a moment as they both stood there quiet, eyes to the view.

She broke the silence in an attempt to break the heaviness in the room. "You hungry? I saw the fridge was packed with all kinds of expensive shit. We didn't get to eat much today with us being on the lam and you doing your magic of getting us this suite, even though that magic took more time than you liked."

He had been barking orders into the phone left and right while he tried to find a place for them to go.

"We're here now and you'll be safe."

Kat wasn't so sure that was true. It was like the stalker had a tracking device on her somehow. And to think he knew about what she and Steel had done. That was creepy in itself. So much for trying to lighten the mood. Right now, it felt impossible. "How did he know?"

"Know where you were?"

"About us. He thinks I'm cheating on him. He's pissed. Because of you."

Kat did not miss the slight flex of his arms around her. "Right. He thinks you belong to him. I'm not sure how he saw us. He had to have climbed the fence. But I couldn't find any evidence he was in the house, so it makes me think he watched from the pool house roof."

"He watched us having sex," Kat whispered with a shudder. "My first time was ruined by that fucker watching us."

"We have about a week, Kat," he said against her ear. Now the shudder that ran through her wasn't out of disgust, it was from the promises held in Steel's voice.

"Unless he's caught. Maybe he left identifiable evidence behind this time."

"Maybe."

"So, we have a week to get me ready for this fight."

"And a week stuck in this room," he reminded her.

"With a large screen TV, all the movies we want to watch and a fridge full of food. Plus, endless room service," she reminded him, trying to look on the bright side.

"That's not really what I had in mind."

"No?" She met his eyes in the window's reflection. "What do you have in mind?"

"Four hours of working out daily, then..."

"Then?"

"Making up for all those years you denied yourself."

"Well, I didn't totally deny myself. I just didn't have anyone else with me."

"Kat," he groaned.

"What?" she whispered, pinning her lips together to keep from grinning.

"You feel that against your back?"

"Is that your gun?"

"Yeah, it's my gun. Which is loaded and ready to shoot."

She bit back her snort. "Sounds dangerous."

"Kitty Kat," he murmured.

She wanted to hate him calling her that, but she didn't. She liked it more than she wanted to admit. Every time he used it in that tone, it twisted something inside of her. In a good way.

This man was much more than a toothpick-chewing asshole. Though, she doubted he showed his true colors to many people.

Suddenly it had her wondering about his family. She put that on her "to-ask" list. But now was not the time to talk of family, fights or even stalkers.

Steel's cock was hard and heavy against the small of her back and his thumbs were brushing back and forth over her forearms as he held her close. Just that little movement made a spark shoot through her and land in her core.

If she had been asked when she first saw him at The Strike Zone whether she thought he'd be a good lover, she would've said no. That he'd be selfish. Only out to get what he needed and then would split. Like the guy who...

She closed her eyes. *That* guy. *Boy*. Whatever.

But Steel, for all his roughness on the outside, turned out not to be like that on the inside. The last two nights he had taken his time and made sure it was she who got what she needed. Even over his own needs.

Was that normal for an asshole?

"Are you always like this with your women?"

Suddenly, his cock wasn't the only thing hard. His whole body went tense. "Say again?"

"How you were with me the last two nights... I have to say, I wasn't expecting it."

"What were you expecting?"

"Hot, hard and heavy. 'Banging one out,' as I've heard other ass— *men* say."

"I've *banged one out* plenty of times. Is that what you wanted?"

"I didn't know what I wanted, that's the problem," she answered truthfully.

"Are you complaining?"

"Not at all."

"Didn't think so," he muttered.

"I just... The way you were on the balcony, giving me orders... I liked that, too," she ended on a whisper.

Every muscle in his body, except for one, softened against her. "Yeah? Didn't think a woman like you would want to be bossed around."

"Normally, I wouldn't. But..."

"But?"

When she didn't continue, he did.

"Kat, some women love to be bossed around in the bedroom but not out of it. Top CEO's running Fortune 500 companies. Powerful fucking women. But in the bedroom, with the right partner, they can give that power up, let someone else be in control. Sometimes they need it. To remember that they aren't stone. That they're soft and passionate, too. It's a time they can let their hair down, so to speak."

"How many Fortune 500 women have you *banged one out* with?"

"At that level? One. Met her at a gym. She used her wicked negotiation skills to get me into her bed, but then once there, gave herself over to me to do with what I wanted. And, fuck, that was hot."

*Wicked negotiation skills. Please, it probably didn't take any negotiation.*

"I bet," Kat murmured, wondering why Steel fucking some rich businesswoman would bother her. It shouldn't, but it did.

"But there are a lot of women out there like you, Kat. Sometimes sex is the perfect time to just let go, let everything around you go. Give up that control to someone else."

"How about you? Do you ever 'let go?'"

"No."

"Not even with the right partner?"

"No, Kat."

"That sounds like a challenge."

"You can think so, but it isn't."

"Can we test that?"

"You can try. But you don't know what you're doing anyway."

*Damn.* That stung a little. "Oh, I see. Another challenge."

"It's not a challenge, Kitty Kat, it's fact."

"Such arrogance," she murmured.

She felt him shrug. "It's confidence."

Kat snorted, jerked both arms up, breaking loose of his hold, but she didn't have a lot of room to work with since she was only a foot from the window, and he was at her back, caging her in.

Before she could slip to the side, he hooked her by the

waist, so she spun the other direction. Snaking an arm around her waist again to stop her movement, he pinned her to his chest with another arm just below her throat.

"Wanna try again?" he growled into her ear.

She swept her hands up, finding the gaps in his grip, managed to loosen his hold and tried to spin.

*Fuck.* He caught her *again.* Where she stood was a disadvantage. This wasn't going to work unless he dropped his guard. "Okay, I give up."

His deep chuckle rumbled through her. "Nice ploy."

*Damn.*

"I'm hungry. Let's grab something to eat," she suggested.

And just like that he let her go.

She spun to face him, but he was waiting.

"Trying to wrestle me next to a large plate glass window isn't smart, Kat."

"Then stop fighting it."

"You got it," he growled. Instead of backing off, he stepped forward, bumping her backward until her back was pressed to the thick glass forty-five stories above the Strip.

"Hey—"

Before she could get the rest out, he had taken her mouth and swallowed her complaint. But then she forgot what she was going to complain about.

Power. Control.

That's right.

Steel was completely controlling the kiss, so she tried to steal it back from him.

He wasn't having any of that, either.

Instead, he broke the kiss, spun her around and shoved her hands to the window so her arms were extended above her head. She didn't think it was his move that made her breathless.

No, it was the anticipation of him doing whatever he wanted to her and her letting him do it.

Just like out on the balcony when he told her to grab the railing.

A trickle of excitement ran through her, which also happened to dampen her panties.

"Keep your hands to the glass," he ordered roughly, "unless I say otherwise."

"Or what?" Damn the shake in her voice.

He slid his nose along the outer shell of her ear. "Or find out. You're strong, I'll give you that, but you're not as strong as me."

She knew that but she'd never willingly admit it.

"I like that you challenge me. So go ahead, Kitty Kat, challenge me, we'll see who comes out on top."

"Maybe I don't want to challenge you this time. Maybe I just want you to do whatever you'd like."

"*Fuuuuck*, Kat," he whispered.

This totally went against her grain to say, "Tell me what you want me to do." But the last two nights with Steel showed her he could be a great lover and she wanted to experience more of that. The challenges could wait for another time.

"Get naked and put your hands back on the window."

"You want me naked in the window? Can... anyone see us up here?"

"Not up here."

She wasn't so sure of that. "Steel..."

"Kat," he said, which sounded like a warning.

She sucked in a breath, removed her hands from window and unfastened her jeans. She shimmied them down, shoving her panties along with them and over her bare feet. When they were clear, she kicked them to the side. The whole time she watched his reaction in the reflection.

He had stepped back a couple steps to watch her, but his face remained neutral.

Crossing her arms in front of her, she snagged the hem of her shirt and pulled it over her head, tossing that aside, too. Then she grabbed the bottom of her sports bra and ripped it up and off, her breasts finally free of their constraints.

Her nipples were already pebbled and the cool air in the suite made them pucker painfully even more. She was tempted to touch them herself. Instead, she stepped again to the glass and saw her own naked body mirrored back at her.

She tried to see herself through Steel's eyes.

Her short dark hair, layered in a way that kept it out of her face but was still cut feminine. Her muscular shoulders. She had worked hard to develop and keep the muscle needed to win fights.

Her sculpted arms. They weren't manly but they were still defined.

Her breasts, now aching. Not huge, but no longer "mosquito bites" like the boys used to say in school to flat-chested girls. They had a little weight and a nice shape when they weren't confined.

Her waist had a noticeable taper but it wasn't narrow due to her developed obliques and her just visible six-pack. Even so, her abs weren't nearly as defined as Steel's. Her hips and thighs weren't thick, but solid.

She was in no way what a man would call "curvy" or "luscious." Toned and muscled, yes. Soft with an hourglass figure, no.

While she liked the way she looked, a lot of men didn't. They didn't find it attractive and weren't afraid to tell her so. As if she asked. She never understood why men—and even women—had to voice their opinions to her when her body didn't affect them one fucking bit.

She didn't give a shit if she wasn't attractive to them. Or her body style wasn't acceptable in their eyes.

But it seemed as if Steel didn't mind. He actually seemed to like it.

Maybe even preferred it.

She in no way wanted to look like a man, even though some have accused her of it. She just wanted to be strong. Successful. Confident.

She had that. So, fuck everyone else.

But it wasn't *everyone else* who stepped up to her again. Not touching but close enough to feel him, his strength, his power. Though, she felt at a disadvantage. She was naked. He was not.

A shiver slipped down her spine and then again when his tongue—just the tip of it—touched a spot at the top of her neck at her hairline and traced the line of her spine, down her neck, where he sucked her skin. His short beard would occasionally scrape her as he moved lower. He licked her from the top of her back, and used her spine as a path between her shoulder blades, to the small of her back. To the top of her crease.

And then even lower.

When her breath rushed out of her, she hadn't even been aware she'd been holding it. Until he was *close*. Right there. Not quite touching but so, so close.

His lips replaced his tongue as he moved back up, following the same path until he reached, once again, where her back and neck met. There, his warm breath blew over her heated skin before he sank his teeth in.

Fireworks exploded through her and she groaned as everything in her body went electric. He sucked her skin where he bit her, his tongue drawing circles over the bite. She doubted it was deep enough to leave a mark, but she still felt it and would for a while.

She watched him in the window's reflection, his large

hands finding her hips, gripping her there as he slid kisses from his bite up her neck once more.

Then he nuzzled his nose behind her ear. The only thing she could hear was his breathing and her own. And just that alone, made everything inside her clench tight.

When she dropped her head forward, he curled his hand around her throat and pulled her head back up.

His only word filling the space around them was a rough and raw, "Watch."

She forced her eyes to remain on the reflection of the two of them. Him much taller and broader. Her shorter and, for once, looking delicate. For once, even breakable.

His thumb pressed for a moment at the thumping pulse in her neck, then his hand moved lower while his other slid up her ribs and they both met at her breasts. Cupping, squeezing, tweaking.

She bucked against him, wanting and needing more than what he was giving her. So much more.

She was losing her patience with how slow he was going. And from what she felt, how hard he was, she couldn't imagine the man behind her had all the patience in the world, either.

"Steel," she forced out when it got caught in her throat.

"You wanted me to do whatever I'd like. Are you backing out of that?"

"You like to go this slow?"

"What I like is watching you, watching your reactions to my touch. Watching you discover yourself. Watching you give yourself to me."

"Is that why you're not naked?"

"We have plenty of time for that."

She wasn't so sure about that. She was ready to crawl out of her skin. She was ready to defy him by taking her palms off the window, turning and tackling him. Even though he'd probably overpower her once more.

"I want to touch you."

"You will," he murmured into her ear.

"Now."

"No."

"When?"

"Later. Patience, Kitty Kat."

She didn't have any more patience. She was fresh out. But she dug deep, blew out a breath and shut her mouth.

"You wet?"

"Yes."

"Show me."

She had no idea how. She was facing the window with him plastered to her back.

"You have ten fingers, Kitty Kat. You only need one."

"You said not to move my hands from the window."

"You have a one-time exemption."

She slipped a hand between her legs and drew one of her fingers through her soaked folds, gathering the proof of how badly she wanted him right now. And once she did, she lifted her hand up to show him.

His back pressed her almost into the glass as he leaned forward and took her slick finger into his mouth, his tongue swirling around it.

*Holy shit.*

She squeezed her thighs together when she almost came. A trickle of wet slipped out of her and a low groan rose from deep within her chest. She had not only felt him suck on her finger but she had watched it in the window.

Every time he did something to her she never expected, it bothered her even more that she'd missed out on all of this. This pleasure. This intimacy.

She had spent years working on pushing her father's doubt out of her head. She should've done the same with sex.

"Kat, stay with me."

His murmur drew her out of her thoughts. Back to the room. Back to him.

"Again, Kitty Kat. Show me how ready you are for me again."

She repeated running her finger through her wetness and offering it to him.

He accepted it, releasing a low growl. After her finger was once again clean, he said, "Now, I want to watch you come. Show me how you do it when you're alone."

*What?*

She wasn't alone. Why did he want that?

"Whatever I'd like," he reminded her.

*That's right.*

*That's right.*

*That's right.*

She could do this.

He took her hand, the one with the wet finger and slid it down her belly, over the strip of hair, and drew that finger through her folds once more, this time with him guiding her.

He stopped at her clit and pressed her finger there, circling it once, twice.

"Now you," he whispered, pulling his hand away.

She took a shaky inhale as he pressed his cheek to the side of her head, cupped her breasts once more and rolled both nipples between his fingers and thumbs. She groaned and fought closing her eyes, what she normally did when she took care of her own needs.

Her fingers moved automatically to his encouraging words which became a blur of sound.

Soon she couldn't keep her eyes open any longer and she let them close, concentrating on what both she and Steel were doing.

"Kat... eyes open. I want you to watch yourself come."

She couldn't. She never watched herself before. Usually

it was late at night when she was in bed, the lights off. She never had a desire to watch.

"Kat," he whispered. "Watch your face when you come. That's what I see. And this is why I take my time. I don't want to miss any of this."

His fingers were rolling and tweaking hard, sending bolts of lightning to her core as she moved her thumb faster while sliding two fingers inside. Wishing it was Steel there. Anxious to feel him inside her again.

Before long, she was there. Falling. A strong arm held her up and against him as everything in, on and around her rippled intensely. She would have collapsed to the floor if he wasn't holding her.

She was semi-aware of him murmuring, "That's it, baby. That's it. Just let go."

Was he breathing as hard as she was?

Was that him struggling for breath?

He pulled her hand from between her legs and pressed it to the glass once more. "Don't move."

*Fuck*, she'd do anything he said right now.

That should scare her.

It should.

It didn't.

He stepped back and in the window she watched him pull out his wallet, dig in it and drop it to the floor. The unmistakable sound of his zipper sent a shudder through her. Then a rustle before the tearing of a condom wrapper.

He didn't get undressed. No. He only dropped his cargos slightly before pushing her head forward until her cheek also pressed to the glass. An arm hooked her hips and yanked them back, encouraging her to tilt them slightly.

Though, no encouragement was needed.

Then the head of his cock was sliding up and down through her slickness. Once. Twice. And once more before catching.

He drove inside her to the hilt. Where he could go no further. His fingers dug deep into the muscles of her hips, securing her just where he wanted her. And then he began to move.

He no longer was taking it slow.

Hell no. He took her hard, deep, fast.

Their skin slapping loudly as he slammed into her. Over and over.

On almost every breath he said her name like a chant.

She might have said his, too. But she lost track of how long it went on. She lost herself in the pleasure he was bringing her.

The pleasure he was taking himself.

He liked to watch her reactions.

She liked to watch his, too.

Their eyes met in the window's reflection and held.

One beat. Two beats.

Until his face began to change. To twist. His breathing stuttered and he powered even deeper, if possible.

And knowing he was about to lose it sent her quickly spiraling toward her own brink. She hovered there, waiting, knowing. Oh so ready.

"With me," he grunted. "With me, Kat."

And on a long, deep grunt, he drove forward once more and she went with him, free-falling down those forty-five stories.

# Chapter Twelve

THEY BOTH LAID on their backs, their breath and hearts pounding, slick with sweat. Trying to recover from their latest bout of exertion. This seemed to be a common thing with them. Whether fucking in bed, or sparring and grappling on the mat. Or even both.

Which was the current situation.

Their attempt at a four-hour workout session this morning was thwarted when after only two hours of grunting, sweating, punching, kicking and tackling, he took her to the ground and pinned her to the mat, not giving her any quarter that time.

So, she tried another tactic.

By licking a bead of sweat that rolled down his neck, then sucking the damp skin of his throat.

She quickly became pinned in another manner. And their practice turned quickly to naked grappling.

But now, with both of them totally exhausted, they needed a shower, a protein shake and at least an hour in the two-person Jacuzzi tub in the insanely enormous suite bathroom.

She'd have to suggest that.

However, neither seemed willing to move, even Steel who had rolled off the spent condom, tied it off and tucked it into a nearby towel temporarily.

They laid there quietly for several minutes, staring up at the ceiling, sexually sated, side by side, until Kat, curious, asked, "Why do you fight?"

She knew it wasn't for the money. They were paying him five thousand a week plus expenses for him to be her body-guard. A few hundred or even a thousand for winning an underground fight was nothing.

And being a bodyguard seemed to be less damaging on the body.

It took him another long moment before answering, "Because I have to." But before she could question that, before she could dig deeper, he echoed her question. "Why do you fight?"

She echoed his answer. "Because I have to."

"You have something to prove."

"In a way." She thought about why she had decided to begin training and competing. She wondered how much she should reveal to him. "I'm proving I can break the cycle of the women in my family. My father told me I couldn't."

"You're proving you can." He ran his fingers over the tattoo on her ribs. *When they say you can't, prove that you can.* Words to live by. She only had two tattoos, one on each side of her ribs and both had meaning.

"Yes. But by doing so, I alienated them."

"What do you have to prove that's worth losing your family over?" He tipped his bearded chin down to study her.

She avoided his searching gaze. "I haven't exactly lost them, but until I give up this 'foolishness,' they want nothing to do with me. When I'm ready to 'toe the line,' I'll be welcomed home."

*Toe the line.* The exact words her father had said to her

before hanging up the phone the very last time they talked. Which was almost ten long years ago.

Ten years of not speaking to her father or mother. And occasionally, her sister. But even those rare conversations were strained.

Her sister had followed her mother's path by becoming a wife and mother fresh out of high school. Now she had three little ones running her ragged and a very demanding husband who struggled to provide for all of them.

More proof that life was not Kat's destiny. She really wondered if having three children and an over-worked husband at twenty-four was her sister's dream. Kat doubted it, though her sister would never admit it.

"What do you have to prove?" she asked him.

"That I'm alive."

Kat sucked in a breath.

She could easily prove Steel was alive. But there was a deeper meaning beyond the surface of his words. And a lot of that had to do with the dog tags he wore and the tattoo he bore on his back.

She wasn't wrong.

"I've seen the light stolen from people's eyes. I've held them while it went out. I've also been the one to take that light. To extinguish the light of someone's father, brother, son... I've been judge and jury. That is a power a single fucking person should not hold. No one should."

Did what he had to do in his past, his present and maybe his future pull at his psyche? How could it not? No one was immune, were they?

"But you do what you have to do. You do what's necessary." She didn't pose it as a question, because she hoped that was true. She doubted the man on the mat with her just killed people for sport, because he enjoyed it.

"Kill or be killed. Or kill one to save many. Sometimes the choice is removed."

"You saved people." Again, she hoped that was true, because there had to be a silver lining somewhere when forced to take someone's life. Even if that silver lining was tarnished.

"At the expense of others."

He ran his finger over the black script on the left side of her ribs. *Strength is what we gain from the madness we survive.* "This quote fits me, too," he said softly. "The world can be complete madness. How we handle it determines how well we can survive."

"What doesn't kill you makes you stronger," Kat murmured the cliché, more to herself than him.

"I can attest to that."

"When I fight... When I'm on the mat sparring, when I'm in the cage fighting, everything else around me disappears. I understand how you feel when you said you fight to feel alive. It's the same for me. I forget everything but what's in front of me, which is my opponent. I focus on her and her alone. And I have one goal."

"To win."

"To win," Kat echoed. "Every win proves to me that I'm following the path I was meant to be on. Not the one expected of me."

His body jerked just slightly when she said that last part. A second later he asked, "What about your losses?"

"Every loss proves I need to work harder."

"You're hard on yourself."

She thought back to her parents' reaction when she wanted to start competing as a teen. At first, they found it amusing. Something to bide her time like field hockey or volleyball, the sports her female classmates were involved in. Then as she began to get more serious, when her chosen "sport" became more expensive, more time consuming, they were no longer amused.

In fact, her father had put his foot down. Outright told

her that she was on the wrong path. Women weren't fighters. They were the weaker sex for a reason. He told her that she needed to put those thoughts out of her head. Settle down. Find a man. Because no man wanted a woman who was muscular or even aggressive.

Women were made for making babies and baking pies.

She needed to concentrate on homecoming and prom, and finding herself a nice boy to take her to the movies or out to eat.

So, they stopped paying for her "hobby," forcing her to get a job after school to continue. While her friends were saving up for a car, she was paying for classes and competitions. To get around, she rode her bike everywhere. Sometimes hitched a ride with someone she knew.

But she did what she had to do because she wasn't giving up her dream because her father—backed by her mother—told her she was being unreasonable.

If she had been a male, they would have been more supportive.

When she blew out a breath, Steel's hand curled around her neck and he pulled her into him. Rolling into his side, she planted her chin on his chest and met his brown eyes which were trained on her, but his expression was blank.

His fingers, which trailed up and down her arm lightly, stilled when she asked, "And you?"

"What about me?"

"What makes you who you are? Special forces man turned paid bodyguard."

"I'm not just a bodyguard. It's one of many things I do."

"Ah yes, your team and their 'special skills.'"

He studied her for a moment and a fleeting look crossed his face. There and then gone. If she had blinked she would have missed it.

"It's not a story I like to repeat."

Interesting. "Why? Did something bad happen to you while you served?"

"Something bad happened to everyone who served in combat zones, Kat. When you do some of the shit I did, you never come home the same. You see and do things you never forget. Shit that's ingrained in you so deeply you can never dig it back out, no matter how hard you try."

"So, the military made you who you are. And is also why you need to prove to yourself that you're alive."

"Partly."

She waited.

And waited some more.

When she was just about to give up on finding what made him tick, his deep voice filled the space around them. "My mother died before I was born."

She jerked against him. *What?* "Impossible."

He ignored her doubt and continued, "She was killed by a drunk driver while she was eight months pregnant with me. They cut me out of her womb on the scene. My father never recovered from losing her. He handed me off as an infant to my grandmother who died when I was three. I ended up in foster care and was passed around from place to place because I was always getting into trouble, mostly into fights. Finally, I ended up in juvie for assault and stayed there until I was eighteen. I was told I'd be nothing, that I'd end up in prison and be a repeat offender. That one day I'd be on death row for murder since I had a temper and no self-control."

"Who told you that?"

"The guards, the warden, the counselors. All of them. Because of that, I had something to prove."

"To those people who thought you'd go nowhere."

"No, Kat, to myself. Fuck those people. They were no one to me. The only person who truly cared about me was myself. That's it. So, I thank them for doubting me, for planting those doubts in my head."

Kat saw his Adam's apple bob once before he continued.

"I was seventeen when I finally paid attention to the commercial I'd seen probably hundreds of times throughout the years, and it hit me. The few. The proud. The Marines. The second I was released from juvie, I thumbed a ride to the nearest Marine recruiting center and fucking enlisted."

"Only you took it further than that." She knew it was no easy feat to become a Special Forces operator. She had seen the documentaries, too. Even considered enlisting herself to fast track her way out of Indiana.

"One thing you'll learn about me, Kitty Kat, is I don't do shit half-assed. Every time a drill instructor told me I couldn't, I fucking did. Don't ever tell me I can't, I'll prove you wrong."

*Damn*, did that sound way too familiar.

"My drill instructors told me I'd fail boot camp. I didn't. I was told there was no fucking way in hell I'd be selected for MARSOC. And if I was lucky enough to be selected, I'd quit. I made it through every fucking phase until I achieved my goal of becoming a Raider. Quitting was not an option."

His fingers dug deeper into her shoulders to the point of almost being painful. Whether he was aware of it, she wasn't sure.

"My foster homes didn't want me. They only wanted the monthly check. And they didn't want to spend a fucking dime of that check on me. Clothes? Food? Just enough to keep me from freezing or starving to death."

He no longer had his head tipped down to her, now he was staring sightlessly at the high ceiling. He was deep within his head and Kat didn't want to pull him out, she needed to hear everything that crossed his lips.

And maybe he also needed to let it go. He didn't seem the type to be open about his past or his feelings which made her wonder who else he'd shared his story with. Her guess? A select few, if even that many.

"The foster home where I stayed the longest—right before juvie—I had a single mattress on the floor that was old, stained and stunk like something had died in it. I had no sheets or pillow, but one blanket. I was lucky if I got to eat. So, I was skinny and at school I was bullied. Until one day I got sick of it. I'd had enough. I became full of fury and the need for revenge. I began to strike back anytime someone put their hands on me. I got into fights. I got suspended. Then expelled. Eventually, it got so bad, I got arrested.

"Thank fuck my foster family didn't give two shits about me and washed their hands of my situation. I had better accommodations and meals at the youth center. While there, I got my high school diploma. I also learned to protect myself and to protect others. I earned extra food as payment to do so. I found ways to work out whenever I could. I developed my mind and my body."

Kat trailed her fingers over his chest, skirting his dog tags to the ridges of his abs. He certainly had developed his body, she thought, as she slid her fingers over each distinct muscle.

And he wasn't dumb at all. He was not a typical meathead, just using his fists and getting into trouble like he did in his youth, but she could see him being a well-honed fighting machine in both mind and body.

Her fingers traveled back up, this time hesitating on the metal tags that rose and fell with each breath he took. She flipped one over and read his name.

*Sterling*

*A.S.*

His initials spelled *A.S.S.*

She pinned her lips together because now was not the time to point that out.

Especially when his next words were serious. "I'm not one to give up, Kat. I do not accept defeat."

She couldn't imagine he would. And she also imagined he was like that in all facets of his life. Not just fighting, but his job, too. Maybe even his relationships.

Unexpectedly, he rolled her until he almost gave her all his weight, staring down at her intently.

She didn't say a word or even move as his eyes roamed her face from her short hair, to her eyes, her nose, her lips. She could almost feel his gaze as if they were his fingers exploring her face.

Then his deep voice rolled out of him. "Scars aren't always visible, Kat, sometimes the ones you can't see are the worst. Words can sometimes hurt more than actions."

Wasn't that the damn truth.

"Jacuzzi?" he asked, catching her off guard with the sudden switch of topic. He was breaking the heaviness of his story and making it clear he was done talking about it.

She'd respect that. "Yes."

"Even though it's big enough for both of us, we're not going to need all that room."

"We're not?" she teased.

He brushed his lips lightly over hers. "No."

That sounded promising.

———

Five days, six nights so far and Steel was ready to climb the walls. Being cooped up in a suite of rooms, even as large and luxurious as the Royal Suite was, still fucking sucked.

He was itching to go for a run. Go hit a heavy bag. Go to another underground fight.

Something, anything to scratch his restless itch.

His sudden urge to suck on a cigarette, to feel that burn fill his lungs was overwhelming. Besides the occasional cigar

189

during poker night, he hadn't smoked in years. Not since he got out of the Marines. And even after all these years, each fucking day was a struggle.

It was an addiction he still fought each and every fucking day.

Because of that, he understood how Ryder fought his alcoholism. How he struggled to stay dry not only for him, but now for his woman, Kelsea, too.

He was almost through the box of toothpicks room service had delivered along with one of their food orders.

Kat watched him curiously as he went through toothpick after toothpick but hadn't asked him what his habit was all about. He liked that about her. She wasn't the kind of woman who needled and dug until she got the info she wanted or drove the man to snap.

His team was used to his toothpick habit and they knew why he almost always had one in his mouth, but he didn't share it with others.

Not that he was embarrassed about it. He wasn't, since it was just fucking slivers of wood stuck between his lips. But still, it wasn't anybody's fucking business but his own.

Just like his past.

That he had surprisingly shared with Kat.

He'd never wanted to share any of that with anyone before. But for some reason, he felt the need to do it with her.

Maybe he was getting soft at his ripe old age of thirty-six.

*Nah. Fuck that.*

He was still young enough to fuck Kat every morning, afternoon and night.

She hadn't once said no. In fact, she'd tackled him several times when he least expected it.

He liked that.

*Fuck*, he loved that.

A woman who loved sex as much as him and wasn't afraid to go for it.

Maybe he'd created a monster.

He snorted.

That was one monster he wouldn't slay. Anytime she wanted to jump on his cock, he'd be happy to hold it in place for her.

But right now, he was struggling.

The suite might be sizable, but it was still a cage. A box he couldn't escape. And there was no fucking way he was leaving Kat alone. Even with the two hired goons standing guard outside their door twenty-four seven, and the limited access elevator to their rooftop suite.

No fucking way was he letting his guard down. Not like back at the house in Boulder City where he was too focused on getting some tail rather than paying attention to a fucking crazy-ass stalker.

Hard lesson learned.

A mistake he wouldn't make again.

He couldn't wait to get this high profile, well-publicized fight over tomorrow night and get their asses on a plane to Shadow Valley. A place where he could hide her away in the Dirty Angels MC compound, a neighborhood filled with not only bikers but his fellow Shadows.

No one was getting to Kat there.

He could guarantee that.

One more night in Sin City and they were going ghost. Paranzino, the owner of the casino hotel, was even lending them his private jet to head back to Pennsylvania.

He had no doubt that "H" was well-aware of Kat's fight with Calamity Jayne tomorrow night. Steel could even imagine that sick fuck would be in the crowd, watching and waiting.

Whether waiting for the opportunity to finally claim his woman or to punish her for fucking Steel.

It still annoyed the fuck out of him that "H" had watched him and Kat their first time.

The fucker had tainted that experience for Kat. And also for him.

He hoped he got the chance to break the motherfucker's neck.

That was one light he wouldn't regret extinguishing.

In fact, he would relish it.

# Chapter Thirteen

THREE ROUNDS of five minutes each. That's all she had to last. Fifteen minutes total. Without getting knocked out. Without getting disqualified. Without tapping out.

He'd done his best to get her ready.

He hoped his best was good enough.

Berger had met them at the venue, which was larger than he expected. It was also packed and noisy as fuck with an audience so wired it was like they had all mainlined Red Bull.

As soon as they'd arrived via limo with two more of Paranzino's goons, Berger had pulled Kat out of Steel's grip and dragged her away to meet with the officials, then when he finally dragged her back to where Steel waited by a private locker room with her name on the door, he locked Steel out.

Just locked him the fuck out.

If it was up to him and it wouldn't upset Kat, Steel would snap the fucker's neck for doing so. But he practiced hard-learned restraint and didn't. Instead, he chomped on his toothpick and waited impatiently by the door as Berger prepped her for the fight.

Berger was her manager and trainer, Steel only her bodyguard, just like Paranzino's hired muscle, he reminded himself over and over again, until the door once again swung open a half hour later. Berger escorted Kat out in her sports bra that was emblazoned with a well-known emblem, her tighter and shorter shorts than he expected, which advertised a major sponsor over her hips and ass, her taped hands and MMA gloves, which left the fingers free for grappling.

Her eyes were focused, her face serious, her thoughts clearly on the fight ahead of her.

But when her gaze landed on him outside her door, her lips curved slightly at the ends and her eyes softened just a touch. But only for a split moment.

And, *fuck*, if that didn't get him in the gut.

That slight smile, that look, did something to him he didn't recognize, and it scared the fuck out of him.

He ignored it and took up the pace behind Kat as Berger led her down a narrow passage toward the arena. The closer they got, the louder it became.

This was a fight for the record books.

If Kat lost this fight...

If she lost it, he'd be there afterward to help pick up the pieces.

She'd survive. She was strong enough to pick herself back up and continue on. He'd seen it. He was confident no matter how the fight ended, she would never give up on her dreams.

He respected that.

And he had the utmost respect for her, too.

If her family didn't appreciate her dreams, her goals, her hard work and determination, then fuck them. They didn't deserve her.

One thing he learned by being around the Dirty Angels MC and working for Diesel, their Sergeant at Arms, was something everyone should not forget: *Blood wasn't always family; family wasn't always blood.*

Because that was damn fucking true.

After joining the Marines, his "family" became fluid, depending where he was stationed. Until he became a Raider, then his battalion became his blood.

And now his teammates from In the Shadows Security were his family. No matter what, they had his six and he had theirs.

But Kat didn't have any of that. She was an island.

A complete fucking island.

That had to get lonely.

He was shaken from his thoughts when Kat stopped dead ahead of him right before stepping out into the arena.

Berger stopped, too, with a frown and urged, "Kat."

She shook her head and gave her manager a *wait-a-minute* finger before grabbing Steel's arm and taking them back a few steps deeper into the shadows of the tunnel.

"Hey," she said, stopping and staring up at him.

"Hey," he returned, unsure what this was about.

"Thank you."

His brows shot up. "For what?"

"For everything."

"Kat..."

"You're only being paid to be my bodyguard. You were so much more."

*How much more?* he wanted to ask. And why did it sound like she was saying goodbye?

"Kat—"

"Take your toothpick out," she cut him off on a murmur while staring at his lips.

He quickly spat it out and grinned.

Then she leaned in and took his mouth hard.

*Fuck.*

He sucked a breath in through his nose as her tongue

swept through his mouth, once, twice, before abruptly ending the kiss.

Berger made a sharp noise at the end of the tunnel but they both ignored him.

"For luck," she whispered just loud enough to hear over the roaring crowd which echoed down the narrow corridor.

"You need luck?" he teased in his own whisper, his lips a fraction away from hers.

"Fuck no," she said louder and with a grin.

"Didn't think so," he said as he took her mouth one more time. This time it was him taking control, their tongues touching briefly but firmly.

He pulled back enough to stare into her eyes. "Kat, I'll be right there. I'll be in your corner."

Her grin disappeared and her face became intent again as she gave him a single, sharp nod. She pounded her gloved knuckles together and then held them out in front of her.

Steel tapped his fists with hers. "You got this, baby. Tonight you're not..." *my*... He quickly corrected, "a Kitty Kat, tonight you're a tiger."

She gave him another sharp nod, then glanced toward Berger who was impatiently waiting, but, lucky for him, giving them space.

Steel grabbed her chin and turned her face back toward him. "Go kick her fucking ass."

"That's my plan," she said, turned and walked away from him.

―――――

STEEL WAS GOING to throw up. Just going to embarrass the fuck out of himself and puke right outside Kat's corner of the cage.

Like a fucking pussy.

A complete fucking pussy.

196

He'd rather be the one in the cage. He'd rather be the one ready to fight.

But instead it was a woman who he'd become attached to more than he ever expected in the last week and a half.

This was no way the same shit that his teammates felt when they met their women, was it?

Fuck no.

He was just nervous for Kat.

Berger was hopping beside him like he was high on cocaine. This fight meant a lot of money for him, too. The more Kat won, the bigger Berger's cut.

And Steel was fucking sure as shit that, since they were in Vegas, Berger also had bet heavily on Kat winning. Because, for fuck's sakes, he better not have bet on Kat losing.

If he did, that would be another good reason for Steel to twist the man's neck like he was removing the bottle cap off a beer.

The knot in Steel's stomach tightened when both Kat and Calamity Jayne moved to the center of the octagon.

*Jesus fuck.* He'd rather be kicking in doors and dodging bullets in Afghanistan right now than watching this.

The male ref stood between them saying his spiel, while the two women eyed each other up. The ref's speech was the typical bullshit of a legal fight. Nothing like one of his underground fights where they didn't have many, if any, standards at all. Especially the no holds barred fights, where the main goal was to leave the building alive with a fistful of cash.

The women touched gloves, went to their "corners" and then Steel just about jumped out of his skin when the bell rung, and the audience became deafening around them. Most of them chanting Jayne's name.

Steel actually heard one asshole behind him shout, "Kill that bitch, Calamity!" which made his trigger finger itchy.

His heart practically pounded out of his chest when he heard "Fight!" yelled out.

Round one.

Steel swallowed down the bile that rose in his throat as both women approached each other from their corners, hands up and bouncing on their toes.

Right now they were fresh and full of energy but it wouldn't take long for that to change. After a round, their own weight would get heavy.

Kat and Jayne circled each other, currently both light on their feet, watching each other carefully. Watching for any sudden moves.

The crowd noise surged with each jab, each punch as the women made contact. Then Jayne kicked high and Kat barely ducked in time.

"Focus!" Steel yelled, earning the side eye from Berger next to him.

Kat kept her fists in front of her face as she circled the larger woman. As Jayne punched with her right, Kat leaned away from it.

Berger was yelling instructions of his own, but his words were quickly swallowed up by the surrounding roar of the crowd.

Kat needed to start striking out. She needed to wear Jayne down and not wear herself down by only avoiding Jayne's hits.

"Get her, Kat!" Steel screamed.

He wasn't sure if she heard him, but after a few more cautious circles, she began to pummel Jayne. Giving her an uppercut to the chin, Jayne's head snapped back and when it did, Kat pivoted on her right foot and her left leg shot out with a side kick, connecting with Jayne's thigh. As the woman's knee flexed involuntarily, Kat quickly regained her balance, and did her high roundhouse kick that always impressed the fuck out of him.

"Fuck yes!" Steel screamed as he watched Jayne take the hit alongside the head. But it didn't take her down.

Kat bounced away to catch her breath, watching Jayne carefully.

It was hard to miss the surprise and the wrath on Jayne's face. An anger which quickly turned into determination.

Steel had no doubt Jayne wanted to take Kat out in the first round. The larger woman was realizing Kat wasn't an opponent who she could play with for a while before taking her down.

Jayne was facing serious fucking competition.

She thought Kat would be easy.

Well, fuck that. Kat wasn't going down easy. And if it was up to Steel, she wasn't going down at all. If anything, her arm was going up in the air at the end when she was declared the winner of this match.

While winning wasn't supposed to be "everything," tonight it was *every-fucking-thing*.

For Kat. For Steel. For—

Fuck Berger.

All week, late at night in bed, he and Kat had watched those YouTube videos of Calamity Jane's fights over and over until Kat wanted to pull her hair out. But they broke down Jayne's movements, her tactics, her ways to get her opponents cornered and, once there, down to the ground.

He had advised Kat, "Fuck the three rounds. Go for a KO. Knock her down and keep her there. That's how you'll win. She'll get the upper hand if she gets you down first."

Jayne was a good ground fighter, but heavy on her feet. More power than grace, which was what Kat had said about his own fighting.

After a few more circles around the cage, Jayne began to press Kat toward the fence by non-stop punching and kicking, then reaching out with her longer arms to try to get Kat in a choke hold.

Kat needed to avoid that.

Finally, the bell rang again, and the first round was over. It was the longest five minutes of Steel's fucking life.

He might not last all fifteen himself.

His blood was humming through his veins, his muscles and joints were locked, and he wanted to jump into the cage to check on Kat. But he wasn't allowed and if he forced his way in, she'd be disqualified.

So, he waited.

Impatiently.

Finally, Berger was back at his side.

"She okay?"

"Good."

"Can she hear me?"

Berger shook his head at him. "She needs to listen to me, not you."

Steel gritted his teeth and his attention went back to the octagon as the bell rang again, indicating the start of the second round.

For the next five minutes, Steel could think of nothing but Kat, how she moved, how Jayne reacted. Their kicks, their punches. Their clinches until one of them slipped free. His throat became raw with him constantly screaming out demands, commands and sometimes even suggestions.

"Protect your head."

"She's getting tired. Keep at her!"

"Stay on your feet."

"That's it, Kat. Fucking knee her."

"Yeah! That's it, baby!"

"Fuck!"

Half the time he had no idea what he was even saying, he was so caught up with the action in the ring.

Jayne attempted to get Kat into a clinch over and over, but between the slipperiness of their sweat and Kat's skills, she was luckily unsuccessful.

When the ending bell of round two rang out, Steel breathed a little easier.

Kat had blood coming from a cut above her right eye. She had blood running from the corner of her mouth and discoloring her mouthguard. Her left eye was already swollen and turning an ugly shade of purple. Red marks, which would turn to bruises, marked her ribs and her legs.

But she was still standing. Still determined to win. Even as exhausted as she looked.

Steel's eyes sliced across the cage to Jayne on the other side of the ring. Kat's opponent didn't look much better.

In fact, she was talking angrily with her trainer or manager, or whoever the fuck was leaning over her.

Fuck yes, Jayne had not expected Kat's will to win.

Steel grinned.

Even if she lost, Kat had won. Kat might not see it as that at first, but Steel would make sure to convince her.

She had held her own with two rounds of going head to head with a well-known, undefeated champion who was bigger than her.

And that right there was a huge win.

The bell for the third round rang out and Steel's body went solid once again as the two tired women approached each other. Neither light on the feet any longer. Both ready to get this over with.

So the fuck was he.

Heartburn seared his chest.

But it was almost over. If she couldn't take Jayne down, all Kat had to do is last five more minutes. Just five. Then it would be up to the judges to choose the winner.

Surprisingly, when Jayne lobbed a few punches at Kat, they looked sloppy. That gave Steel hope.

Until he realized it was Jayne's ploy. She was messing with Kat, who had also believed Jayne was weakening so moved in closer.

And because of that, Jayne's foot made contact with the side of Kat's head.

Steel yelled out a searing curse as Kat stumbled backward, almost lost her balance but barely caught it in the end.

It would have been over if Kat went down. Jayne would've finished her off.

Instead, Kat moved away, recovered for a few seconds, then went back at Jayne in the center of the ring.

She bounced a few times on her toes, faked left, then struck right, nailing Jayne right in the jaw. She followed with a left uppercut, then stepped back and found enough energy to do her high roundhouse kick, cracking Jayne upside the temple.

Steel's jaw had to be on the floor as he watched Jayne crumble to her knees but still remain upright.

Kat executed a perfect spinning back-kick, which took Jayne almost to the ground. But before Jayne completely hit the mat, Kat grabbed Jayne's head and kneed her a good one, busting the woman's nose and knocking her out cold.

Once Jayne was flat on her back, Kat straddled her, cocking her arm back for another punch but the ref pulled her off and flung her out of the way to check on Jayne.

Then the ref stood and called the fight over.

Kat won by a knockout.

A fucking knockout.

*Holy fucking shit.*

It was over.

She fucking did it.

She fucking won and she did it like a champ.

Berger shoved past him and into the cage while Steel struggled to keep himself where he was.

He could barely hear himself screaming along with the rest of the crowd. Only he was celebrating. The rest—all the doubters—were not.

Like at the underground fight, there was a lot of money lost. Millions this time.

He didn't give a flying fuck.

Steel watched as Jayne, with assistance from her manager, and Kat stood once again in the middle of the octagon with the ref between them.

Then the announcement filled the arena. Kat Callahan was officially declared the winner.

From where Steel stood, he could see a couple tears escape her eyes and mix with the blood running down her face, but she quickly brushed that proof of emotion and, most likely relief, away.

She was struggling to keep her shit together, but then so was Steel. His chest swelled with pride and he couldn't wait to hold her.

He got to do that not a minute later as Berger escorted her from the cage and out.

Steel bumped Berger out of the way, grabbed Kat's arm and quickly guided her through the wound-up crowd, back into the tunnel and to her private locker room.

As soon as he got her back inside, he closed the door and locked Berger out.

He turned and they stared at each other, both of them still breathing heavily.

With her eyes not leaving his, he approached and reached out to swipe the blood from her cuts with his finger. Then he streaked it across her forehead, gathered some more, and slowly painted two lines diagonally down both cheeks.

When he stepped back, he whispered, "You're a fucking warrior."

She was sweaty, bloody, her damp hair plastered to her scalp, but he didn't give a fuck. He grabbed her face and crushed his lips to hers, tasting her blood, sweat and determination.

It was a heady combination.

But he didn't want to aggravate the cut on her mouth, so he began to retreat, until she stopped him by wrapping a hand around his head and pulling him back down, kissing him even harder.

A few moments later, she shoved him away and, with their gazes pinned, she yanked her sports bra over her head and shoved her shorts and underwear down to her ankles.

*Fuck*, she was the most goddamn beautiful woman he'd ever seen.

Perfect.

Even bruised, sweaty and bleeding.

This woman did not need fancy clothes, makeup or high heels to turn him on. It was the gleam in her eye, along with her honed body and sharp mind that drove him nuts.

No other woman compared.

Not fucking one.

"I need a shower," she murmured, her voice husky with emotion.

Yeah, she did. But he'd take her just as she was. No complaints.

"Need help to wash your back?" he asked.

"Need more than that."

"I might be able to accommodate," he said.

Her lips twitched just slightly. "That would be good."

"I think, Kitty Kat, it will be more than good."

"I'll go start the shower while you strip down and unstrap your arsenal of weapons."

"That would be good," he echoed her.

"More than good," she whispered and disappeared into the shower area of the small locker room.

As soon as he heard the water run, he snapped into action, yanking off his boots, his clothes, his guns and knife, before double-checking to make sure the door was locked.

Then he joined Kat in the shower. And it was a long one.

————

AN HOUR LATER, he was finishing lacing up his boots and waiting for a text from Paranzino confirming the jet was fueled and ready to go when they heard a pounding on the locker room door.

His eyes sliced to Kat, who was still getting dressed because she was moving much slower than him due to exhaustion and her body taking a pounding. Not only from Calamity Jayne but from him.

That last part should make him grin, but instead the interruption made him growl, "I got it. You finish getting ready. As soon as you are, we're heading home."

It did not escape him that Kat lifted a dark eyebrow sharply when he mentioned "home."

He unlocked the door and slipped out, shutting it firmly behind him to face Berger, a look of impatience clearly on the man's face.

Too fucking bad.

Kat's manager handed him an envelope.

"Have you been out here the whole fucking time?" Steel growled, accepting it reluctantly.

Berger simply gave him a look, which was easy to read. He had and he'd probably heard. Not that Steel surprised, but still...

He glanced down at what Berger handed him. "What's in the envelope?"

"Her locker room bonus. Apparently the organizer was very happy with her performance."

Well, no fucking shit. Her "performance" was stellar. One for the record books.

"Locker room bonus?" Steel already gave Kat her "locker room bonus."

"Just give it to her."

"We're out, Berger. From here, we're on a plane and heading..." Steel shook his head. "Heading somewhere safe. I'll text you when we arrive and everything will be on a need-to-know basis until that fucker is caught. You get me?"

Berger's face tightened, but after a moment, he nodded. "I hear you."

"I'm going to find him since the cops haven't done shit."

Berger frowned. "You need to guard her, that's what we're paying you for."

"She'll be in good hands."

Berger jerked his chin toward the closed door behind Steel, who was blocking it from Kat's manager. "Yeah, sounded like it." He sighed and slid a hand through his blond hair. "Just keep her safe."

"You got my promise on that."

Berger nodded, hesitated, then stuck out his hand.

Steel stared at it for a moment, confused. *What the fuck?* He reluctantly took Berger's hand in a tight grip and shook it.

"She won because of you."

*Jesus fuck*, that had to kill Berger to admit.

Steel dropped his hand and leaned forward. "Kat won because of Kat."

Berger tilted his head, stared at Steel for a moment, then nodded once more. "Right. Text me when you get wherever you're going. And keep me updated. I'll do the same on my end if I hear anything on the investigation. I'm heading home to LA for now." With that, Kat's manager turned and headed down the corridor toward the exit.

Steel turned, too, but to face the door. As he shoved it open, he hoped Kat was ready. They had a plane to catch.

# Chapter Fourteen

Kat wandered through the first floor of the large, expensively furnished house. She had no idea who owned it, but it was quiet and Steel said no one lived there. So, that meant it wasn't his.

His matte army-green, military-looking Jeep had been waiting in the short term parking lot when they landed at the Pittsburgh airport and he had quickly taken them from there south, through a remote-controlled gate to this house toward the rear of the enclosed neighborhood.

He informed her as they drove through the quiet streets that the "compound" was full of bikers who had built the neighborhood to keep their families close and safe, and some of his fellow "Shadows" also lived within the walled community.

It was secure and he sounded confident that "H" couldn't find her there.

She wasn't so confident.

For being a biker compound, she was surprised at how it looked like some upper-middle class neighborhood.

Instead of MC members, you'd think bankers, lawyers and doctors lived behind the closed doors of the large, beautiful homes with well-maintained yards and three car garages.

Weird.

He also said a cop and his wife lived in the compound, which surprised the shit out of her. What little she knew about MCs, she didn't think bikers and cops mixed.

At least not without bloodshed.

But, even so, they had a place to stay for a while until her stalker was caught by police and she could head back home to LA.

*Home to LA.*

It had been so long since she'd been home, she was starting not to miss it. California was great, but expensive, and her money would go much farther somewhere else.

She was pretty sure the mortgage on her small condo was more than the mortgage on two of the large homes in the neighborhood they were currently in.

With a sigh, she returned to the kitchen, the last place she'd seen Steel, who had been making several calls. From what it sounded like, notifying his teammates of their current status.

As she sidled up to him, his brown eyes landed on her and his mention of "finding that fucker" trailed off.

She had no doubt that Steel would make it his personal mission to find "H" since the police had failed to do so.

Now that she was in a place he deemed safe and surrounded by people he trusted to protect her, he was determined to track "that fucker" down.

In one way, Kat was relieved by that news, in another, not.

Her fear of "H" no longer being locked up, but Steel instead because of doing something illegal, ate at her. She didn't want to be the cause of him being arrested for "dispatching"—the term she heard him use—"H."

Steel's deep but quiet, "Gotta go," caught her attention.

He disconnected, shoved his cell into the side pocket of his cargo pants and then lifted a hand to her face.

She stepped into him and his thumb brushed lightly over the bruise on her cheek while his eyes stared at her swollen, black eye. His lips flattened out and his jaw turned to concrete.

"I won," she reminded him.

"But you still got hurt."

She lifted one shoulder in what she hoped looked like a casual move. "It happens. It's called fighting for a reason."

His lips, pressed in a grim line, barely twitched. "Yeah, I know. My face has been fucked up plenty of times. Doesn't mean I like to see you like this."

"Again, it's part of the game."

"Game," Steel repeated in a murmur, curling his fingers around the back of her neck and pulling her into his side.

"You know what I mean."

He said nothing but she could read his thoughts just by the sudden lift and fall of his chest as he took a long, deep breath.

She turned her face up to his. He was staring sightlessly across the well-appointed kitchen. "So, now what?"

Steel tipped his chin down to meet her eyes. "Now we end this." A puff of breath escaped her parted lips, but before she could say anything, he continued. "We're going to find that fucker and end this whole thing."

"At what cost?" she whispered.

"Hopefully none."

"There's always a cost to end something." And that was so damn true.

His thumb traveled along her jawline. She winced slightly when it touched a sore spot. Leaning over, he followed his thumb with his lips, then pressed a kiss to her forehead, tightening his arm around her hips.

How could an asshole show such tenderness?

Easy. Because deep down he wasn't one. It was his façade. The shield he donned from his troubled youth. A way to protect himself. Just like she had used MMA to build walls around herself, too.

Walls to protect her from rejection. From her family. From her first crush who not only disappointed her, but embarrassed her.

"Steel..."

"Yeah?"

"I was wrong, you're not an asshole."

His lips twitched as he lowered them to just above hers. "Yeah, Kitty Kat, I am. You were right."

"An asshole wouldn't be doing as much as you are for me. Going above and beyond your duties."

His warm breath swept over her lips. "Kat. Just because I'm doing it for you, doesn't mean I'd do it for anyone else."

"Bullshit." She didn't believe that now that she knew him a lot better. He had a good soul. It might be buried deep, but it was there. "Then why me?"

Instead of answering her, he closed the slight gap between them and took her mouth. Kat groaned not only from her swollen and healing lip but the intensity of his kiss. Their tongues touched and tangled; their breaths mingled.

Yeah, *so* not an asshole.

She expected him to drag her upstairs to test out the bed in the master bedroom, but he didn't. Instead, he released her and tucked the toothpick he'd been holding between his fingers back into the corner of his mouth.

Since they started sleeping together, she didn't remember a hot kiss like that between them that hadn't ended with them both naked.

Because of that, she looked at him in surprise.

He must have read her thoughts because he said, "The guys are headed over here. We're going to have a little meeting."

"About me?"

"About 'H.'"

"I'll get to meet your team."

Steel tilted his head as he searched her face. "Yeah. Just a warning, they're all assholes."

"I doubt it."

He smirked. "Then you'd be wrong."

"Tell me something," she began, garnering a cocked eyebrow in her direction. "What's with the toothpicks?"

"Just a habit." The narrow sliver of wood jiggled in the corner of his mouth. "One habit replacing another."

"What was the original habit?"

"Tobacco."

She nodded. "How long ago did you quit?"

"Six years ago. The day I put my boots back on American soil."

Kat found that curious. "Why then?"

"I needed a change. It was a good place to start."

"I'm glad you quit."

"Why?"

She gave him a small smile. "I hate smoking and I'm glad you don't taste like an ashtray. If you did, I'd miss out on your kisses and they're too good to miss out on."

"Have much to compare it to?"

"You already know that answer."

His brow rose. "Even kissing?"

She gave him a nod. "Even kissing."

His grin got so big, she swore it would blind her.

"Okay, rein in the asshole."

He chuckled. "Told you I was one."

"You don't need to convince me."

She turned away and moved deeper into the kitchen and headed toward the fridge. She opened it and was shocked to find out how well stocked it was.

"Damn," she whispered, then shut it and turned. "Who normally lives here?"

"No one. Jesse stocked the house with food and the necessities."

"Jesse?"

"She works in the neighborhood, cleaning houses, sometimes cooking. Running errands. It's a full-time job for her. She's cleared a background check and has unlimited access to the compound."

"So, not just anyone can get past those gates."

"No. Not even delivery people."

"Is there a reason for it?"

"There was. And while that reason is gone, it's just better to keep everyone secure."

Kat frowned. "What was the reason?"

"The MC had enemies."

"And no longer?"

"Not now. Hopefully, not in the future. But the club's expanded to wives, ol' ladies, kids. Both the prez and my boss, Diesel, the club's enforcer, want to keep everyone safe."

"Ol' lady," Kat murmured.

"Yeah, same as a wife without the legal paperwork. You'll probably meet some of them."

"How will they take a stranger within their midst?"

"Since you're with me, you're not a stranger."

Kat found that curious. "I'm not *with* you. I'm your job."

"Same shit."

She doubted that was true.

"Since we don't have time for you to eat me as a snack, you want me to make you one?" She turned with a smile when she heard Steel burst out laughing.

"Yeah, Kitty Kat, I could eat, even if it's not you."

———

*HOLY SHIT.*

Kat had seen a lot of hot, muscular men in her day. Especially when it came to her career. But what sat around the dining room table just was...

Pure testosterone.

With an edge.

A dangerous one.

The tension in the room was thick even though she was standing right outside the entryway to the room. *Maaaybe* snooping.

How could she not?

The men who worked with Steel were in a class of their own.

She had been introduced quickly as they entered the house and each had paused, gave her a good once over—especially the bruises and Steri-Strips that held her skin together over her eye and cheek—scowled at the injuries and then moved on to where they were convening for their intense discussion about her stalker.

Seeing those six men together, former special forces and who totally fit the term "badass," Kat had no doubt "H" would soon be caught.

She would not want to be their target. At least in the way "H" would be.

Their deep voices circled the table as they discussed how they were going to hunt that "fucker" down and who would do what.

Two had laptops in front of them, Hunter and Walker, if she remembered their names correctly. The tall one sitting at the end of the table, Mercy, looked scary as fuck, especially with a scar marring his handsome face. The man was too intense for Kat. Especially when he had stopped in front of her earlier, didn't say a freaking word and just stared at the injuries on her face.

His silver eyes had become ice. Cold. Intense. And they had sent a chill down her spine.

If Steel could snap a man's neck with one twist, what could a man named Mercy do?

Kat didn't want to know, and she was glad he wasn't the man she pulled when she was at the underground fight. If she had, she might have actually backed out. And she was in no way a quitter.

Ryder and Brick seemed to be the friendliest of the bunch when she was introduced to them. At least until Steel shoved Brick away from her after the man scoped her out, not only her face but *everywhere* thoroughly, not hiding his perusal of her chest for longer than he should have.

Steel had practically growled Brick's name while his fingers curled into fists.

The man had only grinned, elbowed Steel, and followed the rest of them into the dining room.

Kat *did* notice Brick was hot as hell. But then they all were. The only one who didn't show up was Steel's boss, Diesel, who was dealing with three baby girls. One a newborn, apparently.

She felt like her own stalker as she listened in, but her eyes were focused on Steel, who sat facing away from her. He had changed into worn Levi's, which fit him perfectly, his signature white tank top, which hugged his muscles, and old, worn cowboy boots. He was the reason she was having a hard time concentrating on their conversation.

Or at least until she heard a snicker come from one of them, possibly Brick, and the words, "She's like a fucking female version of Steel. It's scary."

"Yeah, asshole, if you wanted to fuck yourself, it would be easier to keep using your fist. No strings. No drama."

The blood drained from Kat's face and she pinned her back flatter to the wall just outside the dining room.

She should move. She shouldn't be listening in.

"D'you see her fucking muscles? Jesus. She's a regular Sarah Connor, isn't she? That shit turn you on, man?"

Kat waited to hear his answer, but Steel remained silent.

She peeked around the corner to see Brick chicken-necking while saying in a high-pitched voice, "I don't need no man! Everything a man can do, I can do better!"

"She one of those?" came Mercy's unmistakable deep voice.

"Does it matter what the fuck she's like?" Steel asked, his tone holding obvious irritation as he sat back in his chair and scrubbed a hand over his hair. "She's just a fucking job."

The whole table went perfectly silent before it broke out in snorts and laughter. Kat even heard the table being slapped.

"Get the fuck outta here," one of the men crowed.

"Jesus, keep your fucking voice down," Steel growled.

"Brother, she's perfect for you. You can punch each other as foreplay. Give each other black eyes instead of rings."

"Shut the fuck up," Steel grumbled. "Can we concentrate on finding this fucker so Kat can go back to LA?"

"She's not goin' back to LA," Ryder murmured, his eyes pinned on Steel.

She wasn't?

Her gaze landed on Steel, too, waiting for his response.

And waited.

Finally, he blew out a breath and said, "Kat will do what Kat wants to do."

"Damn," whispered Walker, who was sitting next to Steel.

"Guess I need to lend you the cock cage you bought me," Ryder responded.

"I don't need a cock cage, dickhead, and if I did, yours wouldn't be big enough. I said she's just a fucking job."

Ryder snorted. "Someone's a bit cranky."

"Yeah, because we're discussing Kat instead of this fucker who's stalking her and wants to come all over her fucking face."

The room went silent at that and they quickly got down to business.

Kat snuck away and left them to it.

# Chapter Fifteen

STEEL ROLLED OVER, surprised to find Kat's side of the bed empty. He jackknifed straight up, ignoring his morning wood.

Though, he wouldn't be ignoring it if Kat was still in bed.

While staying in the compound, he didn't feel the need to shadow her as much as out in Nevada, but how she slipped from the bed without him knowing it bothered him. He must have been more exhausted than he realized.

He stroked a hand over his aching erection, regretfully advising it that it would have to wait, as would his bladder, and got out of bed, pulling on the jeans he'd shucked last night before fucking Kat breathless.

She had been more quiet than usual after his team left with a plan in place. He just thought she was tired from traveling, especially since she was still recovering from the fight.

But maybe he was wrong and it was more than that.

Leaving his jeans unfastened to give his dick some space until it decided to calm down, he hoofed it barefoot downstairs. After searching the rooms, he ended up in the kitchen where his eyes landed on something on the counter.

She did *not* leave this fucking house and leave a note, did she?

He moved closer to see it was the white envelope Berger had handed him after the fight. Kat's locker room bonus.

The top of the envelope was ripped open carelessly and the torn opening gaped slightly. He snagged it and peeked inside.

He slid the check out. A cool fifty grand. That meant, in the end, that win had brought in two hundred K.

One night. One fight. Two hundred thousand.

He was sure some professional boxers brought in millions per fight, but for Kat's level of MMA fighting, a couple hundred grand was nothing to sneeze about.

He wondered what she did with her winnings. Invest? Sock it away in a savings account?

She wasn't high maintenance so he knew she didn't blow it on material things, like jewelry—she wore none—or clothes—sports bras and workout pants couldn't set her back much. And definitely no mani/pedis. She kept her nails short for fighting and there wasn't a bit of color on her fingers or toes.

He stuffed the check back into the envelope and tossed it onto the counter. Beside the envelope, there was no sign of her being in the room. The coffeemaker was empty and the counters were, too.

He sighed.

Something was up her ass and he needed to find out what.

When the sliding glass door from the deck opened and she stepped inside, she had her arms wrapped tightly around her middle. She came to an abrupt halt when she spotted him. Without a word, she closed the slider behind her and then turned, her bruised and partially swollen face unreadable.

"Kat," he began softly, disturbed by this crazy need to touch her. He curled his fingers into his palms instead.

"This certainly isn't California or Nevada weather. I don't have anything to wear for this colder climate." She vigorously rubbed her hands up and down her arms as if trying to warm up, avoiding his gaze.

"It's only October. PA gets much colder than this."

"I'm sure," she murmured as she headed toward the coffeemaker.

Unable to stop himself, he snaked out a hand and snagged her wrist, pulling her to a stop. "Kat."

She didn't fight him. Instead, she allowed him to pull her closer and met his gaze.

Hers was cautious. Which made his the same.

"What the fuck is going on?"

"What do you mean?"

His jaw tightened. "You wanna play games?"

Something behind her eyes flickered before it was quickly hidden. "I'm just tired. Tired from the flight. Tired from the fight. Tired of moving..."

"If you're tired, why weren't you in bed when I woke up?"

Her own jaw shifted, and her amber eyes hit his hard when she said, "Maybe I'm just tired of this whole fucking thing."

He searched her face a moment longer, then let her go. He watched her carefully as she moved to the coffeemaker. "Don't make coffee yet."

She glanced over her shoulder at him. "Why not?"

"'Cause I want to go for a run." Without a pool at Nash's unoccupied house in the compound, he had no choice but to run to rid himself of the frustration he was feeling. Because he certainly wasn't going to the gym right now.

She shrugged. "So, go."

"I can't leave you until we have someone to watch you."

"Like a child."

He gritted his teeth. "Like a job," he reminded her.

She turned away but he still caught the soft, "Right."

"We're going to get someone set up while we search for your stalker, but in the meantime, I'm not leaving you alone." He stared at her back, which was stiff as shit. "You run?"

He hadn't seen her run or even mention it during the last couple weeks but that didn't mean she didn't.

She turned again, this time with her hands on her hips, which were encased in tight, black spats. She probably didn't have a lot of long pants with her and the Pennsylvania weather was definitely different from where they just came from. "Not by choice. Only when Berg thinks I need to drop a few pounds because he's afraid I won't make my weight class."

"Basically, the short answer is, you run."

She lifted a shoulder. She wore a worn Tapout brand T-shirt instead of her normal loose tank or sports bra like she had worn in Boulder City. "Reluctantly."

"I need to stretch my legs and, *like I just said*," he emphasized, "I'm not leaving you alone while I do it."

"I'll be fine."

"It wasn't a suggestion. You need to figure out when what I say *is* one and when it's not." For fuck's sake, he hadn't meant to cram that down her throat. He felt like they were going backwards. Him simply being the bossy asshole and her only his job.

Her next comment cemented that. "I bet you get a lot of women with your charm."

"That's what got you in my bed."

"It wasn't your charm."

"Yeah? What was it?"

220

"Stupidity," she said way too quickly, then added, "On my part."

"Regretting it, Kitty Kat?"

Instead of answering, she spun and headed toward the stairs. "I'll grab my sneakers."

He stared at the empty space where she'd been previously standing, his chest tight as fuck, his brain spinning. His frustration kicked up another ten notches.

He wanted to follow her upstairs and drag out whatever was bothering her, but he didn't. Even though he needed to go up anyway to change into running gear, he waited until she was finished.

When she finally came back down, ready to run, he went upstairs without a word.

Especially since his mouth was already full of his own fucking foot.

———

"He's a complete asshole!" Kat grumbled, frowning at her wine glass that was somehow once again empty. She grabbed the nearest open bottle and filled it back to the brim. She wouldn't be surprised if she spent half the night puking up both the wine and cupcakes she'd shoved down her throat. She wasn't used to eating so many sweets or even drinking like this. In fact, it was rare she ever drank.

She shrugged to herself.

*Fuck it.*

She took another long swallow of the pinot noir and then glanced around the table to the women who stared at her with knowing looks. "No one is going to argue that?"

Pursed lips, *uh-huhs*, head shakes circled the table instead.

Kelsea, a blonde-haired woman close to Kat's age, raised

both palms up. "You're certainly not going to get an argument from me."

"Great."

"Welcome to our world," Sophie grumbled as she shifted uncomfortably in an Adirondack chair near Kat.

Her belly was huge, and Kat bet the woman couldn't get out of that chair if she tried. The woman with the long dark hair and stunning green eyes said she was carrying twins. Then Kat got lost when Sophie explained how the twins weren't hers and she was just the incubator because the eggs had come from Ivy.

It turns out Ivy was the redhead sitting down at the other end of the table who had announced she couldn't carry the twins because her womb was reserved for Jag's baby.

What Kat figured out was Sophie was actually carrying her niece and nephew for her brother-in-law, Axel, who was the cop Steel said lived in the compound, and his wife, Bella, who was unable to have babies.

While Kat found that selfless and also impressive, she would not be volunteering to be a surrogate for anyone.

Kat had just shaken her head and then decided not to ask questions to clarify any of that. She wasn't going to be in Shadow Valley long enough to keep everyone's name straight or who was incubating whose baby.

Sophie continued, "Just give him time, they eventually stop fighting it."

Kat's eyebrows pinned together. "Stop fighting what?"

"What they're feeling," Rissa, a tall curvy woman with dark blonde hair, said. Mercy's wife, girlfriend, woman, ol' lady, Kat wasn't sure how she identified with being tied to the tall man with the icy eyes and scary features. Rissa was the total opposite. Warm and welcoming, had a great sense of humor and she smiled a lot. Especially after her second glass of wine.

"About what?" Kat asked her, still confused.

"About you," Rissa stated.

Kat picked up her stemless wine glass and lifted it to her lips, careful not to spill even a fucking drop. She'd need every one of them.

"I don't understand," she announced loudly after taking a healthy gulp of the red wine. The fermented grapes may be going to her head. She was starting to feel a bit fuzzy around the brain.

"Steel probably doesn't, either," Kelsea said with a snort.

It was time to divert the topic of conversation since all eyes were now on her and they all held a "knowing" look that Kat did not like. At all.

"How many women are in this," she waved a hand around, indicating the huge multi-level deck on the back of Sophie and Zak's house, "*sisterhood*, as you call it?"

"So many that the guys are beginning to get nervous when we all gather," Frankie, Hunter's wife or girlfriend, or *whatever*, said.

"Is this all of you?" Kat asked.

"No. Bella, Jewel, Ellie, Emma, Kiki, Jayde, Jazz and Brooke aren't here," the woman named Diamond spoke up. Apparently, she was Slade's wife or girlfriend or ol' lady... gah... woman. Slade and Diamond also owned or managed, or *whatever*, Shadow Valley Fitness.

"Too bad you're not allowed to leave the compound while he's gone. I'd love to take you to our gym. Slade, my ol' man, is Steel's sparring partner and they're close. I also teach kickboxing. I'd love to learn some moves from you."

"Have you done any competitions?"

The gorgeous dark-haired woman nodded, "Some local events when I was younger. I began kickboxing more for self-preservation than competition, but I love it. I had to hide it from just about everyone for years."

Kat's ears perked. "Hide it? Why?"

"I grew up in the MC. It was the club's job to keep us all protected. Females..."

Kat lifted a hand already knowing that same old song and dance. "I get it. Females are good for one thing, right?"

"Women—or girls—in an MC are considered property. The men—especially the Sergeant at Arms—are supposed to protect us. I'm not saying the women aren't capable. Fuck yes, we are. But bikers have a different type of mentality. It's a bit more archaic than the rest of the world. To put it simply, they're behind the times."

That sounded way too familiar.

"It's getting better," Sophie said, her hands massaging her belly.

"Thank fuck," Ivy muttered at the end of the table.

"And you all accept that?" Kat asked, surprised.

Her question was answered with smiles and chuckles.

"You all don't accept that," she answered herself, thankful that this group of women didn't just allow the men to rule their worlds.

"It's getting better," Sophie repeated. "What happens behind closed doors is sometimes different from what others see."

"It's a game," Kat said.

"It's a way of life," Sophie said simply.

Kat could understand that. "I came from a family very set in their ways, set in traditions. Women had—*have*—their place. I broke the mold. I wanted nothing to do with it. I watched my mother, and also my sister, conform and I didn't want that life."

"Did that cause tension with your family?" Rissa asked.

Kat stared at her now half-empty wine glass, running the tip of her finger around the rim. "Let's just say that until I see the error of my ways, I'm no longer invited home for Christmas dinner."

Murmurs surrounded her. Kat glanced around the deck

at the women. She hadn't told them that for sympathy, but because they made her feel comfortable enough to do so. She hadn't been comfortable around a group of women in a long time. If ever.

"We are a huge family. Not just the MC, but the Shadows," Frankie stated. "I never felt so welcomed anywhere before like here in Shadow Valley. And I'm relatively a newcomer."

"You fit right in," Kelsea told Frankie. The blonde turned toward Kat. "And so would you."

That caught Kat off guard. While that was flattering... "Oh... I... I'm just here until they catch my stalker."

"And then what?" Sophie asked.

"And then I head home to LA and continue my training and career."

"I've been to LA and I've lived in Vegas most of my life. I can attest that Shadow Valley is so much nicer," Rissa said carefully, her eyes on Kat.

"I'm sure it is," Kat murmured. "But I have no reason to stay here."

The deck became dead quiet.

"Damn," Diamond whispered. But when she opened her mouth to say whatever she was going to say next, Rissa clamped a hand on her arm, making Diamond's mouth snap shut. The two women shared a look, which Kat did not like, and suddenly the whole subject was dropped.

All of that made the hair on the back of Kat's neck prickle. Why did they act like they knew something she didn't?

"When are your boys getting back?" Ivy asked, also catching that exchange while sipping on seltzer since her "stomach was upset."

Apparently, upset stomachs in the sisterhood meant another baby amongst them but Ivy insisted over the yelling of the other women when they had all first arrived, while she *could* be pregnant, it wasn't definite yet. She also announced they'd all be the first to know, after her husband, of course. Husband, boyfriend, ol' man, *whatever*.

Though, she did call the biker named Jag her husband and not ol' man.

This whole MC life was far too complicated to figure out in the hour they'd been sitting out on the deck enjoying the fall weather and the colorful leaves of the surrounding woods.

Kat had to admit the area was beautiful, the women were great and the neighborhood peaceful. But it was not for her. It was too laid back. She enjoyed the hustle and bustle of both LA and Vegas. And she wasn't sure if sitting in a rocking chair on a deck in Pennsylvania staring at trees while drinking wine was in her future any time soon.

But again, there was no reason for that even to be an option. Especially after what she heard—and also did not hear—around that dining room table the other day.

"They're trying to track down Kat's stalker," Rissa was saying, drawing Kat's attention back to the group.

"Then that fucker has no chance," Diamond announced with a knowing smirk. "Especially since Steel is good with his hands." She made a twisting gesture with her hands in the air like she was breaking someone's neck. "Right, Kat? Steel's good with his hands?"

Once again all eyes were on her. Most of them holding amusement. "Well, he hasn't tried to break my neck. Yet, anyway. But he's a good boxer."

A few snickers and *mmm hmm's* rose around the deck. Which bristled those little hairs on the back of her neck again.

"I'm not sure what you ladies think is going on between us, but did I not mention that he's a complete asshole earlier?" she asked after draining the last of her wine.

"He brought you home," Sophie said softly.

*He brought you home.* Way too much meaning was behind those simple words.

"That's not his home and he only brought me here to keep me safe while they hunt 'H' down since the cops haven't been successful."

*Uh huh's* and *sures* filled the fall air.

"You think he needed to bring you here when they all went back out to Vegas, anyway? It would've been easier for the rest of them to just meet you two out there. One could've guarded you while the others hunted."

*Guarded. Hunted.* Like she was helpless.

She was not a fucking helpless woman who needed a man to handle her problems.

Kat pushed to her feet, pressing a hand to her stomach, which was churning and not from wine and cupcakes. "I'm not feeling well. I need to go... I... I just... need to go."

Diamond jumped to her feet, too. "You can't leave until Slade comes back to get you."

"I don't need a fucking babysitter." Kat squeezed her eyes shut when she realized how irritated she sounded. These women had been nothing but nice to her, she shouldn't take her frustration out on them. She lifted a hand. "Sorry. This situation has me on edge. I've never had to rely on anyone and it makes me feel helpless. I didn't mean to snap."

"Understandable," murmured Rissa.

"I thank you for inviting me today. I was going a bit stir-crazy stuck in the house." Three days of being locked in that house with only the DAMC bikers Slade, Linc, and Dawg as company, each one of them taking shifts to "babysit" her, was enough to drive her off a cliff.

She was so done with all of this.

Her life was no longer her own. She needed to get back to her regularly scheduled programming. Not going to the gym and unable to work out her frustration with the situation made everything worse.

She didn't even have Steel to mess with. And he was cranky as hell before he left to head back to Vegas. She should've insisted she went with him.

When she suggested that, he said no. That 'H' wouldn't find her here in Shadow Valley, even though the fucker had been finding her everywhere else. Apparently here in the Valley, she was off the grid.

"But now I need to go lay down, the wine is getting to me." Sort of the truth, sort of not. She was a bit buzzed but not to the point of not being able to think straight.

"I'll call Slade," Diamond said quickly.

"I'll be fine. I can walk back. It's only around the corner. Just have him meet me at the house."

"Kat," Diamond said, her phone already to her ear, "at least let me walk with you."

A few of the other women insisted on that, too. To keep the peace, Kat nodded her head in agreement, forcing out a laugh. "Fine. With the two of us, no stalker has a chance, right?"

Diamond returned the stiff, humorless laugh. "Right. No chance." She glanced at her phone with a frown. "He's not answering. I'll keep trying."

Sophie called out, "I'll call D and give him a head's up," as Kat and Diamond made their way down the deck into the grass.

Diamond yelled, "Do that," over her shoulder, rushing to keep up with Kat's impatient pace.

And as they walked together back toward Nash's house, Diamond sent a text to her husband, boyfriend, ol' man, *whatever.*

## Chapter Sixteen

STEEL WORE a path in the carpet at the airport, his cell phone glued to his ear.

A familiar answering grunt greeted him.

"We have an issue," he started. "We found out who 'H' is."

"Get 'em, then," his boss responded.

"There's a problem, which is why I'm calling your ass right now, D. Henry McGill, aka 'H,' got on a red eye last night."

"Lemme fuckin' guess to where," Diesel responded.

"Yeah. And, fuck me, we're all out here," Steel growled into the phone.

"Slade's with her, ain't he?"

"He's supposed to be. But I need you on it, too. Between you and Slade, he's got no chance to get to her."

Diesel grunted.

Steel took that as agreement, so he continued. "We're getting on Paranzino's jet as soon as it lands and they refuel it. It was on its way back from dropping Paranzino and his husband off in Tahiti or some such shit. Mercy made it crystal fucking clear we needed it right away. Next commercial flight into the Burgh isn't until tomorrow morning."

"Fuck. Good thing that fucker has turned into Mercy's lil' fuckin' bitch."

"Well, I'm not sure how long that's going to last. He wasn't happy about sending his jet home just for us and also made that quite fucking clear."

"Fuck 'im."

"That's pretty much what Mercy's response was."

Diesel grunted again.

"So, you got it covered on your end?" Steel asked his boss, trying to keep the alarm out of his voice as he walked away from the rest of the Shadows so they wouldn't overhear.

"Yeah."

"D..."

"Yeah."

"Make sure nothing happens to her."

The long hesitation on the other end of the phone wasn't unexpected. D finally barked out a laugh. Again, not unexpected. Steel also expected D to ride his ass without any lube.

"'Cause she's your woman? Or 'cause she's your fuckin' job?"

Steel scrubbed a hand down his beard. "Does it matter?"

"Just answered my fuckin' question."

"D..."

"Yeah, asshole, got it. That fucker shows up in our territory, we got 'im. Nobody fucks with our women."

The phone went dead.

He stared at it for a second before heading back to his waiting teammates. "I want to know how the fuck he knows where she's at?"

"Her manager?" Hunter asked, sprawled across three seats and using his duffel bag as his pillow.

Steel chomped down on his toothpick and shook his head. "I didn't let Berger know where I was taking her solely for that fucking reason."

"Think he got a bead from her phone?" Walker asked, slouched in a seat across from Hunter, his boots planted on the floor, his knees cocked and spread.

"Berger had switched her phone out a couple times. Last one, her current phone, is in a cousin's name."

"Berger did," Mercy emphasized in a low grumble. "But did you?"

He cocked a brow toward Mercy. "You think her manager is somehow tied to this? Why would he want to risk his cash cow?"

"Is she?" Ryder asked, his baseball cap pulled so low, Steel couldn't see the man's eyes.

"Is she what?"

"A cash cow to Berger."

"Fuck yeah. She earned two hundred grand off that last fight alone."

Ryder let out a long, low whistle.

Steel continued, "I have no idea what his cut was, but she was the one taking the hits and losing blood in the cage. He stood outside the ring with me while looking pretty."

"What's it like watching your woman get knocked around?" Brick asked. He was sitting on the ground, his back against a large column, his wrists resting on his bent knees, his eyes hidden by dark sunglasses even though they were inside.

Steel took a breath before answering, "She isn't my woman."

"You two are mirrored images, Steel," Ryder said.

"You couldn't find anyone more perfect for you," Hunter told him.

"I'm not looking," he reminded them.

"Sure?" Hunter asked. "You brought her back to Shadow Valley. You didn't have to do that."

"To keep her safe," Steel insisted.

One of them snorted.

"Keep telling yourself that," Brick said with a grin.

"You sleepin' with her?" Ryder asked, tipping his hat up enough for their gazes to lock.

"How soon's that plane landing?" Steel asked Mercy, avoiding Ryder's searching gaze.

"Not before you answer that question," the big man answered.

"We need to get back ASAP."

"And we will," Ryder said. "D will hold shit together in the meantime."

"I sure as fuck hope so."

"Unless you're about to sprout wings, we aren't getting there any fucking faster than Paranzino's private jet," Mercy said.

"We still need to find out how the fucker keeps locating Kat."

"And we wanna know why you're avoidin' the question," Ryder said, sitting up.

"What question?" Steel asked, wondering how he could get them to drop this interrogation.

"Ah, fuck," Ryder laughed. "You got it fuckin' bad. The asshole got his toe caught in the trap."

"Or dick locked in a cock cage," Walker added with a grin.

"Or both," Brick said.

Then they all laughed. Except for Steel.

Yeah, it was real fucking funny.

"Just because all of you got your dicks caught in a cage doesn't mean I will."

More fucking laughter.

"Except me," Brick announced, still chuckling.

"Your dick isn't in anyone long enough to get stuck," Ryder reminded him.

"Yep. And that's the reason I keep moving," Brick answered with a grin.

"That's his life. Swipe right," Walker said seriously.

"That's right. Swipe and go, fuckers," Brick said. "No fuss. No muss. No clingers." His eyes hit Steel's. "No cock cages."

Steel grabbed his crotch. "Cage free, brother."

"Wouldn't it be a pisser if it was Kat who didn't want Steel?" Ryder asked, watching him closely.

Then they all laughed again.

*Great.*

"I'm irresistible," he grumbled.

More laughter. Louder this time.

"What-fucking-ever, assholes. Can we use this down time to figure out how McGill keeps finding Kat?"

Laughter died and grins flattened.

There was a time to work and a time to play. Right now they needed to work.

"I'm saying it's her phone," Walker said. "No other way."

"Maybe," Steel mumbled.

"Okay, then," Walker ran a hand down his cheek, "what other electronics does she have?"

Steel shrugged. "I think a tablet and a laptop."

"I wonder if any of them were in her place when he broke in? Could he have put an app or program on her tablet or computer without her knowing?" Mercy asked Walker, who was their resident tracker.

"Anything's possible when someone's determined," Walker replied.

"We know that all too well," Hunter said.

"We could test that theory by gathering her electronics

and using them as a trap. Then we know for sure. And, bonus," Brick shouted, "we get the fucker."

"That sounds like a plan, but in the meantime—"

Steel cut Mercy off. "In the meantime, we need to get those electronics away from Kat."

Mercy added, "And out of the fucking compound."

"We don't want that sick fuck anywhere near the women or kids," Hunter agreed, especially since he had a woman and kid in that very compound.

"A-fuckin'-men to that," Ryder muttered.

"I'll text D and get Slade to give her shit to him," Steel said. "Then he can put them in one of those bags that blocks the signal until we're ready for the trap."

"Yeah, but if McGill can't pick up the signal, won't he go to the last known location anyway?" Ryder asked.

"Are you worried about him getting into the compound?" Hunter asked. "We can give Slade, Dawg and Linc the heads up. It's still the most secure place for her."

Mercy spoke up again. "I think we need to have the boss man give everyone in the compound the heads up. Anything suspicious, they notify him."

"Agreed."

"Lot more eyes there than if we move her elsewhere."

Steel agreed once again with Mercy who approached him and slapped him on the back. "Don't worry, asshole. Your woman will be okay, and we'll get that fucker. Guaranteed."

He sure as fuck hoped so.

But Mercy's words didn't relieve the churn in his gut due to knowing "H," aka Henry McGill, was on his way to Shadow Valley and had a head start.

---

ONE OF THE bikers had brought some kind of special bags to put her cell phone, tablet and laptop into. Dawg explained they were RFID-blocking. The younger biker named Linc said they blocked radio frequencies in case "H" was using her electronics to track her.

It would make sense since "H" kept finding her. But so far, none of the big men in leather vests with patches proclaiming them members of the Dirty Angels MC, had mentioned that "H" had found her this time. Though, all of them seemed suspiciously alert.

Really alert. And it was rare that in the last few days all three of them were in Nash's house at the same time.

Even Steel's boss, Diesel, occasionally stopped in. Each time he'd been wearing an infant in one of those carriers that strapped the baby to his massive chest. If seeing a beast of a biker, covered in tattoos, wearing what was explained as "colors," also wearing a tiny baby girl wouldn't stop traffic, nothing would.

It was like King Kong cuddling a newborn kitten, which made it hard not to stare. Or rub her eyes to make sure she was seeing what she was seeing.

But this new activity within the house set her on edge and no one gave her an explanation beside a placating, "Just bein' cautious," until the Shadows returned.

They apparently were on their way as soon as they caught a flight.

Which hopefully meant that they'd found "H," and this would all soon be over. But she'd heard nothing from Steel the whole time he was gone. Not a call, not a text, nothing.

If he wanted to play it like that, so could she. Even though her fingers had itched to call or text him.

To get an update on the situation.

That's all.

Nothing else.

She had no other reason to talk to him since she was simply his "job."

A financial transaction.

She had given him more than any man. She should've known better.

Her mistake. One she wouldn't make again.

Her attention was drawn to the closing of the front door. Was he back?

Her heart began to pound like the traitor it was.

Fuck him, the toothpick-chewing asshole.

She blew out a breath.

Her eyes slid to the king-sized bed. She had been distant with him before he left. But, even so, she hadn't been able to resist sleeping with him.

More than *sleeping* with him.

Not that they had spoken much during the run he insisted she take with him. Or later that night when they worked up a sweat again between the sheets.

He was good in bed. She reluctantly gave the man that. Not that she had a lot to compare to. But he sure knew how to light her on fire and bring her to orgasm.

And his mouth, his fingers... His fucking addictive cock.

*Fuck.*

Now that she knew what she'd been missing, when she got back to LA, she'd be more open to finding a man to...

A man to...

She closed her eyes and tried to imagine a man—any man—other than Steel doing what he'd done.

She couldn't.

But she had no choice.

"You okay up there?" Slade yelled from what sounded like the main floor.

She moved to the bedroom doorway. "Yes, just resting." Sort of the truth. But not really, since she'd been pacing the floor restlessly.

"Dawg had to go open the gun shop an' Linc had to go open The Iron Horse."

Both businesses owned by their MC. Kat was surprised how extensive their club was, with not only members but businesses. It was run like a well-oiled machine from the conversations she'd had with her biker babysitters. For some reason they had felt the need to give her the run-down on all things club related.

"They'll be back later if Steel ain't back by then."

So, it wasn't Steel walking in the front door. It was two of the bikers walking out.

She fought her disappointment. Which made her even more disappointed at herself for being disappointed.

*Damn it.*

A few minutes later, Slade once again yelled up the steps. "You smell smoke? Gonna check the perimeter. Stay put."

Where the fuck was she going to go? The only transportation she had was her two legs. She highly doubted Slade would let her get far. He was a good guard dog. And while she was in shape, he was in even better shape, just about as built as Steel and Kat wasn't about to go a few rounds with him.

Though, he looked nothing like a biker, except for the excessive tats. If anything, he looked more military-like. Just like the Shadows with short, cropped hair, and Kat had noticed the faint outline of dog tags under his worn T-shirts and leather vest.

Kat had always had the impression that bikers were scruffy, smelly, dirty, and had beer guts. So far, none she'd met in the DAMC looked like that. No wonder their women were hot. And smart. Seemingly well-educated.

Caught up in her thoughts, she realized she never answered Slade. "Okay."

When all she got was silence as an answer, Kat decided

to stop hiding upstairs like a pouting child and see if she could help Slade search for the source of the smoke.

She didn't smell it until she hit the foyer. She headed toward the back of the house where the kitchen and the sliding glass doors to the deck were.

She was surprised to see one of the sliders wide open, which meant the alarm was off. She poked her head out and called, "Slade?"

Nothing.

She leaned out farther. "Slade?" she called even louder. He was probably circling the outside perimeter like Steel had done on many occasions in Boulder City.

She stepped out onto the deck, wrapping her arms around herself since the temp had dropped again and there was a cool breeze rattling the dried leaves in the trees. Good thing this was all coming to an end soon, since she'd need warmer clothes if she was stuck in Pennsylvania any longer. She was ready to head back to a warmer climate.

Her eyes scanned the area and the woods directly behind the house, not seeing any fire or source of smoke, but she still could smell it faintly in the air. She stepped farther out onto the deck, her bare feet quickly turning to ice on the vinyl decking. She glanced at the house two lots down to the right. Nothing.

The lot to the left was empty, too.

Still no sign of the biker.

"Slade!"

The eerie sound of the breeze through the leaves was her only answer. She shivered and wrapped her arms around herself tighter.

She needed to put on a pair of shoes and search for him. She also couldn't call or text him since the house didn't have a landline and her cell phone had been taken from her by Dawg.

"Fuck," she muttered under her breath. Before she could

turn to go back inside, a movement around the corner of the house caught her attention. It was a brown-haired man, tall, thin, with glasses, but wearing a familiar leather vest. The DAMC colors. "Hey! Have you seen Slade? He was checking to see where the smoke was coming from and—"

As the man rushed toward her, he said, "He wants you to come with me. There's a fire and I'm supposed to get you somewhere safe."

This guy didn't look like a biker, but then the others hadn't fit the mold, either. Well, except for Diesel and Dawg, somewhat. So, she shouldn't be surprised that this one looked like a librarian. An accountant, maybe? A nerd, for sure.

As he closed in on her, her gaze dropped to the patch with his name.

*Slade.*

Her chest compressed, making it hard to breathe. He was wearing Slade's cut.

Where the fuck was Slade?

"I... uh... need to grab some shoes first. I'll be right back out," she managed to say.

"No, Katheryn. You're not going anywhere but with me."

Her spine stiffened and she became hyper-focused on the man only steps away from her now.

She readied herself by softening her knees and curling her fingers into fists.

She was ready for the fight of her life.

Right here. In Shadow Valley. On the deck of an unoccupied house.

"I'm not going anywhere with you," she answered as calmly as she could.

"We'll see."

"Yes, we will," she agreed. Instead of retreating, she met him across the deck and as she launched into her first roundhouse kick, something black and compact appeared in his hand.

Her brain began to spin as her body did.

Gun?

Was she going to die right there?

Then whatever he held made contact with her calf. As fifty thousand volts of what she now knew was a stun gun hit her, she dropped instantly to the deck as her weight-bearing leg crumpled beneath her and her body was no longer her own.

She had zero control as he kept the voltage flowing through her body and he dropped over top of her. She could do nothing as a needle was pulled from somewhere on his person and was jammed into her thigh through her thin spats.

She couldn't resist, she couldn't scream, she couldn't escape.

She was fucking helpless.

Goddamn helpless.

All the training she'd gone through; all the skills she had honed; all the blood, sweat and tears she'd endured to become a champion. All of that meant nothing in those few moments as her body betrayed her due to the electrical current running through it.

And eventually, whatever was in that syringe switched her world to "off."

———

KAT'S VISION WAS BLURRED. Not just from whatever her stalker had shot into her bloodstream, but from whatever was covering her head. White lightweight cloth. Possibly a pillowcase.

Her wrists were bound, as were her ankles, and she knew she was in a vehicle. Most likely the back seat of one since she was laying down.

She needed to puke.

Her head was foggy but her brain was still spinning, her gut twisted in knots.

Bile threatened to rise from her stomach. But if she threw up, it would get caught in the pillowcase. So, she sucked air in through her nose as best as she could to fight the nausea. Unfortunately, the bumpy ride wasn't helping.

She tried to speak, but her throat felt raw, her tongue thick, her lips dry. Even so, she forced herself to ask, "What did you give me?"

Her body hurt everywhere, and her muscles felt weak.

Still helpless.

"Why, Katheryn? Why? Why? Why? Why didn't you just do as I asked and come to me? We could've had a good life together. Why did you have to fight what we have? Why did you give your innocence to that man? He doesn't love you like I do. Why? Why did you make me do this to you?"

"What did you inject me with?"

"You were supposed to be mine!" came the shriek, making Kat wince since her head was still throbbing.

"Where are we going?"

"Home. Where you belong."

Her heart, already racing, kicked up a notch. "Where is home?" Was it somewhere where she'd never be found? Would her stalker win?

"You don't have to worry about anything, Katheryn. I'll handle everything. I'll make sure you're happy and our children are happy. I'll provide for you and our family."

*Fuck.*

*Fuck.*

*Fuck.*

"If you want to make me happy, you'll let me go."

"Then you'll continue to be lonely. I saw it. Your life is

empty. You have no one but yourself. I saw it in your eyes. They were vacant. I want to fill them with joy."

"Drugging and kidnapping me doesn't fill me with joy," she whispered.

"You'll see. You'll see the error of your thinking. You'll thank me later. When you're holding our firstborn in your arms."

Kat quickly did a mental body scan. Had he raped her while she was unconscious?

Her spats were still in place and she didn't feel any fluids between her thighs. That was a good sign, wasn't it?

She shuddered at the thought of "H" sexually assaulting her while she was drugged.

She tested her bindings which felt like zip ties. Secure and just tight enough so she couldn't slip them.

She needed to figure out a way to get out of this situation. She had no idea where "H" was taking her and she had no idea how long they'd been driving. She just knew the farther he took her from Shadow Valley, the harder it would be for Steel to find her.

In the meantime, she had to play along with "H's" fantasies. By being compliant, she could buy time and hopefully keep the man on an even keel, so he didn't do anything rash.

She needed to play his game.

She also needed to win it.

# Chapter Seventeen

As THEY DISEMBARKED from the small Cessna, everyone's phone binged or vibrated. All at the same time.

Which was not a good sign since all the Shadows were on the jet together. That meant it was a mass text from Diesel.

As one, they glanced down at their phones.

*Warehouse. Now.*

Diesel was never chatty, but his short and to the point message made a bead of sweat pop out on Steel's forehead and his asshole squeeze tight.

Something was wrong.

And it could only be one thing.

His nightmare of McGill getting to Kat came true.

They were still a half hour away from the warehouse. On a good day with light traffic.

There was no way he was waiting a thirty-minute drive to find out what the fuck happened.

"Let's get to our vehicles ASAP," Mercy grumbled as they hoofed it across the tarmac.

Steel hit Call and was greeted with Diesel's signature grunt.

"ETA in thirty. Talk to me," Steel barked into the phone, trying to keep from sprinting to the two vehicles they'd left in short-term parking.

"Gotta keep your shit together," D warned him.

For fuck's sake, that just made him even more wired. "Tell me!" he exploded.

Mercy yelled, "Keep your shit together," over his shoulder but was now almost at a jog himself.

Everyone else picked up the pace, too.

"You were supposed to be on it, D. What happened?"

"Fucker set fire to the house."

"Fuck! Is she okay?"

"Fire was a distraction, got Slade outta the house an' her alone."

"Jesus fuck. Is she okay?"

Now all six of them were jogging toward the parking area.

"D, is she okay?" he shouted into the phone.

"Don't fuckin' know. The fucker tased Slade, injected him with something to knock him out, stole his fuckin' cut. Slade's got no fuckin' clue what happened after that."

His fist tightening around his phone, Steel almost stumbled as he got the urge to shut his eyes and scream. He forced them to remain open and began to run even faster. "Double-time," he shouted to the rest of them. "He got her?" he asked D.

"Yeah, he got her."

"How long ago?"

"Maybe three hours from what we can figure. Slade's thinkin' the fucker used his cut to trick her."

"Any signs of a struggle?"

"No."

Steel was about to lose his shit. "What's he driving?"

"Stole a vehicle from the compound so he could get out of the gate. Thinkin' he climbed the wall to get in."

244

That meant they needed to install razor wire along the top of the wall. *Fucking motherfucker.*

"Whose vehicle?"

"Yours."

Steel almost fell to his knees. "Thank fuck!" he yelled to the sky. "I've got an EVTS on it. We can track them."

"Got no fuckin' clue what the fuck that is," D barked into the phone.

"We're on our way. We can track it once we get there."

"Fuck that," Walker yelled out as he arrived at Mercy's Terradyne RPV. "I've got my laptop. We're tracking it now."

"No point in heading to the warehouse if we can get a bead on them now. Just wasting time," Mercy seconded.

"You hear that?" Steel asked.

Diesel grunted his answer. "Keep me updated."

Steel quickly got into Mercy's SUV on steroids, sitting on pins and needles in the back seat next to Walker.

Mercy yelled out, "Follow us," to Brick who was climbing into his just as obnoxious Rezvani Tank. *Crazy motherfuckers.*

Ryder rode with Brick, while Hunter rode shotgun with Mercy.

"Three hours' head start," Steel said to no one in particular, his knee bouncing a mile a minute. "Three fucking hours. So fucking glad I sprang for that tracking system on my Jeep."

"You're normally such a cheap fuck," Hunter said. "Aren't you glad you weren't this time?"

Steel ignored him and watched Walker do his thing, his fingers flying over the laptop's keyboard. "You got the identifying info for your vehicle?"

Steel pulled up an app on his cell phone where he kept all his important info.

Walker just gave him a look and shook his head.

"What?"

"I could hack your phone and get all that shit from you."

"But you won't."

"*I* won't. Doesn't mean anybody else won't."

He handed Walker his phone. "Just find her."

Walker grabbed it, found the Jeep's identification number he needed and went to work, hacking into the system's site.

It was a long fucking ten minutes until he lifted his head and grinned. "Got the fucker."

"Where?" Steel leaned over and looked at the coordinates that had been pulled up. "Can we shut the vehicle down?"

"No," Mercy chimed in from the driver's seat. "We shut that vehicle down and he'll find another that we can't track. Is he moving?"

"Yeah," Walker answered.

Mercy started his RPV and pulled out. "Where we going?"

"West. He's almost through Ohio already."

"Guess we're heading west. He has to stop sometime," Hunter said.

"I fucking swear we're going to be stopping for gas every fifteen minutes for these ridiculous tanks you and Brick have," Steel growled.

"Oh, yours is much better on fuel?" Mercy asked, his silver eyes hitting Steel's in the rearview mirror.

Steel's lips flattened out. "Better than this."

"Do we want to rent a faster, more fuel-efficient vehicle while we're here at the airport?" Hunter asked.

"Do we want to waste the time and BS of dealing with a rental car company?" Walker asked.

"Fuck no," Mercy grumbled and jammed his foot on the gas pedal.

"That fucker Paranzino have a helicopter?" Steel asked.

"No," Mercy grunted.

"Does any of us know anyone with a chopper? I still got my pilot's license," Walker stated. "Fuck it, I'd still fly it even if it was expired. That's not something that I'll ever forget how to do."

"Like riding a fucking bike," Mercy said.

"With rotor blades," Walker added.

"A helicopter would be way faster. Who do we know?" Steel asked. "Anyone with access to one nearby?" Steel's head twisted toward Walker. "But how are we going to track the fucker while we're in it? Will you have service?"

"Can use a hotspot on my phone."

"That'll work?" Steel asked him. If they lost the signal, they'd lose McGill and Kat. They couldn't risk that.

"Hopefully."

Walker's answer wasn't good enough. "Hopefully is not what I want to fucking hear. Fuck!" Steel shouted.

"While you assholes figure it out, I'll just keep driving."

"I'm sure he'll stop at a motel or something. Do you have any idea why he's headed west?" Walker asked.

"Home to LA is my only guess," Steel said.

"That's a hell of a drive, which means he'll definitely need to stop for breaks," Hunter concluded.

"And we won't stop," Mercy announced.

"Fuck no," Steel whispered. He raised his voice. "But my concern is what he'll do to Kat once he does."

No one said anything for a few moments after that.

Hunter faced the windshield when he muttered, "Just gotta get her back in one piece."

Just like that. That easy. "One piece. Yeah, right." Steel shook his head and blew out a breath. "How long did it take Jazz to be put back together? How long did Kelsea fucking deal with the shit done to her? How about Diamond?"

"We can get law enforcement involved," Hunter

suggested, turning around again in the front passenger seat to look at Steel. "Put out a BOLO. Let them track the Jeep at the same time we do."

"Brother, did you want them involved when Leo was taken by Taz?" Steel asked Hunter, then turned to Walker. "Did you want them involved when Ellie was snagged by the cartel?"

Neither said a word.

"How about you, Mercy? Did you want us to handle that fucknut who took Rissa or did you want to hand him over to the cops?"

Mercy's silver eyes met Steel's again in the mirror. "I hear you, brother."

Steel jerked his chin up. "Cops get him, he's gonna live. I get him, he won't. He'll never do this shit again. To Kat. To anyone."

"So, we're chasing him," Walker concluded.

"We're fucking chasing him," Steel confirmed. "A chopper's a great idea but we're three hours behind him and it'll take longer to find one."

"Copy that," Mercy said up front.

Walker turned his laptop to show Steel a map with his vehicle's signal. "Not three hours behind, maybe two. And if Brick and Mercy can get their beasts moving faster, we can shorten that window."

"Let's hope that fucker's going the speed limit, afraid of getting pulled over," Hunter said to the windshield.

"Let's hope that we don't get fucking pulled over ourselves," Steel added. "That'll delay us."

Steel could already feel his fingers wrapped around McGill's neck. But the reality was they were about two hours behind, which meant her stalker could do what he wanted to her in that time before Steel and his team could arrive.

He only hoped his taste for revenge turned out to be sweet and not bitter.

Because if something happened to her because of his decisions, he'd never forgive himself.

And she probably wouldn't forgive him, either.

———

KAT SLOWED her breathing as the vehicle rolled to a stop.

"Where are we?"

No answer.

"I need to go to the bathroom," she insisted.

"You can't."

"Do you want me to piss my pants? Is this how you're going to treat the mother of your future children?" *Asshole.*

Again, nothing.

She wished she could see him. This Henry. That's what he told her his name was, even though she hadn't asked. She'd rather know where they were and where they were going.

Of course, that he hadn't shared.

"I'm hungry, too. I need food. I need water. I need to relieve myself."

"I need you to be quiet, Katheryn."

*Oh no. Fuck that.* "No, Henry. You took my freedom from me. I'm not going to be quiet. Sorry, but I'm not going to suffer in silence. If you don't like it, too bad."

She grimaced as she heard the emergency brake get pulled.

"I can't let you out of the Jeep."

Jeep? Were they in Steel's vehicle?

"Why not?"

"Because I'd have to remove the pillowcase and ties. Otherwise, it'll draw attention."

Kat wanted to scream, *"You think?"*

She didn't.

"How about you remove them, and I promise to cooperate. I just need a quick bathroom break and then to eat something. *Please*."

"I'm not stupid, Katheryn."

"Are you going to keep me bound and blindfolded for the rest of my life? How am I going to raise our children like that?" She was struggling to hide her impatience with him and losing that battle.

"Once I get you home and you see how well you have it, it'll be unnecessary."

Which proved he *was* stupid.

No, maybe not stupid, but delusional. Definitely delusional.

"I'm already resigned to the fact that we're meant to be together, Henry. You and me. Forever. True love."

"Now you're mocking me."

*Fuck.*

"I just wanted you to give me a chance, to see what we have together. How good it could be."

His whininess grated on her nerves. "I can't see that with a pillowcase over my head!" she yelled, then desperately reined in her temper.

Getting angry would do her no good and only agitate him.

"I'm sorry, Henry, I didn't mean to lose my patience. But, please, I need to relieve myself before I make an embarrassing mess."

"Katheryn, you'll have to promise me that you'll behave yourself."

"I promise." *I promise to kick your fucking ass when you let me go,* she added silently.

"I'll gas up the Jeep, grab drinks and food in the store

and then find out where their restroom is. If it's not on the outside of the building, I'll have to take you somewhere else. I can't risk you talking to anyone inside."

*Damn it.* "Okay, Henry. I appreciate it."

Ten minutes later, Henry was back in the vehicle with what sounded like plastic bags.

And he drove the fuck away!

"Henry..."

"I'll find you somewhere else. It's too risky here."

Kat was not a crier, but tears stung her eyes. She had hoped to get an opportunity to get free of Henry.

She hated feeling helpless!

"Henry, soon, yes?"

"Yes, Katheryn, soon. I promise."

He broke his promise and drove for way longer than Kat had hoped. By the time he stopped again, her bladder was screaming and so were her thoughts.

"We'll stop for the night. Since it's dark, I can get you inside the motel room without anyone seeing you and we'll leave before dawn. I need some rest and you do, too. I'll uncover your head so you can eat and drink, and we can talk."

*Great.* Just what she wanted, a meal and conversation with her stalker.

He got out of the vehicle and was back quickly, so she assumed he had stopped in a motel office to register and get a room key.

*More good news.*

Then he drove again, most likely to the farthest room.

"We'll have privacy here," he said as he parked the Jeep and shut it off. "The motel is empty, and we have the room farthest from the office. It's perfect."

Kat disagreed.

She groaned when Henry finally helped her off the

uncomfortable backseat of the Jeep and onto her feet. It felt good to finally be upright again, but she was stiff as hell.

She had no idea how she was going to walk since her feet were still bound. "Henry, I can't move since I'm tied up."

In truth, the last place she wanted to go was inside a room with her stalker, who had masturbated on her things.

That didn't bode well for her. Especially since he wanted her to have his children. And the only way for her to get pregnant was...

She squeezed her eyes shut, trying not to imagine what that would entail.

At least with Henry.

A shudder went through her and her heart began to race.

She needed to convince him to untie her, then she could get the upper hand. As long as he didn't have that damn taser.

Which, of course, he did when he jammed it into her back like a gun before pulling off her "hood."

It was true, it was dark. The motel lot badly lit. But from what she could see, it was some fleabag motel that probably rented rooms by the hour. *If* they were lucky to get customers. She couldn't see much past the motel, but it looked like it was surrounded by fields and alongside a quiet road.

None of that was to her benefit.

But she'd worry about that once she got free. She needed to take Henry out and get Steel's keys.

Henry tossed the pillowcase into the Jeep and slammed the door shut.

"You have to untie my feet so I can walk, Henry."

"If I untie your feet, you'll kick me like you tried to do back at that house. I've watched all of your competitions, Katheryn. I know how capable you are."

*More fucktacular news.*

"Then how are you getting me inside?"

Kat gasped as Henry drove his shoulder into her painfully empty stomach and somehow—though, a bit wobbly—threw her over his shoulder. She didn't think the painfully thin man had that kind of strength.

He made his way to the door, used the key, almost dropping her in the process, and shoved the door open.

The smell that hit her as he made his way into the room and over to the bed, singed her nose and made her want to gag.

With a grunt and a groan, he dropped her onto the bed. He went back to close and lock the door, draw the curtains and turn on the dingy overhead light.

The room was old, outdated and disgusting.

Perfect movie location for a kidnapping or murder scene.

Only this wasn't a movie. "Really? This is the best you can do for your future spouse?" Her eyes narrowed on him, annoyed.

Frustration filled his face as he looked around. "It's the best I can do for now. I'm sorry you have to deal with this, but you forced my hand. You kept moving. I had to do something."

"You could've left me alone," she suggested.

His pale blue eyes landed on her. "You're mine, Katheryn. No one else's but mine. It's bad enough that you let *him* touch you. Soil you. He took what was meant to be mine. Why?"

Suddenly Kat saw the man switch from a calm psycho to a manic one. He dragged his fingernails over his cheeks and then he began pulling at his hair, his face twisting. "Why? Why? Why? Why? Why? Why?"

Each "why" became louder and louder until he was screaming and Kat was wincing.

Had he snapped?

"Why did you let him do that to you?"

Kat attempted to swallow but her throat was too dry. She wouldn't have an answer that was acceptable to him, anyway.

"I need to use the rest room, Henry. I can't wait any longer," she forced out in a low, what she hoped, calming tone. "Henry, please, I'm in pain."

"I'm so disappointed in you. Now you need to be scrubbed clean before I give you my seed."

Kat's mouth opened and then snapped shut. She couldn't even begin to fathom how disturbing those words were. What did he mean? Was she safe for tonight? Was he going to drag her into the bathroom and scrub her skin raw, then rape her?

He gave her one more wide-eyed, crazed look, then opened the door, slamming it behind him after stepping outside. He was back in under a minute, a satchel in his hand.

He dug in it, pulling out the taser and a large knife.

*Jesus.* She was going to die in this rat trap.

"Henry..." she started.

"Stay still. I'll free you so you can relieve yourself, but I'll be by your side with the taser. If you try anything, I'll zap you again and give you another shot of ketamine. And I don't want to have to do that. Please don't make me do that, Katheryn."

*Ketamine.*

That's what he had injected her with. Had he done the same with Slade? She had no idea what happened to him.

"Is Slade okay?" she asked as he began to saw at the plastic zip ties used to bind her ankles.

She watched him carefully as he did so, anticipating her freedom.

"Who?"

"The biker. Is he okay? Did you hurt him?"

"I'm sure he's fine."

He finished cutting through the thick plastic band and her legs were finally free.

*Fucking free!*

All she had to do was plan. He still held the taser. She needed to kick that out of his hand and then knock him down and out.

But she needed her hands free first.

"Go," he said, jabbing the taser against her thigh. Even though it wasn't engaged, Kat still flinched.

"I can't go without the use of my hands."

"I'll help you."

*What?*

*Fuck!*

"Henry, I need privacy—"

"You'll get what I give you, Katheryn!" he barked impatiently.

Kat rolled off the bed to her feet, feeling a bit lightheaded as she stood. She gathered her wits and turned until her bound hands were in his direction. "Cut my hands free. You can bind me again afterward."

"No, Katheryn."

"Please." She had to convince him somehow, someway. "Henry, I'll make a deal with you." She glanced over her shoulder to see him studying her hands. "You cut me free, I'll go to the bathroom and then take a shower and scrub myself clean from... from him. Then I will be fresh and ready to be yours. Deal?"

"You're not on any kind of birth control, are you?" His cheeks were flushed and his eyes beginning to gleam at her suggestion, which creeped her the fuck out.

She needed to do something to get out of this situation.

Whatever it took.

She needed to do it.

She would grin and bear whatever it was.

She inhaled a deep breath and bolstered herself. "No."

His face turned hard for a moment. "You're not with child? With him?"

Kat's heart skipped a beat.

"Because that would be even more disappointing, Katheryn. Because he can't have you. No one else can."

"I'm not pregnant. No."

Then the fucker smiled. "When was your last cycle?"

*WHAT?*

"When was your last cycle?" he screamed when she didn't answer fast enough.

"I... I..." She couldn't tell him that she had irregular cycles due to the amount she worked out. She simply had to lie. "I think I'm fertile right now."

Anything, *anything* to get out of this situation, she reminded herself.

Henry hissed out a breath and then a smile once again filled his face.

A horrifying smile that Kat wanted to wipe off his face. With her fist. Or her knee.

"Katheryn," he whispered in a way that made her want to vomit.

"Henry, I can't wait any longer," she reminded him gently. "Then I will shower and scrub him away. There will be nothing but us left, I promise. That's what you want, right? Just us? And babies? The family you've always wanted?"

"Yes. That's what I want. You. Me. Our lovely children. Two at least. Maybe three. We can start making them tonight once you're clean."

Cold, invisible fingers slid down her spine.

"I'll be clean," she promised, turning her back again to him. "As soon as you cut me free so I can do that for you. The sooner you do that, the sooner you can make me yours. All yours. I'll want no one but you. But I can't be happy bound like this and filthy from his touches. I need to come to you clean and pure. Help me do that."

"Katheryn," Henry groaned, leaning forward and brushing his nose along her hair. "I want you so badly."

Kat did her best not to shudder and pull away. Instead, she fought her instinct and leaned back into him. "I want you so badly, too. But not like this. Henry, I'm ready to start a family. It's what I always wanted, too, but could never find the right man."

"Then why did you stand me up?"

"Because I didn't know how strong you were until today. You've proven yourself to me with your dominance. That's something I need in my life. You have what I need, Henry. I see it now. I was wrong and you were right."

He inhaled deeply, his hands now gripping her shoulders, holding her against him. Her bound hands were pinned below his waist and pressed against his erection.

"You're so beautiful when you're compliant. You don't need to be hard. You don't need to fight. You need to let your man fight your battles for you, solve all your problems. I'll do that."

*Jesus*, it was her upbringing all over again.

*You need a husband. A man to take care of you.*

*You need to get married and have children.*

*Your purpose in life is to have a family. To serve them.*

She swallowed down the bile bubbling up. "You're right. I need someone like you to provide for me and take care of me. I've been fighting it, but now I see the truth."

She wanted to puke, but she needed to play the game. To convince him she was cooperative and willing. Not a threat. Maybe then he'd cut the bindings on her wrists, giving her a chance to escape.

Without warning, he jerked against her and grabbed her elbow, dragging her in the direction of the tiny bathroom at the back of the room. He shoved her inside without turning on the light, then cut the plastic cuffs from her wrists before shoving her forward, making her catch her balance. The door slammed shut with him on the outside.

"I'll be waiting out here, Katheryn. Do what you need to do. But don't betray me. Or I won't be so forgiving next time."

Kat released a shaky breath and felt around for the switch. Finding it, she flipped it on and wrinkled her nose at the condition of the puke green tiled bathroom. But that was the least of her problems.

The bathroom had no window, so she had only one way out of there. Through Henry. Through Henry with a taser and possibly another syringe of Special K. And if she ended up knocked out again...

She could easily end up knocked up against her will.

She did the first thing she could no longer avoid. Emptying her bladder. Then she cupped handfuls of water and drank as much as she could since she was dehydrated. The water was awful, but it was something.

She eyed the shower and the moldy shower curtain.

"I don't hear the shower running, Katheryn."

*No shit.*

She rubbed a hand over her eyes, trying to keep herself together, then turned on the shower. She stared sightlessly at the falling water, the sound of it hitting the tub filling the tiny room, filling her head, calming her.

She needed a plan.

A better one than just kicking and punching the crap out of Henry, getting tased again and being knocked out with a drug.

She needed to win this time. Not him.

And she also needed to buy some time. She turned toward the door and saw it had a lock on the doorknob. She twisted it slowly, trying not to catch Henry's attention. Then she stripped out of her clothes and took her time taking that lukewarm shower.

To get her clean.

Pure.

Free of Steel's touches.

Just how Henry wanted her.

# Chapter Eighteen

WALKER SLAPPED a palm against Steel's chest. Whether it was in excitement or a sign for Steel to keep his shit together, he didn't know, because he was too focused on the only vehicle in the lot—beside an old rusty Oldsmobile parked in front of the office—to care. The familiar army-green Jeep was parked in front of the room at the very end of the seedy motel.

The first thing he noticed was that the license plate had been swapped out, which meant the fucker wasn't dumb. If the cops had put out a BOLO, it would've been with Steel's registration.

But his missing plate wasn't important. Kat was.

Mercy and Brick had turned off their vehicles' lights once they had pulled off the road in the middle of Nowhere, Indiana. Ironically, Kat's home state.

A sliver of light escaped from between drawn drapes, so there was no doubt which room she was in.

But what was in doubt was her current physical and mental status.

He only hoped she was alive.

Anything else could be and would be dealt with.

It had taken an hour and fifty-three minutes to catch up to them. And once the Jeep had stopped moving in the tracking system, Steel had been beside himself.

With worry. With anger.

With thoughts that death for McGill would be too good for the bastard. Especially if he violated her in any way.

No matter what, the man had signed his death warrant the second he had boarded a plane to Pittsburgh.

As soon as Mercy stopped the vehicle, Steel jumped from it, sprinting across the narrow lot, his focus solely on his destination.

He didn't even waste time trying the doorknob. He lifted his boot and immediately kicked the door so hard, it splintered as it broke free. Even the chain lock snapped.

He felt like Godzilla as he rammed his body through the remaining pieces of door and launched himself into the room, almost falling to his knees as his eyes landed on the bed.

Where Kat was.

Where Henry was.

Kat's eyes were shut, and she didn't even react to his arrival.

But Henry did.

His hand which was wrapped around his dick ceased its movements and his eyes were wide behind black plastic rimmed glasses.

It took a fraction of a second for Steel to assess the situation.

It took a fraction of a second to see nothing else but his target.

The naked man who was kneeling above Kat's similarly naked body sprawled lifeless over a dingy bedspread.

She wore nothing but black panties and those were marked with blotches of what Steel knew were cum.

The same which marked her bare chest and breasts.

McGill had ejaculated all over her and was attempting to do it again.

Before he could unglue his feet, his team was at his back and Mercy stepped beside him, aiming his Sig Sauer at the center of McGill's melon.

That melon was twisted so McGill could see them all. And it did not go unnoticed that the fucker had a massive bruise on one cheek, a black, swollen eye and blood crusting one nostril.

Kat did not go down easy.

*Thank fuck.*

Ryder pushed past him, hooked McGill around the neck with his arm and yanked him right off the bed into a heap on the floor. He used his boot to smash his glasses where they landed.

Brick rushed forward to throw his jacket over Kat's chest and when he turned, he drop-kicked McGill right in the ribs, causing the fucker to cry out and curl up into a ball, groaning.

"That's nothin', fucker," Ryder leaned over and shouted in his face. "That's fuckin' NOTHIN'!" He stepped away, his nostrils flared, his fists clenched.

The tension in the room between the six of them was thick, the air crackled. And Steel could do nothing but stare at Kat. On that bed.

Vulnerable. Violated.

But alive.

*Thank fuck. Thank fuck. Thank fuck.*

"Take care of your woman," Mercy ordered, tucking his gun back into its holster and moving toward McGill.

That spurred Steel into action. "Don't you take him. He's mine."

"Steel." Mercy jerked his chin toward Kat. "Take care of your woman."

"I'm about to by taking care of that motherfucker," Steel growled.

Their eyes met and Mercy gave him a single nod. "Do what you do best. We'll get your woman out of here."

Walker stood with his feet spread, hands on his hips, looking down at McGill, who was now strangely quiet.

He knew his time was limited. It was written all over his pale face.

"I'll grab her clothes," Hunter said, searching the room and ending up in the bathroom, coming out seconds later with them. He jerked his head toward Brick. "Grab towels and a couple of wet washcloths. She's going to need them."

Brick nodded, his jaw tight, as he pushed past Hunter into the bathroom.

Steel watched, completely detached, as if viewing everything from above, when Mercy tucked Brick's jacket around Kat more securely and picked her limp body up in his arms.

Steel's eyes followed her as Mercy moved past him, then his gaze landed back on the sick fuck who was still on the floor in a ball, now crying silently.

Yep, McGill knew what the fuck was coming. If it wasn't for the fact that he wanted to get Kat out of there ASAP, he'd take his time and make the man suffer slowly.

"Did she cry? Did you make her cry?" Steel asked him.

No answer.

"Want me to stay?" Ryder asked next to him.

Steel looked at his best friend and shook his head. "No. I got this."

Ryder squeezed his shoulder. "We'll come back in to clean up afterward."

Steel didn't bother to respond as Ryder followed the rest of the Shadows outside and stood guard with Hunter, blocking the doorway.

Just in case there were any curious eyes nearby.

Steel took a step closer to McGill who cringed and

pulled himself into a tighter ball with his arms wrapped around his knees.

"She beg for you to let her go?"

"No," came the shaky answer.

"Did she want to be drugged and stripped naked? Did she ask for you to come all over her?"

Again, McGill didn't answer and he wouldn't meet Steel's eyes.

Steel stood with the tips of his boots just inches from McGill's face. "Did you fuck her?"

"She wanted to bear my children."

His palms began to itch. "She told you that?"

"Yes."

His fingers began to twitch. "Before or after you stole her from me?"

McGill lifted his head. The tears had stopped. Now he looked defiant. Steel had touched a nerve.

"She was never yours," McGill hissed. "She was always mine. We were meant to be together. She scrubbed herself clean of you so she could give herself to me free and clear."

"She was never yours, motherfucker. You made her mine. Do you want to know how?" Steel didn't wait for an answer. "It was your bullshit. You stalking her, unable to let her go, is what brought me into her life. *You* gave her to *me*. It was all you, McGill. Your psycho tendencies put me in her path. I never would have met her if it wasn't for you. So, I have to thank you for giving her to me. Because of that, she's mine. Not yours. You'll never have her. Unlike you, I never had to force her."

"I didn't have to force her."

"No?" His eyes moved to the taser and the empty syringe on the chipped nightstand. "Funny, when she asked me... no, *begged* me to fuck her, I didn't need a taser or a sedative. She came to me willingly. You can't say the same."

"From the moment I saw her, I knew it was destiny. I loved her."

Steel squeezed his eyes shut, absorbed those words, then spit them back out, knowing each word McGill had uttered was the same for him. "From the moment I saw her, I knew it was destiny."

"But you don't love her like I do!" McGill shouted.

"You're right." Steel opened his eyes. "I love her more."

McGill's gaze finally met his. "We'll have to agree to disagree. But I will never willingly let you have her."

One side of Steel's mouth lifted. "You'll have no choice."

McGill inhaled a shaky breath. "What are you going to do to me?"

"Put you to sleep like you did to Kat with whatever you had in that fucking syringe."

Only, unlike Kat, McGill would never wake up.

Steel tilted his head as he considered the monster at his feet. "Why don't you fucking beg me to let you go like Kat probably did with you."

"Her name is Katheryn, not Kat. And if I can't have her, I don't want to live."

"Then I'll be glad to accommodate you."

He glanced over his shoulder to make sure Ryder and Hunter still stood guard, then he reached down and snagged McGill by the throat, lifting him to his feet. Once they were eye to eye, Steel said, "She would've beaten the fuck out of you if you didn't have an unfair advantage. And I would've paid to see it."

Releasing the man's throat, he quickly repositioned his hands and, with one clean jerk, snapped the man's neck. He let McGill go, letting him crumple to the ground. Once Steel confirmed the man was no longer breathing, he wiped his hands off on his cargo pants.

He sneered at a lifeless McGill, fighting the urge to do so much more to the body.

But it was pointless. And Kat needed help.

Lingering would just feed his anger and waste time.

When he turned, Ryder and Hunter were already stepping back inside the small room, their eyes glued on McGill.

Ryder spoke first. "We'll stay with Brick and do cleanup. You go with Mercy and Walker and get Kat out of here. She'll probably be out for a while yet. Just keep her on her side in case she vomits."

"Did he..." Hunter began, not needing to finish the question. A question that was on all their minds.

"I don't know. He didn't answer that question."

"She wouldn't remember if he did," Ryder said softly. "Maybe head to the nearest ER and get a rape kit done."

Steel closed his eyes and took a sharp inhale through his nostrils. He wanted to say no, it wasn't needed. But he couldn't say that. Because it very well may be needed. However, if they did that, the cops would get involved. And if it had happened, McGill's DNA would be detected and they would be searching for him.

*Jesus*, they were fucked if they did, fucked if they didn't.

"We take her there, cops will get involved. Then this cleanup might not be so... clean."

Ryder jerked the bill of his baseball cap lower.

Hunter scrubbed a hand over his hair. "Do you want to know?" He shook his head. "Forget you. Don't you think Kat would want to know?"

"I don't know," Steel murmured, torn.

Ryder stepped up to him, squeezed his shoulder, and said, "Brother, I think she'll wanna know."

Steel met the man's eyes. After a moment, he nodded. "Yeah. You're right. We'll figure out a story."

"We got shit handled here," Hunter announced, toeing the dead man at his feet. "At least this cleanup will be easier than when Frankie hit a home run using Taz's head. Now *that* was a fucking cleanup."

"But oh so fuckin' worth it," Ryder said, turning away from Steel.

Steel took one last look at the man who would never bother Kat again and then turned on his heels and walked out of the dingy rural Indiana motel room.

If Kat ever came back to this state, he'd be surprised.

———

HOURS. And hours. And more fucking hours.

It took hours at the hospital to find out McGill had not done what they feared.

It took hours for them to get her back to Shadow Valley.

It took hours for Steel to bring her home to his condo, lock the door and set the alarm. Finally giving himself a chance to breathe easy.

Kat had purple half-moons under her eyes. They were dull, her hair out of order, her face drawn and pale.

She no longer wore Brick's jacket but was now wearing what she had been when she'd been snagged by McGill. Steel was sure that she wanted to rid herself of those clothes and that memory.

But the woman was tough. Not a tear was shed once she came to. Not a tear was shed in the ER. Or during the exam with the rape kit, through which he stood sentry outside her room until it was over. Not a tear was shed in the excruciating long ride back to his place.

But then, not much was said, either.

Ryder was right. Kat had wanted to know. Now she knew. Now they all did.

Their relief was undermined by exhaustion. For all of them.

Between the flight from Las Vegas to Pittsburgh and then the chase from Pittsburgh to Indiana, they were all dead on their feet. Barely running on vapors and a constant stream of black coffee.

Steel had wanted to hold Kat on the trip back from Indiana. But once she was conscious and upright, she kept to her side of Mercy's RPV, keeping a distance between him and her.

It was only a couple feet but to Steel it felt like miles.

Even so, he gave her that space. He respected her need for it.

She didn't ask once about McGill.

She didn't need to. She knew.

How could she not?

The fact was she was now safe, free from her stalker, and that was all that mattered.

She was whole and unharmed, and he hoped what happened wouldn't have any long-term effects.

She was strong. And had more grit than any woman he knew.

She'd be fine.

He'd help make it so.

He realized he'd do anything for her. Anything.

And the intensity of that instinct bothered him more than he wanted to admit.

He could ignore it, or he could accept it.

He wasn't sure which direction he'd take yet.

He had time to decide. They had time.

He hoped to fuck they had time.

He had really wanted to carry her from his Jeep into his condo, but he knew she'd never allow it.

Instead, he just made sure she made it up the stairs without stumbling and got inside safely.

Her only words uttered were about how filthy she was

and how she needed a shower. He needed to wash away the last thirty-six or so hours, too.

He led her into his master bedroom and left her perched on the edge of his bed while he started it. When he came back out of the bathroom, she was slowly stripping off her spats. Her sneakers, T-shirt and sports bra already discarded in a pile on the floor.

She did nothing to hide her nakedness as she slogged past him like her feet were mired in quicksand. He followed her, pausing in the doorway to watch her enter the shower stall, then he stood there undecided.

After seeing her unmoving under the stream of water through the frosted glass, he kicked off his boots, stripped off his socks and dropped his cargo pants, leaving them where they landed. He opened the stall door and stepped inside, still wearing his tank top and boxer briefs.

This shower wasn't for him. It was for her.

She needed to wash away the day, too. Grabbing his body wash and a washcloth, he began to swipe it over her neck, her arms, her back and the rest of her. He took his time, the water beating down on both of them, the steam filling the room and fogging up the glass.

After running the sudsy washcloth over her legs and feet, he stood just in time as she began to crumble, every bone in her body disintegrating before his eyes.

Catching her with an arm under her breasts, he held her up and against him, the warm water still sliding over them both, soaking his hair and clothes, washing away any soap still clinging to her skin.

Her head dropped forward and he felt, rather than heard, the first sob wrack her body, then the next and he continued to hold her until they were all gone, even though they seemed endless. And once they stopped, he turned her in his arms, wrapped her arms around his neck, hoping she'd take hold. When she finally did, he grabbed her face and pinned their foreheads together.

He breathed, "Fuck, Kitty Kat."

Spikey dark wet lashes separated, and tired, empty amber eyes met his.

"Fuck," he whispered once more. Not sure how to help her besides simply being there for her. "It's over. You're safe. It's all fucking over. He won't fuck with you again."

When she tried to pull out of his arms, he held on tighter, tipping her chin with his thumb so she'd meet his gaze. But her eyes slid to the side to avoid it.

"I don't ever cry," she said flatly.

Her words, her confession and her raw voice twisted his gut. Never, ever had he cared about anyone as much as he did the woman in his arms.

It was foreign to him. This need to protect and help her, not because she was a job, because she was so much more.

He reached behind her and shut off the cooling water, but kept them there, in the shower, in their cocoon. "Baby, you're so strong, but you're exhausted. Let yourself have a moment of weakness. We all have them. It's what makes us human."

His weakness was her. He knew that now.

There wasn't anything he wouldn't do for her.

But this was not a discussion to be had at this point.

They needed sleep and clear heads. She needed to reset. So did he.

And he also wasn't sure what he'd do with these unfamiliar feelings. Or how she'd react to them. He had no idea how she felt about him. If anything.

Her distance might be proof of her feeling nothing for him. And if that was true, he'd have no choice but to accept it.

He wasn't McGill.

After he helped her from the shower and they both dried off, he guided her back into the bedroom where he dug out a pair of old Silkies he had, giving her those and one of his tanks to wear. He yanked on a dry tank and a pair of boxer briefs himself.

He urged her to lie on the bed and he followed her, pulling the covers over them both, then tucked her face into his neck, holding her close.

She hadn't resisted and curled into him willingly. But she said nothing.

He stroked her back mindlessly, and the motion soothed them both. Now was not the time to replay everything that happened in his mind. How things should've been done so McGill couldn't have gotten her.

No one was to blame but a man with a mental issue. It wasn't Kat's fault and it certainly wasn't Slade's. The DAMC member had been tricked and disabled the same way Kat was.

Steel knew Slade would've done whatever he could to protect Kat. He hadn't taken that responsibility lightly.

If anyone was to blame in that situation, it was Steel. For leaving Kat in Shadow Valley to find McGill. He should've stayed behind and let the others go without him. But it was against his nature. He wanted to personally solve the issue with McGill.

Steel wanted to be the one to bring it to an end.

And he did.

But at what cost?

Kat's words came back to haunt him. *There's always a cost to end something.*

His fingers continued on the path along her spine from her neck to the small of her back and eventually her muscles relaxed and he heard her breathing steady. Signs indicating she had fallen asleep.

He only hoped she stayed that way and could rest peacefully. Because unlike her, he wouldn't sleep anytime soon.

Even though he shouldn't keep reliving the past couple days in his mind, he couldn't stop. He analyzed everything and analyzed it again.

He could have lost her.

What he had told Kat was true. McGill's goal wasn't sex, it was control. McGill wanted to crawl inside her and own her soul. But the biggest risk was McGill could have completely snapped and decided to kill her.

And, for fuck's sake, Steel wasn't sure he would've survived that.

Just that thought made his chest ache, his gut burn and his fingers go still in her short, damp hair.

He didn't know if he could live without the woman whose warm breath swept across this throat, whose palm was pressed over his dog tags and whose thigh was thrown over his.

And, fuck him, that was also a feeling he didn't recognize.

That need so strong for a single person, you worry you'd die if you didn't have them.

Kat had become his oxygen.

And he couldn't live without breathing.

## Chapter Nineteen

Sometime during the early morning, he had fallen into a coma-like sleep. Most likely from pure exhaustion. But what he didn't like was waking up with the spot next to him empty.

This wasn't the first time, and he knew it wouldn't be the last.

Kat was independent. It was one thing he loved about her.

Yeah, that. *Love.*

*Fuck me.*

He stared at the ceiling and sucked in a breath as he snaked a hand under the sheet to adjust his morning wood and give his nuts a quick scratch and tug.

He should probably tell her. But again, with all the shit that happened, now was not the time.

And again, he hoped they had time to figure things out.

Because things would definitely need figured out. Like how he was going to convince Kat to move to Shadow Valley.

He was not in the mood for that fight this morning.

But that's what he wanted. Her to move in with him. Or

if she wasn't ready for that, at least move into Nash's empty house in the compound until she was ready to wake up in his bed every morning.

However, he pretty much figured the Valley wouldn't be her choice of places to land. He might have to call in the cavalry to help him in that regard. The DAMC sisterhood was a fucking force to be reckoned with, and Kat may cave to them after some strong convincing. And possibly a lot of wine and cupcakes.

*Fuck*, he hoped so. Because there was no way he was leaving his team, who was his only family, and a job that was perfect for him. There was also no way he was moving out to LA. It might not be the last spot on Earth he'd want to live but it was pretty fucking close.

Kat could be based anywhere, and the Pittsburgh airport was close, so she could easily fly to fights. Plus, with Slade and Diamond running Shadow Valley Fitness, she had a place to continue training. And, *hell*, Steel would even be willing to build her her own training center.

Look at that. He had their future all fucking planned out already.

All she had to do was agree.

"Fuck," he muttered to the ceiling.

Again, that was not a fight he was willing to have this morning. He needed to make sure Kat was okay. That was priority. Then he could test the waters.

If they were still murky, he'd give it time to settle.

Though, his patience was thin because he didn't like shit being up in the air. And now that he knew how he felt about Kat, her not knowing felt as though something important was hanging between them.

He blew out a loud breath and groaned when he rolled out of bed. Being on a plane, then in a car for hours sucked.

The barely two hours of sleep he managed to get had not helped.

Ignoring the cargo pants he'd left on the floor last night, he grabbed a pair of old jeans that were clean and yanked them up his legs before hoofing it out of his bedroom and into his living room where he spotted Kat wrapped up in a blanket sitting in one of his shitty folding chairs outside on his small balcony.

From what he could see, her head was down but he had no idea what she was looking at. If anything, maybe she had dozed off. He figured she'd need a couple days to recover her energy after her ordeal, especially with the ketamine most likely lingering in her system.

He opened one slider and stepped out into the brisk late October air. He should've put on some fucking shoes. And something besides a tank top, possibly something smart like a hoodie.

The first thing he noticed was his tablet in her lap, which reminded him that he should've password protected it and hadn't. Since it was his new non-work tablet, he'd figured there wasn't any important info on it for anyone to steal.

Or he hoped not.

*Fuck.*

He should've known better. Walker would be riding his ass about it, if he knew.

Speaking of... "Walker's going to clean your electronics."

She tipped her pixie-like face up to him. She still looked tired, but he was relieved to see her eyes had more life in them. "Was that how he kept finding me?"

The urge to hold her was so fucking strong, he had to press his palms to his thighs to prevent him from just grabbing her and hauling her out of the chair. "We think so. When he broke into your place in Vegas, he had access to your computer and tablet, didn't he?"

She nodded, then turned to stare through the balcony's metal railing. What she was looking at, he didn't know since his condo only faced another building. That was one reason why he was renting and hadn't bought it. He didn't love his place, but it had four walls and a roof.

"Walker will confirm it this morning," he said, stepping closer. When he was at her side, he leaned over to press a light kiss to her forehead and when she didn't resist, he tipped her face up to him and slid his lips briefly over hers.

She didn't kiss him back, but she also didn't pull away.

His gaze fell to the tablet's screen and he immediately recognized the popular travel website.

A sick feeling turned his stomach as he took a step back and his eyes narrowed on her. "What are you doing?"

"Booking a flight."

His heart skipped a couple beats and he asked a question he already knew the answer to, but, fuck him, he needed to hear it come from her lips. "To where?"

"Back home to LA."

Again, he stated the obvious. "You're leaving." That fight he wanted to avoid this morning might be unavoidable.

"Job's over, Steel. As I heard Mercy say on the phone to your boss, *the threat has been neutralized.* I'll make sure you get paid, don't worry. And that's all I am to you, right? A job. Nothing more."

What the fuck was she talking about? "You're not just a job."

"No? Isn't that what you told your fellow Shadows?"

He tilted his head and jammed his hands on his hips. He wasn't sure if it was anger or bile bubbling up from his gut. "You're going to hold what I said to a table full of men against me?"

"Men you value as your brothers. I can't imagine you would lie to them."

"Are you fucking kidding me?"

She glanced up from the tablet, her expression giving him nothing. Abso-fucking-lutely nothing. "I haven't been back to my condo for months. I'm sure my plants are dead."

"Your plants are dead," he repeated flatly. Her fucking plants were more important to her than him?

She studied his face, her eyes as narrowed as his. "Is something wrong?"

"What the fuck could be wrong?"

"That's what I'm asking *you*."

"You're just going to get on a plane and walk out of—" He blew out a breath and scraped a hand through his hair.

"Well, fly, but—"

He unlocked his set jaws. "Are you fucking serious?"

"I—"

"Kat," he growled.

"*Steel*. I need to get back. I have a career I love. A career I worked hard to build. A career where I earned respect in the industry. My manager and trainer is back in LA. Everything I know is in LA."

"I'm not."

"I..."

He watched her chest rise and fall as she inhaled deeply. Then she pulled the blanket tighter around her. She stared at her bare toes which were peeking out from the bottom of the blanket for a long moment before looking back up at him. And what he saw on her face, he did not like.

There would be no fight.

They wouldn't be going ten rounds.

Not even one.

She'd made up her mind already.

"You're right. You're not. I've always said I'd never give up my dreams or goals for a man. I watched my mother do that. When she married my father, he became the center of her world. She revolved around his axis. If she had dreams and goals, I have no idea what they were."

"Maybe it was to become a wife and mother."

"Maybe. But she lost her voice as an individual. I'm not going to give up the years I've invested in getting where I am, creating who I am, for what? To abandon it all when a man comes along?"

"A man." He was reduced to simply being "a man." Nothing more, nothing less. "I'm not asking you to abandon anything—"

"Not once in this conversation have you said, 'I'll come out to LA with you, Kat.' I don't hear you willing to make any sacrifices, but you want me to make them for you."

"You could stay in Shadow Valley and still compete."

"Are you asking me to stay? Because you haven't. I can see it in your face that it was something you assumed."

"We fit, Kat."

"Do we?"

"You don't think so? I've... Fuck! I've never wanted a woman to stay before. I've never even fucking considered it, Kat. Until now."

"I'm flattered, but..." Her brow furrowed and she still avoided his gaze. "This is not my home."

"You have no family in LA."

"I have no family here."

"I have family here..."

"Your team? Everyone who lives in that compound?"

"Yes. All of them. Blood isn't always family; family isn't always blood," he spat out the saying he'd heard too often between his team and the DAMC. They said it often because it was true.

"I know that all too well, Steel. But this..." She waved a hand between them. "This was a business transaction. You were hired to protect me."

His nostrils flared and he took a step back. *Goddamn it.* She was looking for any excuse to leave. "And I failed."

"That's not what I'm saying. Don't twist my words."

"I failed, Kat. I know I fucking failed. I'm not twisting anything."

"You were hired to be my bodyguard until my stalker was caught. He's been caught. It's over. What's left?"

"If you can't see what's left, then you're blind. You're ignoring what's right in front of your face, Kat."

"Am I?" she whispered. "What I see is a man who wants to make decisions for me. He wants me to change my life to fit with his. I'm not that type of person, Steel. I never have been, never will be. I'm not her."

"Asking you to stay in Shadow Valley is not making decisions for you."

"Again, you didn't ask."

"Fine. You want me to fucking ask? I'll fucking ask. Will you stay in Shadow Valley?"

"And then what, Steel? If I stay, then what? Will you try to bend me to your will? We both have strong personalities; eventually something will have to give. And I know it won't be you. Honestly, I'm not willing to give up my freedom, my choices for anybody."

A muscle in his jaw popped as he ground his teeth. "I'm not just anybody."

"Maybe not. But..." Her voice caught. "But... I can't. Please understand that. I won't lose myself. I will not lose everything I fought to gain because of one person. I promised myself that a long time ago and I need to keep that promise."

"You feel nothing for me?"

"I respect you."

*Damn*, that hurt. Steel rubbed a palm over his chest. A weak attempt at soothing the sharp pain that shot through it.

"Answer me honestly. Would you come to LA and give up everything you have here? Would you come out there to support me and my career?"

He was tempted to say yes, but that would be a lie. And she'd know it. "You've got nothing in LA."

Kat closed her eyes and nodded her head. "Thanks for that answer. That was everything I needed to know."

"The ketamine is probably still in your system. You've been through a trauma. Give it a few days. When you're more rested and thinking straight." Now he was grasping at any straw he could find. He wasn't ready to give her up.

"I wasn't knocked out the whole time I was tied up in the back of your Jeep with Henry. I had hours and hours to think about my life. To reflect on where I came from, where I went, where I was going if I survived. I had a chance to evaluate everything."

"Including us."

"Is there an 'us,' Steel? An 'us' would be Steel and Kat. But you know what I've heard? Men around here—not just your team—call me 'your woman.' Not Kat. *Your woman*."

"You're going to penalize me for that? For something so fucking petty?"

"Maybe it's petty to you, but it's not to me. It tells me what the mindset is. The same mindset I left behind in Indiana. I ran away from that. I refuse to run toward it."

He was done. If she couldn't see what they had, then...

Then, no amount of convincing would remove those blinders.

If she didn't think they were worth fighting for, then he needed to face the fucking truth. Whether he liked it or not.

He kept his voice steady as he said, "I'm not McGill. I won't force you into something you don't want. If you don't want to be with me, I have no choice but to accept it. And I'm not going to beg. I want you here, Kat, but I want you here because *you* want to be here. If you don't want to be here, then I'm not stopping you from leaving."

"My flight is at one."

*Fucking Christ.*

Every cell in his body screamed at him when he said, "I'll take you to the airport."

"I ordered a car."

Steel turned away and stared through the glass into his condo. He needed to go inside because, for fuck's sake, he was about to drop to his knees and do what he didn't want to do, which was fucking beg for her to stay, plead with her to give him a chance.

And if he did that, he might as well cut off his fucking balls and hand them to her on a platter. Or buy himself a locking cock cage and give her the key.

He wanted her, but he was not going to give up himself to have her. Just like she wasn't willing to do the same.

So, they were at a stalemate.

Two fighters, standing in their respective corners across the ring, neither willing to take the first step toward the center.

Neither would win.

But both of them would lose by default.

"Lock the door when you leave," he said, jerking the slider open and slamming it shut behind him.

Without a lot of thought, he gathered his shit, went down to his garage and uncovered his custom Fat Boy.

And he rode until his balls were blue, his tank empty and she was long gone.

## Chapter Twenty

A LOW WHISTLE greeted him as he stepped under the light in one corner of the warehouse.

"Fuck," Ryder muttered, shaking his head.

A few other curses rose around the poker table someone had found at an estate auction and paid twenty bucks for. They had also scrounged six mismatched chairs at a yard sale and now had a permanent place for their poker games.

Somewhere no one gave a fuck if they smoked cigars while they played.

Or drank.

Or came to the table with a black eye, a busted lip, two broken ribs and a *don't-give-a-fuck* attitude.

Or so Steel thought. That last part might not be quite true since he was getting eyeballed hard by the five others sitting around that table.

Before even planting his ass in the only empty chair left, he snagged the bottle of Jack which sat like a beacon in the middle of the table and a red plastic cup from a bag on the floor next to Brick's chair, then filled it to the point so when he was done, he'd be numb to the pain.

"Know better than that," Ryder grumbled with a frown.

"You can't drink, but I can," he said, but regretted it the second it came out.

Luckily, everyone at that table already knew he was a miserable son of a bitch so Ryder didn't take offense.

But maybe he was spoiling for another fight.

He settled into his chair and let about a quarter of what he poured slide down his throat. With a grimace, he waited out the burn and then wiped his hand across his stinging, swollen mouth.

Hunter slid a can of pop in front of him. "Want a little cola to help that shit go down easier?"

No, he wanted to feel the burn, what felt like acid eating at his gut. "Nope."

That got him an answering sigh.

This wasn't the first time he'd shown up at the warehouse wearing the results of a lost underground fight, so he was surprised they were commenting at all.

"Who's dealing?" he asked when no one moved to begin the game. Instead, they continued to stare at him. Like he was a circus monkey or something.

"Not you, apparently," Walker mumbled next to him.

"Didn't want to fucking deal anyway," Steel grumbled, ignoring the obvious double meaning and stacking some chips on the green felt in front of him instead.

"Well, you coming in looking like that *again*, shows you're not dealing with shit."

Seemed like they weren't going to let this shit go.

He knew he wasn't dealing well with Kat going back to LA. He didn't need to hear it from his team.

It had been over a month now. He should be over it.

Should be, but wasn't.

He needed to get the fuck over it.

It was done.

Over.

Finished.

That fact was underlined by the nice chunk of change direct deposited into his account a couple days after Kat had left.

He hadn't touched that fucking money.

Not a fucking dime.

In fact, he should donate it all to the new foundation that Ellie was talking about starting. One that would help amputees.

She'd probably appreciate his help. Unlike Kat.

Steel closed his eyes and swallowed down the "fuck" that almost escaped.

Never did he think that a woman could derail his life, but one did. And he wasn't sure how to get it back on track.

"Can't hide your emotional pain with physical pain, asshole." Mercy's grumble made him open his eyes.

Steel was still the center of attention. *Oh fucking joy.* "Maybe my skills aren't where I thought they were."

Mercy's chair creaked as he leaned forward, his silver eyes narrowed. "Keep lying to yourself. Keep taking those hits. Keep taking the losses. Eventually, you won't feel shit."

Wasn't that the point?

"You can't keep doin' this to yourself, brother," Ryder said softly. "You're gonna end up dead. You don't lose fights. You're too good for that. We all fuckin' know that. You're losin' them on purpose."

"You're really gonna be a stubborn fuck and not go after her?" Walker asked, shaking his head. "Are you going to continue to wallow in your own fucking misery?"

"She's independent. She doesn't want that to change."

He didn't, either. That was one thing he loved about her.

*Jesus fucking Christ.* Here he went with that fucking L word again. It was more dangerous than an IED.

"You two would be perfect together. Two stubborn fucks," Brick announced, finishing off his beer and crushing the can in his fist before tossing it toward a nearby five-gallon bucket and completely missing. The aluminum can bouncing across the concrete echoed through the cavernous warehouse. "You know if you're still mooning after her after a month, it's true *looooooove*." The kissing noises added onto the end of his sing-song words added a nice touch. If you were five.

Apparently, Brick was in the mood for a direct shot to the face. He was too pretty, anyway.

"And anyway, we're tired of seeing your ugly, depressing puss. Those bruises only make it worse," Mercy added.

"You've got no room to talk," Steel said under his breath.

"I've got bionic hearing, asshole," Mercy said.

"Yeah? Well, I meant for you to hear it." He lifted his cup and drained the remainder of the whiskey into his gullet, letting it burn his insides and hoping the numbness would kick in soon.

"For fuck's sake," Mercy exploded. "Was I this wretched when Rissa went back to Vegas?"

A resounding "fuck yes" circled the table.

"You fuckers should have shot me," Mercy grumbled, shaking his head.

"You weren't much better." Brick elbowed Ryder in the ribs. "We were just spared from it because you went to hide in Chicago." He turned toward Hunter. "You had a case of *head-up-the-ass-itis*, too. It only took a baseball bat to make you see reality."

Walker raised both palms before he was next on Brick's list. "Hey, I admitted defeat early. I saved you all from suffering along with me." He turned to Steel, his blue eyes serious. "Go to her, you stupid ass. Kiss her goddamn feet. Tell her you'll be her sex slave. Tell her that when you offer to give her a massage, you'll actually wait ten minutes before trying to stick it in, instead of thirty seconds. That gets them every time."

"Yeah, I can't take much more of this shit," Ryder said, also way too serious. "Either go to her or get the fuck over it."

"If you decide to go to her, you already have that website for cock cages favorited, so that's half the battle," Hunter snickered.

"If I chase after her, I'm no better than McGill."

"That's what you think?" Mercy asked. And the big guy actually rolled his eyes. "Are you that motherfucking dumb? Nobody can be on this team and be that fucking dumb." He glanced around the table. "Can they?"

"You plan on knocking her out before fucking her?" Hunter raised his hand. "No, don't answer that. I could see that being some sort of freaky sex play between the two of you."

"Unless you plan on druggin' her and wearin' her skin as a coat, you're nothin' like McGill," Ryder stated.

"Only McGill's lotion wasn't actual lotion," Brick reminded them.

A few groans circled the table.

"Last thing I need is relationship advice from you fuckers," Steel growled, his neck twisted toward Brick. "Especially you, Mr. Swipe Right, Exit Left."

"Yeah, he has to keep swiping right because no sane woman wants to share his bed with his MK-11, his one true love." Walker added kissing sounds on the end of that.

"More reliable and faithful than pussy," Brick grumbled with a shrug. "And easier to clear a jam."

"Don't be a hopeless fuck like him," Mercy said to Steel as he jerked his chin at Brick. "Look how happy I am with Rissa in my life." He faked an awkward toothy smile.

The man might be bullshitting, but the only time Steel ever saw that block of ice at the end of the table melt was when he looked at his woman.

*Fuck.*

*His woman.*

They thought of Rissa not as Rissa or Parris, but as Mercy's woman. And it was the same for the other women who belonged to the men sitting around the table.

*Jesus fuck.*

*The other women who belonged to the men...*

Kat's point was now smacking him right in the face.

She would be considered Steel's woman. At least by the men sitting around that table. By the bikers living in the compound. And even by some of the sisterhood. Especially the women who grew up in the misogynist community of the MC, where women were considered property.

"You all just want me to suffer like the rest of you," he mumbled because they were all waiting for a response.

"If you think coming home to a warm fucking meal and a willing woman in my bed is suffering..." Hunter trailed off with a grin.

"Kat's never going to do that shit."

Brick snorted. "Well, in your case, coming home and being sucker punched. A little bit of grappling, a couple choke holds later and..."

"Fucked up foreplay," Ryder said. "But, hey, whatever works for you."

"Are you going to ride my ass all night or are we going to play poker?" Steel finally grumbled.

Mercy grinned. A real one this time. "Who said we can't multitask?"

Brick slammed the bottle of Jack in front of Steel. "Buckle up, Buttercup. Game on."

―――――

"You need to get your head on straight, Kat. I never should've let him take you to Pennsylvania. You haven't been the same since."

Berger didn't *let* Steel take her. Steel didn't give Berger a choice. Just like he hadn't given Kat a choice. That was just Steel's way. A take control of the situation type of man.

It was just who he was.

"It's over," she murmured.

"Your career is not fucking over," Berger growled as he double-checked her gloves.

"Not my career." She was done wallowing in self-pity. "But you're right, I need to get my head back on straight."

"This fight's a good start. It'll be an easy win. You need to get your mojo back."

Her *mojo*. The same mojo that went missing the second she stepped on that plane back in Pittsburgh.

She thought getting on that plane and heading home would return her to being Kat Callahan, champion MMA fighter, instead of a victim.

Or a job.

Or Steel's woman.

She grimaced.

But being Kat Callahan right now felt empty. Lonely. The only thing she had to hold onto was her career.

She loved her career. But as she lay in an empty bed one night in her too quiet condo in LA, she realized it wasn't the only thing she loved.

Somehow she had fallen in love with a man nicknamed Steel. Someone who could handle what she did as a living, who she was as a person, and who wasn't turned off by her strength or determination. Or her goals.

*"We fit, Kat."*

She had to admit, he was right.

*"You're ignoring what's right in front of your face, Kat."*

Yes, again he was right, because she had been. At the time, all she could see was the same of what was expected of her from her family when she lived in Indiana.

But not once had Steel asked that of her.

At least at that point. It didn't mean he never would.

Would he ask her to be his wife, the mother of his children? Did he even want that? She never asked. Maybe because she was afraid of the answer. Afraid of the disappointment. Afraid of being labeled 'not normal' for not wanting those things.

Her family saw her as an oddity. Someone who was broken for not wanting to settle down with a family at a young age.

It wasn't like she never wanted a family of her own. Maybe one day. Until she was ready, she refused to be pushed in that direction. It needed to be on her terms.

Not anyone else's. Not her father's.

Not any man's.

*"I'm not just anybody."*

Did she fuck up?

Yes, *damn it*, she fucked up.

She really fucked up. She hadn't even given Steel a chance.

She now realized why.

Fear.

The fear of needing someone. Of relying on someone.

Of someone being everything to her.

The fear of losing herself by being with that someone. Of her disappearing behind someone so much stronger than her. Of her becoming invisible.

"You ready?" Berger asked, interrupting her thoughts. "Get your head in the fight, Kat, or you're going to lose again. You start to lose on a regular basis, you're going to lose your sponsors and your career will collapse. You want that?"

Was that her manager's idea of a pep talk? You lose, you're done?

Though, it *was* strangely motivating...

She met Berger's eyes and inhaled a deep breath to clear her thoughts. "No. I'm not going to lose."

"Good girl," Berger said, knowing she hated that. That it pissed her off.

Steel had used the same tactic, whispering the same into her ear to get her torqued for her underground fight all those weeks ago.

It worked then, it worked now.

She pounded her gloves together and Berger shoved the mouthguard between her lips. She settled it in place and turned to face the center of the ring.

She needed to fight her fear of losing herself just because she loved a man.

She needed to stop fighting her feelings for that man.

She was strong enough to remain her own woman even with him by her side.

That's where he'd have to be. By her side. Because she would never stand in his shadow.

As she moved toward the center of the ring to meet her opponent, she realized she was strong enough to remain Kat Callahan no matter what life threw at her.

Even if she loved a man named Anson Sterling.

*Especially* if she loved a man called Steel.

# Epilogue

STEEL'S HEART thudded heavily as the door to the locker room opened and he heard a surprised, "You're not coming in?" then Berger muttering a "sorry" before the door slammed shut.

"What the fuck, Berg?" Kat yelled. "Why'd you lock the door?"

At least Berger had been smart enough to know why Kat lost her last fight and had agreed to Steel's plan.

Which he hoped didn't backfire.

Everyone back home was tired of the Steel Shit Show. And so was he.

Which meant he was going to do what he never thought he'd ever do and beg if he had to.

Fact: life sucked without Kat.

From what Berger had told him, it seemed like Kat's life sucked without him, too.

He only hoped that was true and Berger wasn't being a total dick and setting him up, then standing outside the locker room door laughing at Steel as he made a fucking fool out of himself.

Because if Berger was, then...

"Berg! I need you to help me with my gloves!" Kat shouted and pounded on the door.

*Shit.*

He didn't want her already pissed when he approached her.

He sucked in a breath, did a quick check to make sure his balls were still there and stepped out of the shower area.

Kat's back was to him, her fists pressed to the door with her head hanging between her outstretched arms. "Berger, why are you doing this?" she whispered.

"I asked him to."

Kat's body snapped like a stretched rubber band and she whipped around to face him, her eyes wide, her mouth that he wanted to kiss hanging open.

"Kitty Kat," he whispered, taking her in. Her short dark brown hair was still plastered to her head from the fight. A sweat stain circled the top of her sports bra and her skin was still slick in spots.

She was beautiful as fuck.

"What are you doing here?"

"I came to watch your fight." A fight she won this time. Her head had been in it tonight, unlike the last one he watched her lose. And lose badly. But then he could see she had no will to win that one, just like the last few underground fights Steel had lost. They had both punished themselves enough.

"You didn't have to fly to San Diego to watch it. Pay-per-view would've been cheaper."

"Strength is what we gain from the madness we survive," Steel quoted her tattoo softly.

Kat sucked in a sharp breath, then carefully schooled her face. With a tilt of her head, she studied him.

Well, fuck that, he wasn't going to do the same. He

wasn't going to hide how he felt about her. That's not why he flew all this fucking way.

Drawing in a deep breath of his own, he stepped up to her and held out his hands, palms up.

She stared at them for a few seconds, then tentatively placed hers in his. He removed her gloves one at a time, then began to unwrap her hands as he talked. As he ripped himself open and laid himself out before her.

"I'm weak without you," he admitted. "I need to be surrounded by strength, Kat. To keep *me* strong. My team, my boss, my woman. Soft is great. For a night. Maybe two. But forever?" He shook his head. "No. I need a woman who can love me as hard as I love her. Fight with me as dirty as I fight with her. Fuck me as hard as I fuck her. A woman who won't break when I don't even realize I'm trying to break her. I need a woman who's not going to cower when I lose my fucking shit. Because I can guarantee there will be days I'll lose my fucking shit. It's one of the reasons why I fight and why I'll continue to fight. I won't ever ask you to stop because I know you won't ask me to stop, either. Your career is yours and I'll never interfere with it. Just like I know you'll never interfere with mine. That's why we fit. We understand each other's needs. I've never had that before and I know neither have you. We can have that, Kat. With each other."

"I... That was a lot for me to process, Steel. Was there a question somewhere in all that for me?"

What he was going to say next would make or break this whole thing. Whether he would go out and punch Berger for lying to him, or shake the motherfucker's hand and thank him.

He thought long and hard about how he would word what he was about to say. And he decided on a way that if she couldn't live with it now, he knew she'd couldn't live with it later. Because if she wanted to be with him, she'd have to get used to being labeled as such. He didn't want to fool himself or her, that people back at home wouldn't use those words to identify her.

It was now or never.

"Kat, I want you to be my woman." When she shook her head, he lifted a hand to stop what she might say next. To shoot him down before he finished. Because he needed to finish and then he would accept whatever her decision was. "But I also want to be your man. I want it to be a claim that works both ways. I swear to fuck that I will never try to bend you to my will or try to break you until you fit the norms. I love you the way you are. I love you because of who you are."

"You love me," she whispered.

"Yeah, and I don't expect—"

Kat shook her head and said, "Shut up."

His head jerked back and his mouth snapped shut.

"If you keep talking and saying those things, I'm going to start crying and then I'm going to have to punch you for making me cry."

He grinned. Then he opened his mouth.

She lifted a hand and shook her head to stop him. "Just fucking kiss me instead. That's all you had to do. Just kiss me and tell me how much you love me. You could've kept it simple."

He frowned. "Are you fucking with me?"

Kat grinned. "Yes. Because the truth is I loved everything you said. Especially because I never expected a man like you to say any of it. I love the fact that you love me as I am. That you aren't threatened by my career. But there's a problem..."

Steel's stomach flipped. "What?"

"You still haven't kissed me."

He dropped the wraps he'd been squeezing so hard his

fingers had cramped to their feet. "Meet me halfway," he whispered.

Both of them took a single step closer until they were toe to toe. Him, over six feet in his boots. Her, barely five-foot-two in bare feet.

Even so, she was a powerhouse.

One that had knocked the fuck out of him.

He dropped his head and she lifted up on her toes until their lips were just a breath apart.

"I love you, Kitty Kat. Will you be my woman?"

"Just by you asking that and me not punching you in the balls as an answer means I already am. I love you, asshole."

He smothered his chuckle by crushing his mouth to hers and, *fuck*, did she taste good. The last month and a half had been torture without her. He never wanted them to be apart for that long again.

He should be scared as fuck that he felt so strongly about another person.

But it didn't scare him. It felt right.

They *were* right.

So fucking right.

A half hour later, after the water had turned cold, Steel led them from the shower and wrapped Kat up in a towel. But before he let her get dressed so they could get the hell out of there to somewhere he could spend more quality time with his woman, he leaned in once more, whispering against her lips, "For luck, Kitty Kat."

When he lifted his head a few moments later, she teased, "You need luck?"

He grinned. "Fuck no, not when I have you."

———

**Turn the page to read the first chapter of book 6 of the In the Shadows Security: Guts & Glory: Brick**

---

**Sign up for Jeanne's newsletter to learn about her upcoming releases, sales and more! http://www. jeannestjames.com/newslettersignup**

# Guts & Glory: Brick

**Turn the page for a sneak peek of
Guts & Glory: Brick
(In the Shadows Security, Book 6)**

# Sneak peak of Guts & Glory: Brick

## Chapter One

THE GLASS-SHAKING slam of the front door had all the Shadows shooting straight up in their chairs. Brick wasn't the only one sitting around the table whose hand automatically fell to the handgun strapped to his ankle.

What sounded like a woman's heels came down the hallway in their direction.

"Shit," Ryder muttered. "You said she was out with the sisterhood tonight."

Mercy's silver eyes slid to him. "Yeah, she's fucking supposed to be out most of the night with the rest of them."

"I knew we should've had poker night at the fucking warehouse," Steel grumbled.

"The motherfucking heat is out," Hunter said. "We would've had to cancel because of blue balls. And all the women are occupied with Bella's baby shower, so it's the perfect time to play."

"We could've worn layers," Walker muttered.

All eyes slid to him. "And your momma could've dressed you up in your fucking snowsuit and mittens, too."

Walker gave Steel the finger.

A stutter of those clicking heels was heard, a stumble, then a bang. Like Rissa had fallen against the wall.

Brick glanced at Mercy. "Jesus, is she drunk? What'd you do wrong to make her get smashed?"

Mercy frowned and surged to his feet. "Nothing. I never do anything wrong, asshole."

Chuckles and snorts circled the dining room table where their chips, cards, ashtrays, cigars and booze were strewn.

Before Mercy could go check on Rissa's condition, a woman burst into the room, her dark blonde hair—the same color and almost the same length as Rissa's—a wreck. Her blue eyes—also the same color as Rissa's—wide as she took them all in.

"Fuck," Mercy muttered and sank back into his seat, scraping a hand down his scarred face.

"You didn't set the alarm?" Ryder asked, grinning.

"You know I fucking did," Mercy grumbled, then turned to face the intruder. "How do you have the fucking code?"

"From the last time I was here. Parris gave it to me." The woman made a face at Mercy. "What? I'm her sister, not a terrorist."

Brick pursed his lips as he took in a younger version of Rissa, but one just as curvy and whose attitude, and other similarities, could make them twins.

Gorgeous, but a pain in the ass.

Or at least, that's what Mercy said. Not the gorgeous part, the pain in the ass part.

Though, Brick never had a chance to meet her in person. And he only half paid attention when Mercy bitched about her during their poker games.

Normally, Mercy wasn't one to bitch. He usually kept shit to himself and let it eat at him like acid. But apparently Rissa's sister liked to do stupid things. Or, at least, make stupid decisions.

The biggest one being, moving across the country to shack up with a man she met on the internet after only talking with him for a month.

Mercy said she was "impulsive."

"She lets you smoke cigars in here?" Not only were Londyn's *S's* slightly slurred, but her balance wasn't so steady, either, as she wrinkled her nose and waved a hand around to break up the smoke. "Yuck."

"Rissa know you're here?" Mercy growled.

Brick read the look on Mercy's face and hoped to hell that Rissa hadn't forgotten to tell Mercy something so important.

"No, I sent her a text when I landed at the airport... For some reason she hasn't responded yet."

Brick swore Mercy rolled his eyes.

Actually, rolled his fucking eyes.

Brick dropped his head and hid his chuckle.

His chuckle died when Londyn stepped up to the table, grabbed the bottle of whiskey sitting next to the pile of poker chips in the center, removed the cap and guzzled straight from it.

While Brick had noticed many similarities between Mercy's woman and her sister, he'd also noted that her chest was just about as big as Rissa's. And Rissa had a *great* rack.

Brick's eyes swung back to Mercy to make sure he wasn't going to die for even thinking those thoughts. He swore the man could read minds.

Luckily, Mercy was too busy scowling at Londyn, so Brick turned back to her. She had dropped the bottle for a second, took a breath and then took another guzzle.

Brick noticed he wasn't the only one whose eyes were glued to her exposed cleavage in the deep V-necked pant-suit thingy she was wearing, or the way her throat moved as she swallowed.

"Bet it would look like that if she was swallowing something else," Brick said under his breath, unable to contain it.

Next to him, Steel stifled a snort and dropped his head.

Mercy surged to his feet and snatched the bottle from Londyn. "Why the fuck are you here?" He slammed the bottle down next to him and out of her reach.

"I had nowhere else to go since you made Parris sell her house in Vegas."

"I didn't—" Mercy's mouth snapped shut and he just shook his head.

"I can't understand why she'd want to leave Vegas when Michael spoiled her. You're just a big ol' grump."

Steel jerked beside Brick, and he had to turn his face away before his laughter got him a .45 bullet smack between the eyes.

Her red-rimmed blue eyes landed on the bottle next to Mercy. "I need a drink."

"How much have you had to drink already?" Ryder asked, looking more concerned than amused.

Londyn lifted a shoulder. "A couple on the plane... And... maybe..."

"Right. We can figure it out on our own," Mercy stated. "No more booze."

Londyn's lips parted as she stared at Mercy for a long, uncomfortable moment, then, as if she shook something loose, she clapped her hands together loudly and yelled, "Then I need ice cream! Your wife have any ice cream?" and beelined right out of the room toward the kitchen.

"Wife?" Brick's head rotated from watching Londyn's thick, but luscious, ass disappear around the corner to Mercy. "You get married and forget to tell us about it?"

Before he could answer, Londyn backed that caboose right up so they could only see her head tilted back, her long hair spilling down her back and the sweet, sweet ass that, if he was a dumb fuck, he'd try to tap.

But, one, he wasn't dumb, and, two, he preferred his balls to not end up on a skewer and served for dinner.

"Oh... That's right. I meant your girlfriend, *Ryan*. Over two years now and my sister still doesn't have a ring on it."

Then she set that train in a forward motion and disappeared.

"Damn," Brick whispered. He picked up his beer and took a sip to hide his smirk.

"No wonder her fucking man left her," Mercy grumbled.

"I heard that!" came from the kitchen.

"That was the fucking point!" Mercy bellowed back.

"Can we get back to the game?" Steel asked.

"Why? This is so much better," Brick said under his breath, though Mercy heard him and shot him a look that could curl wallpaper.

"Should we just call it a night?" Hunter asked.

"I'm not leaving yet," Brick announced. "This is too good."

"And anyway..." Londyn announced as she came back into the dining room in record time, carrying a heaping bowl of ice cream and dragging a chair behind her from the kitchen. She worked it around the table to shove it in between Brick and Steel.

Giving each other a look, they shifted their seats enough to make room.

"He didn't leave me. I kicked him out." She circled her spoon around the table with narrowed eyes. "Doesn't look like any of you eat ice cream."

Before anyone of them could answer her, Mercy barked out, "Notice something?"

"Yeah, a whole bunch of panty-wetting men sitting at a table *not* eating ice cream. But, *helloooo*, I've given them up. All of you. I don't care how hot you are. How skilled your tongues are. I'm done!" She shoved a full spoon into her mouth and closed her eyes like she was having an orgasm. "Damn, that's good."

Yes, it was. Brick watched as she jammed the spoon into the frozen mountain again and lifted it to her mouth. His eyes were glued to her lips as they parted and her tongue darted out. Then the spoon disappeared again, her eyes closed once more, and she made a *mmm* sound.

*Mmm. Yeah. Fuck.*

His hand dropped to his lap as he wondered if she liked to eat cock as much as she liked ice cream. Though by her curvaceous figure, he guessed she liked ice cream a whole lot.

Mercy's shout of, "No women!" pulled Brick out of his ice cream fantasy.

"What?" Londyn asked as the now empty spoon exited her mouth.

"What you apparently hadn't noticed, Londyn, is there are no fucking women sitting at this table."

She raised her brows. "Well, I am." As Mercy's mouth opened and the rest of them sat on the edge of their chairs to watch this all unfold, Londyn cut off whatever he was going to say. "Where's my sister, anyhow?"

"With the rest of the women, where she belongs."

Londyn's raised brows plunged dangerously low and she dropped her spoon into the bowl with a clatter. "Where she belongs?"

Brick crossed his arms over his chest and sat back. This was better than porn. More entertaining than Heaven's Angels Gentlemen's Club.

It was...

"Why the fuck are you here, Londyn? Did your man kick your ass out finally?"

"You know *my man* didn't kick me out. You *know* I kicked his ass out." She dropped the bowl onto the table and a little bit of ice cream landed on Brick's arm.

She noticed it, too. "Sorry." She glanced around the table. "I don't have a napkin." Then she leaned over, giving him a perfect view of her tits, and licked the melting ice cream off his arm.

Rewind.

*She licked the melting ice cream off his arm.*

Who did that?

But that warm, wet tongue on his skin...

*Shit.*

"Why?"

*What?* Was Mercy asking her why she licked his arm?

"Didn't Parris tell you? He hit me."

The room went electric, snapping and popping circled the table. The woman, whose mouth was again full of ice cream, seemed clueless to what she just set off.

"What'd you do?"

Londyn was now licking the back of the spoon like a cat licking its paw.

Brick's fingers twitched near his dick.

"Why do you assume I did anything?" she huffed, then shrugged with a grimace. "I shot him."

Spines snapped. Jaws tightened. Eyes slid around the table. That little tongue on his skin and on the back of the spoon were quickly forgotten.

Did she just say...?

"You shot him," Mercy repeated in a scarier than normal tone.

"Well, yes." She sucked in a breath and launched into, "I first kicked him in the balls, then I shot him."

"Get the fuck out of here," Steel grumbled low. Brick wasn't sure if the man was impressed or surprised.

"He struck you once and you shot him."

"Once was all that was needed."

On the other side of Brick, Hunter released a long *"Fuuuuck"* as he dropped his head in his hands.

Mercy's face turned thunderous. And for him, it took a lot to make it so. He was seriously pissed. The man normally went subzero cold when he was angry, not the other direction.

She leaned forward, jabbing her spoon toward the center of the table. "Okay, here's what happened..."

Everyone—except for Mercy, who rolled his eyes toward the ceiling and kept them there—leaned forward, totally entranced.

"Poker night's over," Mercy muttered.

"Oh no. Fuck no. This is just getting good," Brick announced. He wasn't going anywhere until he heard what happened.

"Okay, so..." Londyn started, ignoring the scary look Mercy was shooting in her direction. "I thought he was my soulmate—"

"Brick meets a new soulmate every time he swipes right," Hunter said.

Brick ignored him and kept his eyes on Londyn's lips as she took a breath to continue her story.

"It turns out he was anything but. Because you can't have two soulmates."

"Says who?" Steel asked, playing along.

"Says me," she spouted.

Brick heard a long *trying-not-to-murder-someone* sigh at the other end of the table. He ignored that, too.

"You can't have a second soulmate when you've married your first one."

Brick shook his head confused.

Londyn turned hers to look directly at him and began to talk, like he was the only one interested in her story. He wasn't pulling his eyes from her to look around to see if that was true. Because fuck the rest of them, he wanted to hear it and she also now had a spot of ice cream on her bottom lip.

And, *for fuck's sake*, he wanted to lick it off, just like she licked his arm.

But just as hot, that little tongue of hers darted out and swept it away.

"Which one are you?" she asked, her eyes narrowed on him.

"Brick."

"I never met you before, have I?"

"No."

"I would've remembered you," she stated.

Before he could ask why, Steel prompted her, "*Soooo*, you found out your soulmate was married."

"Not just married but had a family. It turns out I was his side-bitch! For years! And I never knew."

"So… he then used that as an escape tactic when he finally figured out you were a crazy bitch and decided he'd rather deal with his wife?"

Londyn gave Mercy a look. "No, he didn't use it as anything. I found out by accident."

"Then he slapped you?"

"Actually, he backhanded me."

"Why?" Mercy asked with another impatient sigh.

"Because I threw a lamp at him and hit him in the face, busting open his eye."

"Hold up," Brick said, more humor in his tone than there should be. "You find out he's a cheating dog. You crack open his melon with a lamp. He backhands you. You rearrange his nuts, then shoot him. Do I have that all correct?"

"Close enough," she said around another mouthful of ice cream.

"Are the cops looking for you?" The last thing any of them wanted was the cops anywhere near In the Shadow Security or the compound owned by the Dirty Angels MC. That could bring trouble.

"Why would they be?"

*Jesus.* This woman. Was she for real? "Because you shot a man?"

Londyn waved a hand around in the air. "It was just a scratch. A warning shot."

"What was the warning for?" he asked, still unable to keep the amusement from his voice.

"To never hit me again. *And* to fucking pack up his shit, get the fuck out of our house and go back to his damn wife."

"Goddamn," Walker mumbled under his breath. He wasn't the only one mumbling shit.

"Do you even know how to shoot a gun?" Brick asked, finding all of this so much more entertaining than a poker game.

Londyn lifted a shoulder as the spoon scraped against the bottom of the almost empty bowl. "You point and pull the trigger."

"That you do," Brick said around a chuckle.

"Tell me, if you kicked his cheating, woman-hitting ass out, why the fuck are you here?" Mercy growled.

"Because I don't want to live in New York alone anymore. I only moved there for him. I'd go home to Vegas, but Parris lives here now because of you. So... here I am."

"Here she is," Ryder announced loudly with an accompanying snort-laugh.

"For a visit," Mercy said. "Like a quick layover before you fly somewhere else."

Londyn dropped the spoon into the bowl and pushed it away. "Until I figure out what I'm going to do."

Mercy's lips flattened out. "While in a motel."

Those blue eyes narrowed on the big man at the end of the table. "I doubt my sister will want me staying in a motel when you have a big, beautiful home here."

"Along with that big, beautiful ring she has on her fucking finger, which you apparently had forgotten earlier."

"Oh, is that an actual engagement ring? Or a *just-some-thing-to-appease-her* ring?"

"She isn't fucking needy like you," Mercy said tightly.

"Fine," she surged up, grabbed an empty plastic cup, moved around the table and snagged the bottle from next to Mercy. "Sorry if I'm going through some tough times and I'm *needy*. I'll wait for Parris elsewhere."

"Like at a motel," Mercy yelled over his shoulder as Londyn rushed out of the room. When Brick didn't hear the click of heels, he realized she was now barefoot.

He dropped his head and saw her heels under the table. They were fucking hot as hell. He had no idea how women walked in shoes like that, but he did not care.

Then he pictured Londyn sprawled on his bed, her dark blonde hair spread over his pillow, her blue eyes on him, while wearing a black lace negligee that hugged all her curves and those red fucking heels.

*Fuck yes.*

He lifted his gaze from the shoes to Mercy, just to jerk his chain. "You should be a little more supportive of your future sister-in-law."

"You're welcome to go console her."

Brick pushed to his feet.

Mercy pointed a finger at him. "Sit the fuck down. You're not getting a piece of that. She's buzzed and in a position to being susceptible to your man-ho charms."

Apparently, Mercy hadn't been serious about his suggestion of consoling her.

"His perfect type!" Steel said, laughing and smacking Brick on the back.

"Rissa would kill me. After she killed you. So, sit the fuck down."

"But—"

"Sit the fuck down!" Mercy shouted. "Don't even think of going there."

"I thought you said poker night was over," Brick said.

"It is. It was. *God-fucking-damnit*," he shouted, then scrubbed a hand over his hair. "I need a fucking drink and she took the whiskey."

Brick leaned over, plucked a can from his six-pack of Iron City. "Beer?"

"I'm not drinking that swill," Mercy grumbled.

"Suit yourself," he said and popped open the can, the beer sliding down his throat. His eyes sliced to the doorway where Londyn disappeared. "We playing poker or are we done?"

"Poker," Steel, Hunter and Walker said at the same time. "We're women-free tonight, so we need to take advantage of it."

"A-fuckin'-men," Ryder said, sitting back in his chair and lighting a cigar. "And who knows when the next time we'll get to do this again. Women and children make life complicated."

"You don't even have kids yet," Hunter said. "I'm the only one sitting at this table with kids."

"Kid," Steel corrected him.

Hunter smiled.

Walker whacked him on the back and laughed. "I was starting to think you were shooting blanks, old man. Congrats."

"It's getting to the point where we only have poker games when they're all at a baby shower," Steel complained.

"As long as one of them in the sisterhood keeps getting knocked up, that should be pretty fucking often," Mercy grumbled.

"I keep saying that the club needs to start a fucking daycare," Ryder stated, watching the smoke roll toward the ceiling from the tip of his cigar.

"Soon they're going to need their own school district," Steel said.

"A-fuckin'-men to that, too," Ryder answered.

"Z's talking about the club running a daycare," Mercy said, shaking his head. "A fucking strip club and a daycare. Not in the same building. Thank fuck."

"Well, Moose's strippers could probably use it, too."

"We all could," Hunter said.

"Speak for yourself," Mercy stated.

"Okay, Frankie and I could."

"Jesus fuck, we're turning into the fucking women here! Can we just play fucking poker, smoke cigars and scratch our damn balls like the men we are?"

A few grunts were heard in response to Mercy's outburst, and Brick began to shuffle the deck of cards that had been abandoned in front of him. "I'm dealing, fuckers. Ante up."

**Get Brick and Londyn's story here:
mybook.to/Shadows-Brick**

## If You Enjoyed This Book

Thank you for reading Guts & Glory: Steel. If you enjoyed Steel and Kat's story, please consider leaving a review at your favorite retailer and/or Goodreads to let other readers know. Reviews are always appreciated and just a few words can help an independent author like me tremendously!

Want to read a sample of my work? Download a sampler book here: BookHip.com/MTQQKK

# Also by Jeanne St. James

**Find my complete reading order here:**

**https://www.jeannestjames.com/reading-order**

\* Available in Audiobook

### Stand-alone Books:

Made Maleen: A Modern Twist on a Fairy Tale \*

Damaged \*

Rip Cord: The Complete Trilogy \*

Everything About You (A Second Chance Gay Romance) \*

Reigniting Chase (An M/M Standalone)

### Brothers in Blue Series:

Brothers in Blue: Max \*

Brothers in Blue: Marc \*

Brothers in Blue: Matt \*

Teddy: A Brothers in Blue Novelette \*

Brothers in Blue: A Bryson Family Christmas \*

### The Dare Ménage Series:

Double Dare \*

Daring Proposal \*

Dare to Be Three \*

A Daring Desire \*

Dare to Surrender \*

A Daring Journey *

**The Obsessed Novellas:**

Forever Him *

Only Him *

Needing Him *

Loving Her *

Tempting Him *

**Down & Dirty: Dirty Angels MC Series®:**

Down & Dirty: Zak *

Down & Dirty: Jag *

Down & Dirty: Hawk *

Down & Dirty: Diesel *

Down & Dirty: Axel *

Down & Dirty: Slade *

Down & Dirty: Dawg *

Down & Dirty: Dex *

Down & Dirty: Linc *

Down & Dirty: Crow *

Crossing the Line (A DAMC/Blue Avengers MC Crossover) *

Magnum: A Dark Knights MC/Dirty Angels MC Crossover *

Crash: A Dirty Angels MC/Blood Fury MC Crossover *

**Guts & Glory Series:**

(In the Shadows Security)

Guts & Glory: Mercy *

Guts & Glory: Ryder *

Guts & Glory: Hunter *

Guts & Glory: Walker *

Guts & Glory: Steel *

Guts & Glory: Brick *

**Blood & Bones: Blood Fury MC®:**

Blood & Bones: Trip *

Blood & Bones: Sig *

Blood & Bones: Judge *

Blood & Bones: Deacon *

Blood & Bones: Cage *

Blood & Bones: Shade *

Blood & Bones: Rook *

Blood & Bones: Rev *

Blood & Bones: Ozzy

Blood & Bones: Dodge

Blood & Bones: Whip

Blood & Bones: Easy

**Beyond the Badge: Blue Avengers MC™:**

Beyond the Badge: Fletch

Beyond the Badge: Finn

Beyond the Badge: Decker

Beyond the Badge: Rez

Beyond the Badge: Crew

Beyond the Badge: Nox

**COMING SOON!**

Double D Ranch (An MMF Ménage Series)

Dirty Angels MC: The Next Generation

## About the Author

JEANNE ST. JAMES is a USA Today bestselling romance author who loves an alpha male (or two). She was only thirteen when she started writing and her first paid published piece was an erotic story in Playgirl magazine. Her first romance novel, Banged Up, was published in 2009. She is happily owned by farting French bulldogs. She writes M/F, M/M, and M/M/F ménages.

Want to read a sample of her work? Download a sampler book here: BookHip.com/MTQQKK

To keep up with her busy release schedule check her website at www.jeannestjames.com or sign up for her newsletter: http://www.jeannestjames.com/newslettersignup

**www.jeannestjames.com**
**jeanne@jeannestjames.com**

Newsletter: http://www.jeannestjames.com/newslettersignup
Jeanne's Down & Dirty Book Crew: https://www.facebook.com/groups/JeannesReviewCrew/
TikTok: https://www.tiktok.com/@jeannestjames

facebook.com/JeanneStJamesAuthor

amazon.com/author/jeannestjames

instagram.com/JeanneStJames

bookbub.com/authors/jeanne-st-james

goodreads.com/JeanneStJames

pinterest.com/JeanneStJames

## Get a FREE Erotic Romance Sampler Book

This book contains the first chapter of a variety of my books. This will give you a taste of the type of books I write and if you enjoy the first chapter, I hope you'll be interested in reading the rest of the book.

Each book I list in the sampler will include the description of the book, the genre, and the first chapter, along with links to find out more. I hope you find a book you will enjoy curling up with!

Get it here: BookHip.com/MTQQKK